Tell me everything

Josie N. Winters

Legal deposit: June 2025

D/2025/Josie N. Winters, editor

Copyright © 2025 by Josie N Winters

All rights reserved.

No parts of this book may be reproduced in any form or by any electronic or mechanical means, including information storage and retrieval systems, without written permission from the author, except for the use of brief quotation in a book review.

Cover by Fleurie

ISBN-13: 978-9-0834-8863-9 (Paperback edition)
ISBN-13: 978-9-0834-8865-3 (Ebook edition)

To my younger self: you did it.
Be happy

PLAYLIST

Lovely – Billie Eillish, Khalid
Stressed Out – Twenty One Pilots
Alien – Cary Brothers
Uptown Girl – Billy Joel
GUNSHOT – KARD
Child at Heart – Hanson
Spring – Ballad ver. – Park Bom, Park Goeun
Skinny Love – Birdy
Here With Me – Dido
Ghost Of You – 5 Seconds of Summer
Family portrait (2020) – Kim Jin Ho
The Feels – TWICE
Demons – imagine Dragons
Sugar – Maroon 5
Supalonely – BENEE, Gus Dapperton
Sorry – The Rose
Kill My Time – 5 Seconds of Summer
Nobody Like You – Little Mix
She Will Be Love – Maroon 5
Feel Special – TWICE
Give Me Love – Ed Sheeran
Cruel Summer – Taylor Swift
Distance – Christina Perri
The Little Things – Colbie Caillat
How You Get The Girl (Taylor's Version) – Taylor Swift
Middle Of The Night – Monsta X

In the Name of Love – Martin Garrix, Bebe Rexha
Best Of Me – BTS
Umbrella – Rihanna, JAY-Z
Bad Liar – Imagine Dragons
Love Poem – IU
Monsters – Katie Sky
Sugar Sugar – The Archies
Euphoria – BTS
Holiday – Little Mix
Just My Type – The Vamps
Alcohol-Free – TWICE
This Love – Maroon5
Style (Taylor's Version) – Taylor Swift
To My Youth – BOL4
My Sea – IU
Elastic Heart – Sia
Stereo Hearts – Gym Class Hero, Adam Lavine
High Hopes – Panic! At The Disco
Travel – BOL4
Birds of a Feather – The Rosenbergs
Blueming – IU
Wings – Birdy
Ready Or Not – Puggy
Animals – Maroon 5
Need You Now – Lady A
Symphony – Clean Bandit, Zara Larsson
You In Me – KARD
My Star – MAMAMOO
You Found Me – The Fray
Fine – TAEYEON
Last First Kiss – One Direction

Find the full playlist on Spotify:
https://rb.gy/r1bem

CHAPTER 1

Elena

A little boy was building a castle in the park sandbox. Although his construction crumbled down many times, he didn't give up and started again until it held. Once he succeeded, his father congratulated him and offered to go for ice cream. The child and his father walked hand in hand towards the ice cream shop, not a cloud in their sky. I felt a twinge of sadness at the sight, and couldn't help wondering whether my life would ever regain that carefree spirit that children have.

Every Tuesday, I waited in the park near the school for my mother to pick me up and drop me off at one of my ballet classes. Like clockwork, her silver Audi A3 approached. I took a deep breath and tried to chase away my unease. The image of that boy with his dad stayed with me, just like it reminded me of everything I'd lost. *Breathe, Lena.*

I climbed into the car and looked out of the window. The weather was mild and sunny for a late September afternoon. Which was surprising, given Belgium's fickle weather.

Mom was tapping away at her steering wheel, impatient as ever. She had always been a rather nervous person. "Time is money", as she so loved to say. Usually, I didn't like wasting my time either, like being stuck in Brussels traffic jams, for example, but I'd much rather waste my time in traffic than go home. The place that was supposed to be my home, but was in truth my pandemonium. Once we returned, hell on earth would start again, as it had for far too long. And yet, nothing changed. We'd have to put up with my alcoholic father for yet another day. Another week. Another month. Without ever breaking the pattern.

"How was school?"

"Fine, as always," I replied, keeping my eyes on the road.

"Good."

Communicating with my mother wasn't easy. Although I loved her, we were never on the same wavelength. She didn't understand me, and I understood her even less. Sometimes I felt like we were just strangers with familiar faces, not a mother and a daughter. We hardly spoke at all. In fact, *I* hardly spoke at all. Nothing on earth would change if I expressed my feelings.

The more time passed, the more I resented what we were going through. Despite trying to forget what I'd seen in the park, the image of that smiling child was now engraved in my mind. And it made me sad. I had to know.

"Mom, why don't you ask for a divorce?"

I held my breath while she reacted to the grenade I'd just thrown at her. My heart was pounding in my ears.

"What kind of question is that?" she asked, suddenly alarmed.

I let out a breath. I inhaled deeply, trying to put my

thoughts together, not quite believing I actually asked *that* question. Now I had to face up to it and go through with it, didn't I? *Oh, Lord...*

"Well..." I began, unsure. "Aren't you tired of being treated like trash by a nobody? We'd be so much happier without him."

On top of that, he didn't participate when it came to paying bills, so he was simply useless. Except for ruining our lives with his negative, aggressive attitude. Might as well put the trash in the garbage can where it belongs.

"Don't talk about your father like that."

"I don't think of him as my father... I'm sure as soon as we get home, we'll have another tantrum."

She stopped tapping on her poor steering wheel and checked her nail polish, just so she wouldn't have to look me in the face. My mother was a weak woman. Was it her nature, or because of her life experience? I couldn't remember. To be honest, I couldn't think of many happy memories that included my mother.

"I've already tried, you know... But I just can't seem to get away from him. Remember that in a few months you'll be an adult and you'll be able to go to your dance school in Saint Petersburg. You'll be away from him for good."

If I passed the entrance exams. That was another story.

"What about you?"

"I'll manage..."

Mom parked in front of the ballet conservatory. She finally turned to me and looked at me with a sad smile. This was just frustrating me. This conversation had been for nothing. I grabbed my bag and got out of the car—staying with her in such a small space was stifling. I had to put on my pointe shoes and get my mind off things.

Several dancers greeted me. My house hadn't been my home in years, but the dance studio was my haven. Like everyone else, I did my stretching and let myself fall back into a familiar routine. Dancing was like breathing, and it was only when I danced that I felt alive. Although I was in my element and had done this choreography hundreds of times, my performance was sloppy. My movements were less fluid, and I was having trouble keeping up with the rhythm. This didn't go unnoticed by my teacher.

"Elena, focus."

By the time it was my turn to do a grand jeté, I could feel my balance was off, but it was too late. The moment my foot touched the ground, I collapsed. There was a dull crack, then sharp pain spread through my right knee. The people around me stirred.

"What happened to her leg?"

"Call an ambulance, quick!"

White dots blurred my vision. Someone shook my shoulder, but I couldn't focus on my surroundings. In the blink of an eye, the world was gone.

***

A strange buzzing drew me out of the void. My consciousness struggled to manifest itself, as if a heavy sleep tried to keep me in its clutches. The noise seemed to get louder and louder, and the strange lethargy I found myself in finally dissipated. When I opened my eyes, a powerful LED light blinded me. I had to blink several times before my vision cleared. Pain was pounding inside my skull, while my body was still asleep. It was as if I'd turned into a giant marshmallow. Why couldn't my mind focus?

Mom was sitting next to me, holding my hand, but *where was I?* Light blue walls, a bed with metal bars, white sheets that looked like they'd been washed a thousand times... *The hospital?*

I tried to get up fast, but my body was screaming at me not to move. It resisted the slightest movement. My heart missed a beat, and panic rose inside my chest. Mom leapt to her feet to try and hold me back. It was no use; I couldn't get out of that horrible bed. *What is happening?*

"Calm down, love. You just woke up from surgery."

Despite all my efforts to concentrate, pain made my head spin. I tried to use my voice several times, without much success. My mouth was as dry as parchment.

"What happened?" I asked hoarsely.

Mom gave me a glass of water and waited for me to finish before speaking. "You fell during dance practice. The impact was brutal, but you were lucky. You only have a few ill effects."

Why couldn't I remember anything? My mind couldn't pick up the pieces on its own. The sedative in my system prevented me from functioning properly. I fought the drug coursing through my bloodstream and did my best to stay awake. I had to know.

"Ill effects?"

She gave me an apologetic look before lowering her eyes. No further explanation was needed; I knew what she wanted meant. I sat down despite my mother's and my limbs' protests. My right leg was cast in plaster from my toes to the top of my thigh. *It's not possible, it's not possible, it's not possible!* How was I supposed to dance now? How was I going to train for my graduation show or the entrance exams? My panic kept increasing.

"Elena, calm down."

Just then, Doctor Petit entered the room. His hair had greyed slightly since I'd last seen him, but he still had that warm smile. My anxiety subsided, giving way to the sadness he evoked.

"Elena, it's been a while."

Indeed, the last time I'd been in a hospital for myself was because I'd broken my wrist after jumping off a swing. At that time, it had seemed like a good idea. Until I hit the ground. All to impress Ella, my cousin. It was Doctor Petit who had taken care of me. We'd also met again in the same hospital when Mick, my older brother, had fallen ill. I shook my head. I didn't want to think about that now.

"Do you have good news?"

The doctor sat down in the chair opposite me. "Don't worry. You have a fractured tibia and a ruptured anterior cruciate ligament, but both are treatable. And your knee operation went very well."

His smile faltered a little, just enough to bring my anxiety back in full force. I played with the seams of the bed sheet.

"I feel a 'but' coming on."

"More like a 'however'. However, it was a nasty fall. As you know, healing from a ligament rupture takes time. Physical rehabilitation will take time."

For a few seconds, I waited. Was that *all?* I needed more than that.

"Will I still be able to dance?"

Doctor Petit and my mother exchanged a look that didn't bode well.

"Maybe. I can't tell you that just yet. As I said, your operation went well, but I'm not going to hide from you that in rare cases, healing isn't one hundred percent guaranteed."

A sob formed in my chest. In less than a second, all my dreams and plans for the future had become unattainable, leaving nothing but sadness in their wake. My whole life had gone up in smoke in the blink of an eye.

CHAPTER 2

Alex

A new rumour was making its way through the school halls when Alex arrived. The only surprising thing was that, for once, it wasn't about him. Knowing that most of the time rumours were more fantastic than reality, he tried not to listen to them. If the ones about him were anything to go by, Alex was a vampire who only drank the blood of virgins. His pale skin and dark hair didn't work in his favour. Or he was mixed up with a gang. It was absurd, of course, but he'd heard it before.

"Alex."

Alex turned to Yves and shook his hand.

"Is it true what they say?" asked his friend, a morbid curiosity shining in his brown eyes.

"What are they saying?"

"That a girl in our year had an accident. Elena."

This news left Alex speechless. He didn't know her that well, but she was a sweet girl. Since they'd been in high school, they'd only spoken once. At a wedding, no less. Even though they'd never spoken again after that, Alex had always felt a certain sympathy for the girl who, despite her shy looks, had a funny, energetic personality. He'd never admitted it to anyone, but Alex had had a crush on Elena when they were in elementary school. He couldn't help feeling sorry for her if the rumour was true.

Yves gave him a funny look, so Alex shrugged. It didn't matter if it was true or not; it wasn't his business. He couldn't start worrying about someone else. He could barely manage his own life and problems.

Throughout the morning, Alex managed to carry on as if nothing had happened until he was approached by a petite brunette at lunchtime.

"Hi, Alex!"

It was Kelsey, Elena's best friend. She had big green eyes that always seemed to sparkle with mischief. For someone whose best friend was in the hospital, she was in an oddly good mood. Unless it was really just a rumour. He hoped so. Kelsey tucked a strand of hair behind her ear with the greatest carelessness one could summon.

"Can I ask you a favour? I'm supposed to bring Elena's notes to the hospital, but I can't make it. Could you go in my stead? Your mothers are close, so she knows you better than the rest of the class."

What could be more important than seeing her best friend in the hospital? Alex shook his head and decided not to judge her too harshly. He agreed to go, even if he had a funny feeling about it.

***

"Hi."

Elena looked up from her magazine before raising an eyebrow. She hadn't expected Alex to show up at the hospital. He hadn't expected to be here, either.

Her complexion was slightly greyish, and dark circles dug into the skin below her blue eyes. The ballerina looked terrible. Once, she'd been so smiley and full of life. Now she just looked irritated and hollow.

"To what do I owe this honour?"

Her voice was deeper and colder than the last time they'd spoken, which was over a year ago.

"I came to bring your notes."

"Why are you the one bringing them?"

"Why not?" Alex shot back.

Elena clicked her tongue, shaking her head. "We're not friends, so I don't see why you're going to all this trouble. Don't you have anything better to do?" She turned her attention back to her magazine and pretended he wasn't there.

Alex was caught off guard. Unlike the young Elena of a few years ago, the person in front of him was angry. Aggressive. He let it go and decided to stay positive. She'd just had an accident; a little compassion for her wouldn't hurt. He could do it. As long as she stayed calm, too.

"We could be friends, if you want."

The words were out before Alex even had time to think them through.

With calculated slowness, Elena turned a page. "You're telling me this now that I'm in the hospital, when we used to see each other at school every day without ever talking to each other? Save your pity, I don't want it."

"It's called compassion."

"It's the same."

For a moment, Alex hesitated to simply hand over the notes and walk away as if nothing had happened. "Could you try to see the glass as half full instead of half empty?"

Seeing the young woman's attitude change, Alex knew he'd gone too far.

"They told me I may never fully heal, and you expect me to be positive? That's what you're saying?"

Alex sighed, running a hand through his hair. He'd known it was a bad idea to come. He should have followed his intuition and pretended nothing had happened. Why had he agreed to come when he knew full well he couldn't waste time on other people's bullshit? He could barely handle his own. Then again, he didn't manage that well, did he? Alex drew a deep breath to keep his cool.

"Sorry, I didn't know."

"Of course, you didn't know. You don't know anything about me!"

Angered, Elena threw away the magazine. Coming here had been a mistake. He'd thought that because they knew each other, his visit might not bother her too much. But Alex was facing a caged lion who wasn't going to hesitate to rip him to shreds. He placed the teachers' papers on the table and headed for the exit.

"Get well soon."

CHAPTER 3

Elena

The next day, Kelsey was the one who came to visit. As always, she was radiant. Seeing her smiling like that when I was at my lowest immediately put me in a bad mood. Deep down, I knew it was wrong to want the whole world to suffer with me, so I kept quiet. But all I wanted to do was scream at the top of my lungs.

"Hello, gorgeous!" she exclaimed.

Her optimism was exhausting.

"S'up."

She sat down in the chair Alex had sat in the day before. For several seconds, she stared at her freshly manicured nails. When I'd seen Alex, I'd realized she had better things to do than visit me. I'd hoped it would be for something more important than a stupid manicure, but apparently, I was worth less than that.

"Nice nails."

"Thank you!" she said, a big smile on her face.

"Is that why you asked Alex to come instead?"

I should have had more respect for him. He hadn't asked for anything, and yet I'd been horrible to him. He'd deserved better.

Kelsey's eyebrows went up in surprise. We'd known each other since kindergarten. Obviously, I would figure her out. What astonished me was that she thought her candy-pink nails would go unnoticed. I was naive, but I wasn't stupid. The fact that I was being taken for a fool made my bad mood increase. I took a deep breath, trying not to spit venom.

"Oh, I'm so sorry! But you know, this appointment had already been scheduled for two weeks. I couldn't cancel. But I promise I'll make it up to you!"

Kelsey put her two hands together like she was begging for forgiveness. Of course, she wouldn't make it up to me. I knew her all too well. At this point, that was the least of my concerns. The only thing I wanted was to disappear into a hole and not come out again for a few months. Or longer.

"Anyway, how are you?"

"Bad," I admitted.

What was the point of lying? I didn't want pity or "compassion", but pretending wasn't something I cared about right now.

"What did the doctor say?"

"He says I'll heal, but I may not fully recover. This could jeopardize my dancing career."

"I'm so sorry." Kelsey took my hand and placed a sweet kiss on it. It was a gentle, affectionate gesture if you ignored her cheerful air.

"What about you?" I asked, faking interest.

"I've got a date with Tiago tonight!"

Tiago. Of course... He was one of Alex's best friends and one of the best players on our school soccer team. Alex was a part of the team, too. She'd been circling this guy for months just to get so much as a glance from him. Deep down, I couldn't judge her. I, too, had been crazy about a guy in my dance class for years, even though he'd never shown the slightest sign of interest. Kelsey was the same way with Tiago, just as I'd been with Robin. Except this was how it went: guys like that didn't see invisible girls like us. Until today, it seemed. All the girls were after him, as if a guy chasing a ball would automatically attract the ladies. Alex was also coveted by three-quarters of those girls. They were both handsome and good sportsmen. But where Tiago was known as a real flirt, Alex had the reputation of a dangerous and mysterious young man. Physical attraction was a strange thing. Let's just say the hormones were to blame.

"I'm happy for you. Tell me, did you put your plan into action and pester him to answer you?"

"I didn't even need to!"

Like a child about to be offered ice cream, she was clapping her hands. I understood her enthusiasm. Going to see the boy you've been in love with for months was much more exciting than hanging around the hospital. Even if it was to visit your "best friend". Who was I trying to fool at this point? A gap had opened between us since my brother's death three years earlier. I'd lost my best friend and my older brother at the same time. The only difference was that one body lay six feet under, while the other stood next to me.

"Gotta go. Don't do anything stupid while I'm gone!"

Boy, was that funny. Look at me laughing my ass off. God, when had I become so bitter?

"I don't think you need to worry."

She placed a quick kiss on my forehead before leaving the room. And I felt even more alone than before.

***

Alex

"Hey, Alex! It's been a while."

Alex was surprised to see Elena's mother in the candy aisle of the supermarket. He'd been used to seeing her as a child. After all, Maura was one of his own mother's childhood friends. About three years ago, she stopped coming. The last time he'd seen her was at Jennifer's wedding, another of his mother's childhood friends.

"Hello, Mrs Fleureau."

"Call me Maura. I've known you since you were born."

In the past, he might have considered her a member of his family. That was years ago. He'd shut a lot of people out of his life since then. Not knowing what to say, Alex simply smiled at her. Hopefully, she wouldn't keep him too long. With a tournament this weekend, he couldn't afford to miss his kickboxing training.

"You went to see Elena at the hospital, didn't you?"

He watched as people hurried to grab their products from the shelves before rushing to the checkouts. Alex didn't like wasting his time. Patience was a virtue he didn't always control. "I did."

"Are you getting on well?"

Images from a few days earlier flashed through his mind. Elena had accepted his presence at the hospital just as she had accepted her broken leg. Needless to say, they didn't get along particularly well. "Not really. We hardly know each other."

"According to your mother, you're very honest and direct.

Is that true?"

This conversation was going to last forever.

"I guess so," he replied on guard. "Why all the questions?"

"Can I ask you a favour?"

"It depends on the favour."

Maura pondered, as if she saw in him the solution to all her problems. He had another bad feeling.

"Would you like to spend some time with Lena once in a while?"

For a moment, Alex wondered what was in it for him. He didn't feel like babysitting. Especially since the person in question didn't even want to see him again. Not that he was jumping at the idea of seeing her again either. Maura sensed his hesitation.

"Let's grab a coffee. My treat."

Alex realized she wasn't going to let go of him and nodded reluctantly. It was better to go with the flow and listen to what she had to say if he wanted things to go as quickly as possible. He headed for the checkout and grabbed a pack of cigarettes.

Once they were in the café in front of the supermarket, Maura clicked her tongue. "You shouldn't be smoking at your age."

Alex grew irritated. He didn't feel like being here to begin with, so he could do without unnecessary comments. Everyone knew it was unhealthy. He just couldn't find the motivation to stop. "Can you get to the point, please?"

Maura pursed her lips at his abrupt tone. If she had been aware of his reputation, she would've known that he wasn't appreciated by the older generations. Alex was trouble and not the type of guy you'd want your daughter to associate with. And trouble was an understatement. He didn't want people to see him that way—as worthless or a thug—but certain events had made that image stick to his skin.

"I'll get right to the point, then. I'd like you to spend some time with my daughter."

That had already been established.

"Why?"

"Did you know Elena was mute for a time because of a trauma?"

Alex shook his head. He'd never associated with her since they left elementary school, so he knew almost nothing about her. Alex had spent one evening with her because they were the only ones their age stuck at a wedding they weren't interested in. Elena had been kind and funny, but they hadn't spoken to each other after that. Knowing that this same smiling, cheerful person had been mute was a whole different picture.

Maura ran a finger along the rim of her coffee cup. "You see, her life isn't easy, which is probably my fault. Dancing was her safe haven. With the accident she's just had, I'm afraid she'll relapse. Maybe she won't talk to anyone now that she can't dance anymore, and I can't reach her. It feels like I hit a wall when I try to talk to her."

Her eyes were desperate. She was losing her daughter, a little more every day. Every second, Elena lost the will to keep going. She was losing herself, becoming a shadow of her former self. It all seemed too familiar. Alex felt sorry for the girl who'd had to say goodbye to the one thing that had kept her holding on.

"Why me? A therapist would be much wiser."

"She's already seeing one. But I think talking to someone her age can help. Especially someone who understands what she's going through."

Alex sighed. Without having asked for anything, he felt like he'd found himself in a snake's nest. He wasn't convinced that forcing Elena to spend time with him would help. On the other hand, Alex knew that if he refused, he'd feel guilty. *What a mess.*

"I'll come by tomorrow. Goodbye, Mrs. Fleureau. Thank you for the coffee."

Tomorrow was going to be a long, long day.

CHAPTER 4

Alex

Pulling up in front of the Fleureau house, Alex realized just how large their home was. Even though this was still the same town, he felt a certain shock. There were no mansion-sized houses in his neighbourhood.

Maura let him in, but her smile was forced. Alex felt as if he'd appeared at a terrible time. He already regretted being there.

Alex entered the hall. This house was supposed to be so many people's dream home: spacious with big windows. Yet it was cold and unwelcoming. He shook his head and climbed the stairs. His presence was not going to be appreciated; he already knew that much. As long as things went better than the disaster at the hospital.

Elena's bedroom was open. The ballerina was lying on her king-size bed, staring at the ceiling. Alex knocked on her door; she didn't react. It was almost as if she wasn't breathing. Seconds passed, and Alex feared she'd leave him on the doorstep. It was the first time a girl made him wait like that, and he wasn't sure he liked it. After what seemed like forever, she waved, and Alex entered the room. It was large and spacious, like the rest of this place. The walls were painted a pale pink with black silhouettes of ballet positions. Audrey, his little sister, would love this room.

"How much?" she asked.

"What?" Alex tilted his head slightly to the side.

She hesitated for a brief moment before resuming. "How much did she give you?"

"Who?"

"My mother. How much did she pay you to spend time with me?"

She was quite perceptive. Alex sat down on the black velvet Chesterfield under the window. Even the air here seemed expensive. "Nothing. I don't want money."

"Then what do you want?" Elena snapped.

"I don't know."

Elena sat up. Her fingers tapped nervously on her arm. What was she thinking? This time, she looked more docile than when he'd visited her a few days ago.

"You can go. All I want is a little peace and quiet."

God, she was stubborn. Alex wanted to take his bag and leave. But he'd made Maura a promise, and this annoying girl would eventually give in. If neither of them wanted to be here, they could at least try to make the best of this ridiculous situation they found themselves in. If only for an hour. Then they could get on with their lives as if nothing had happened.

"What you need is therapy and a friend."

"You're going to force me to become your friend? Is that how it works now?"

She's good. Maura had spoken of a fragile, shy girl, but Alex was faced with a raging lioness. Most of the girls he met never went against him. They were afraid. None of them contradicted him, which tended to be annoying. As for Elena, she was either unaware of Alex's reputation or she couldn't care less. And if he was starting to get her right, it was the second option. Maybe this was all going to be more fun than he'd anticipated.

"No, I'm not going to force you, but before you slam the door, can you at least give me a chance?"

He felt stupid asking her to be his friend. Elena lowered her eyes. She looked so sad and lonely. Maura was right, she needed someone. Alex wasn't sure he was up to it, but he didn't feel like giving up.

"Trust me, you don't want to be friends with someone like me."

"Someone like you?"

"Please leave! It's better for you if I'm not part of your life."

She implored him with her eyes. Elena felt powerless, just like he had a few years earlier. Back when he'd felt there was no light at the end of the tunnel. Alex had suffered, alone and misunderstood, feeling like there was no way out. Elena experienced the same thing now. He didn't want her to feel that way. Alex wanted to answer, but a strange noise came from the hall. Elena's eyes widened, and her body tensed like a bow. Irregular footsteps approached, then a medium-sized man in his forties with a vaguely familiar face staggered into the room. He reeked of alcohol. Alex glanced at the young woman. She was petrified.

"There you are!" slurred the man. "The biggest mistake of my life. Just look at you!"

His blood ran cold. The man moved closer to Elena, and

Alex placed himself between them before he could think it through. Something inside him was screaming not to let this man get any closer. If Elena was paralyzed, she must've had a good reason. Alex forced himself to smile and held out his hand. The man frowned in confusion but accepted his hand.

"Hi, I'm Alex."

"Frank."

Alex had crossed paths with him many times when he was a child. Except that the person in Alex's memories didn't match the man in front of him. Frank left the room without a word. Elena tried to be strong, but Alex noticed how her hands shook. He didn't know what to say to break the silence. He'd just been sucked into this family's woes. Maybe Elena had been right—he should have left. Now that he knew what was going on here, he couldn't leave and pretend everything was fine.

"That's why I didn't want you to come."

"I'm sorry."

"Not as much as I am."

CHAPTER 5

Elena

"Tell me, Lena, how are you?"

My heart was beating loudly in my temples. How was I? In all honesty, I didn't know what I was supposed to say. It was a simple question that required few words: okay, or not okay. Still, I couldn't answer. I didn't remember the last time someone had asked me this, wanting to know how I really was.

Stacey, my therapist, watched me in silence, her big brown eyes hopeful. I swallowed. What could I possibly tell her? Deep down, I knew I wasn't doing well. I hadn't been since... since Mick had been diagnosed with leukaemia. But after years of trying not to feel anything, admitting I was hurting seemed like a betrayal to myself. I'd tried so hard to convince myself I was fine, and yet here I was, a weak, pathetic girl about to break down in front of a therapist who'd never been able to make me talk before.

No therapist had ever been able to get me to talk, but Stacey was kind. She was also the only one who believed I'd make it. Everyone else had classified me as beyond repair. But this was a delusion. The only reason she believed I'd pull through was because she only knew bits and pieces of my reality, not the whole truth.

After the tragedy that had shattered my family, Stacey had given me a diary when my mother realized that I had become mute. For a while, I'd thought that letting my feelings and thoughts out on paper would be safe and without consequence. How wrong I had been. The day my father discovered the diary, I learned the hard way that lying was my best option. My *only* option.

I couldn't fool anyone anymore. Alex knew. And if he knew, someone else would find out too. I was so scared. What was going to happen to me now? I had to keep my head straight. I would not fall apart. I looked up at Stacey. She was still waiting for my answer.

"You want me to be honest?"

She raised an eyebrow. "That is the purpose of therapy."

I ran my hands through my hair and took a deep breath. *Stop lying, Lena.* "Things could be better."

Stacey smiled at me and nodded. I let my head fall back. My heart was still pounding in my temples. I just hoped I wouldn't regret this.

"How is your relationship with your father these days?"

I could hardly swallow my tears back, the disappointment about to drag me down. After all this time, I should have been used to it. So why did it still upset me so much?

"He never came to see me in the hospital."

"And how did you feel?"

Being honest was terrifying. This time, I knew I couldn't lie. The lies were becoming too much to bear. "Abandoned and worthless."

"Have you heard from your family?"

I shook my head, unable to answer. If I opened my mouth, I'd either burst into tears or vomit my guts out. I missed my family so much. I thought I'd miss them less after a while, but the more time passed, the more it became clear I had no one left. Between my older brother, who passed away, my mother, who couldn't look me in the eye since she knew my father had tried to strangle me a few years earlier, or my family, who had stopped contacting us, I knew I was alone. But the worst of all, was that I was surrounded by people who made me feel alone. As if I were invisible. And I didn't know how to get through all of this.

***

For long minutes, I waited in the doctor's office. After what seemed like an eternity, but was only six weeks, my cast was finally removed. Goodbye, awkward crutching from one classroom to the next, and hello, slow, painful rehabilitation.

I bit my thumbnail, waiting for the doctor to come back with the results. I'd asked Mom to wait for me in the hallway. I'd been surprised when she'd offered to accompany me to the doctor's office. For years, I'd had the impression that she'd left me on the sidelines, so having her near me at this moment only added to my discomfort.

"Your leg is healing nicely, Elena," Doctor Petit announced as he entered the room.

"Does this mean I can dance again?"

I had to know. For the past few weeks, I'd spent my time worrying. Would my dream end here? Did I still have a chance of succeeding as a dancer? Would I be able to dance professionally? So many questions were racing through my head, making me dizzy. Doctor Petit removed his small round glasses and stared at me. He had a receding hairline, which strangely accentuated his sympathetic aura.

"That's a question I can't answer yet. As long as you haven't started rehabilitating your knee, I can't make any promises. If you follow your physiotherapist's instructions to the letter, I think you will."

It was a relief. But even though I felt a little better, there was still something that bothered me. Even if I could restart my life as a ballet dancer, I was set to lose another year of my life. Another year in that house, with a drunkard and an absent mother.

"I lost a year for nothing..."

"Don't see this break as an obstacle, but as an opportunity. Maybe it's the perfect time to focus on other things you'd like to accomplish or improve."

Yeah, right... I had nowhere else to go. My mother had made sure of that when she'd decided I couldn't see my family after my brother died. This good news wasn't enough to erase all the pain that had been lodged in my chest.

On the way home, Mom talked about anything and everything to fill the void. Her concern wasn't doing me as much good as I'd hoped.

When I arrived home, I was surprised to see Alex waiting on our porch. He looked up from his iPhone and stared at my leg in amazement. You'd think that now that I could walk again on my own and go to school, he'd stop coming. He didn't.

"I see you don't need crutches anymore."

"About time," I mumbled as I entered the house.

I didn't bother closing the door, knowing full well that he was going to follow me. Walking without a cast and crutches was still very uncomfortable. I was still limping slightly, which was bothersome. I was tired of feeling like a broken doll.

Alex placed some notes on my desk and sat down on my couch. He kept bringing me his notes, as if I couldn't go back to class without him. I was beginning to think this was just an excuse to come over.

"So, how did the visit to the doctor go?"

"Good."

I dropped onto my bed, head first into the pillows. I hoped this day would be over soon. After the session with the therapist and the visit to the hospital, I was exhausted. And as always, Alex's presence put me on edge. There was no reason for him to bother me anymore.

"What did he say?"

"Stop bugging me," I said with a sigh. "I'm fine, I don't need you."

"You live with an alcoholic and violent father; your brother is dead, and you just had an accident that may put an end to the career of your dreams. I don't think you're fine."

Is he serious? I glared at him. Was this his way of making me feel better? If it were, it would be better if he just shut up. "Thanks for summing up my life. Do you feel better now?"

Alex ran his hands over his face, exasperated. I was unbearable with him; I was well aware of that. But all I wanted was for him to leave me alone. His green irises pierced holes in my skull. Alex always gave me the impression he could read me as if I were an open book. The idea frightened me. He already knew too much.

"Elena, when are you going to stop lying to everyone? You're not okay."

"If I accept that, I'll fall apart. And there'll be no one to help me up."

That was the sad truth. I had to make it on my own.

"I'll help you."

A shiver ran down my spine. I rubbed my arms nervously and shook my head. He had to stop this *now*. He had to go. "No, you won't. Nobody does. Right now, you believe that you will be there, but you'll leave me. *Everyone* leaves. So don't let me believe in something that won't happen. That's just cruel."

I waited for Alex to argue. My expectations flew out the window when his gaze turned kind. This guy was way too wise and mature for someone our age.

"Maybe you should see this healing period as an opportunity to get better, not as a punishment."

I'd heard that sermon before. I raised an eyebrow, unconvinced. Doctor Petit had told me the same thing a few hours earlier. Needless to say, I didn't believe it. Besides, why had he come to my house to play preacher?

Seeing that I wasn't answering, Alex continued, "This would be the perfect time to solve some issues."

"What do you care?" I looked at him in disbelief. For a brief moment, I hesitated to throw a pillow at him.

Alex let out a quiet laugh. "Don't give me that look. Actually, I'm just telling you what my therapist once told me."

"You..." I began, unsure. "Are you seeing a shrink?"

"Not anymore, but I've seen one for years."

My curiosity was piqued. I had to see one because,

supposedly, I had several traumas to overcome. Which meant Alex was like me. This revelation took me aback. I wanted to hate him so he could get out of my life. But maybe he was broken too. I felt sad for him. As much as I wanted him to leave and never come back, I couldn't help wishing he hadn't had to see a shrink for the same reasons I had: death, denial, self-destructive behaviour... Or worse. Whatever that implied.

"Don't look at me with those sad eyes. I'm all right."

Oh no. I couldn't let my mask slip in front of him. I couldn't bear it. I sniffed and looked the other way, pretending not to care.

"I didn't ask."

Alex let his head fall back. He saw me as a puzzle he was desperate to solve. There was nothing mysterious about me. I was just a girl trying to show others that I was okay. Not that I was convincing anyone these days. Especially not myself.

"You really do have a heart of stone sometimes."

It was the illusion I'd tried to show for years. Now that someone had confirmed that I was made of stone, my heart sank. I didn't want to be like this—I'd never wanted to be like this. But how could I protect myself if I let people in? The only thing that comes from trust is pain and deception. I knew that. I'd learned that lesson a long time ago. So even though Alex looked at me with those gentle, patient eyes, I couldn't let myself get dragged into this mess. I wasn't strong enough to get back up if he decided I wasn't good enough. And I wasn't good enough. That, too, had been established long ago.

CHAPTER 6

Elena

The moment Alex walked through the door, I wanted to scratch his eyes out. He hadn't done anything wrong; it didn't change the fact that his mere presence irritated me. His pity made me nauseous. Even if he was here willingly, I couldn't stand the way he looked at me. That sad, helpless look... He made me feel weak and like I was stuck, and I abhorred that feeling. Even though, objectively speaking, yes, I was weak and pretty much stuck. But I didn't want to feel that way. And yet when Alex was around, I couldn't help feeling useless and powerless.

He sat across from me at the kitchen table, and I did my best to ignore him. Maybe if I ignored him long enough, Alex would eventually grow bored and leave. And so, our paths would part, and everything would return to normal. *Normal.* Sadness gnawed at me. Why did thinking about normality make me feel so lonely?

"Let's go to the Botanical Gardens," Alex suggested, snapping me out of my head. "The weather's nice today."

He gave me a sweet smile, and the urge to scream

consumed me. Alex always looked like he could read me. But he couldn't read me, right? I could feel my pulse quickening and my palms getting sweaty. He had to get out of here. *Now*.

"Go away!"

My biting tone shocked me, but Alex kept smiling. Why was he staying? No one was that patient and kind. *No one*. Especially not him. I didn't know why he was so stubborn about helping me. Alex wasn't known to be a nice person. If I annoyed him long enough, he'd eventually give up. There was no room in my life for him and his pity. It would only cause more pain. My eyes burned. Why was I so weak? For God's sake, I wasn't going to cry in front of him! My mother came into the kitchen and I lowered my eyes. Great, just what I needed.

"Maura, I was thinking of taking Elena to the Botanical Gardens. What do you think?"

"What a wonderful idea! Elena, get dressed. Some fresh air will do you good."

Is this a joke to him? I left the kitchen without saying a word, wondering why life kept testing me like that, but I was getting used to things never going according to plan.

I splashed cold water on my face. No wonder Alex looked at me with such pity; I looked pathetic. I hopped in a pair of jeans and ankle boots before heading downstairs. No matter how low I felt, I wasn't going to show him any more weaknesses. I wouldn't let another person walk over me like my father did.

Alex was waiting for me by the front door. Without glancing his way, I left the house.

"Involving my mother was a low blow."

"You left me no choice."

Just great.

"There shouldn't even be a choice. Just leave me alone and get out of my life. Then you can go on pretending I don't exist."

"Where's the fun in that?"

My blood ran cold. I saw red.

"What?" I yelled. "Am I a joke to you? You're spending time with me because you want to be *entertained*? So what, you want to get me into bed? Don't think I'm not aware of your reputation. I know what kind of person you are, and I don't have the time or the energy for that."

Was this just a game to him? It was, wasn't it? There was no way he was here because he cared about me. I already knew that. But playing games... No. I'd hoped he was better than that. I'd been wrong.

Alex laughed as if I'd just told a really funny joke, while I felt my anger boiling. I clenched my fists.

"I'd like to think I'm a little more than just an asshole who sleeps with every girl he meets... Don't get any ideas, love. Uptight girls like you aren't my type."

And now he was insulting me. *Perfect*. He patted my shoulder, a small, satisfied smile on his lips. Killing him was oh so tempting. "Oh, really? I feel so much better now. Thanks." I turned and walked down the street. *Let's go to this stupid park so I can move on.*

"Hey, where are you going?"

"To the Botanical Gardens," I grumbled, raising my palms to the sky. "Where else would I go?"

"Let's drive. It's a few miles from here."

Alex opened the door of his dark blue Polo, and I climbed in, rolling my eyes. Could this day get any weirder? Once in the car, Alex huffed out a laugh. I silently fastened my seatbelt. I hoped he'd leave me alone.

"You sound so jaded. I only asked you to get in my car, not to have sex with me."

Charming, really.

"We hardly know each other, Alex. For all I know, you could very well be a serial killer, and getting me into your car is the first step in your diabolical plan. Kind of like Ted Bundy used to do with his victims."

"If you think I'm a serial killer, why did you get in without fighting me?"

I shrugged. At this point, I might as well die in an alley. Even if it wasn't a glamorous ending. "Yolo."

For the rest of the drive, Alex stayed silent, focused on the road ahead. I watched the landscape go by. Alex hadn't lied; it was a beautiful day. Under different circumstances, I might have enjoyed this. Alex parked his car and opened the door for me. I had to admit: his manners were impeccable. That didn't change that I still wanted to get as far away from him as possible.

We stopped in front of a small shop selling drinks and ice cream. Alex tried to convince me to have something. He was "inviting" me. In other words, this was a bribe. *Nice try, buddy, but I don't like sweets.* I shook my head. I just wanted to go home and wrap myself up in my blanket, but that was too much to ask.

"What do you want? Ice cream? Iced coffee?"

I kept shaking my head. Eventually, he'd figure out I wasn't interested. The woman behind the counter grew impatient while Alex continued to offer me drinks with unparalleled calm. I had to give him points for all his efforts.

It almost made me regret acting like a bitch. Almost.

"Bubble tea?"

I hesitated a second too long before shaking my head.

Alex noticed and smiled. "I knew it."

At this point, I let him. The woman prepared a bubble tea with milk and an iced coffee. When the drinks were ready, Alex beckoned me to follow him into the Botanical Gardens. Not knowing what to say, I followed in silence. A few meters further on, some tourists were taking photos, and I stopped to be a photobomb. A duck face and a triple chin later, I continued on my way. Alex looked at me, clearly confused. I shrugged.

"You gotta give them something to remember the locals."

"Didn't expect that."

I accepted the bubble tea he handed me. Bubble tea was my guilty pleasure. The only sweet drink I allow myself to have every now and then. Alright, most of the time.

"What?" I asked, taking a sip. "Because I'm so 'uptight', you think I can only take myself seriously?"

Alex was distraught. I didn't know why, but I loved seeing his increasing confusion. "Uptight girls like you aren't my type." *You'll see.* Okay, where was this pettiness coming from? Usually, I didn't care what people thought of me. But I was pretty, and rather hot. The only qualities I could give myself. *Uptight girls like you aren't my type. Yeah, right.* The way he'd said it had rubbed me the wrong way more than I cared to admit.

Alex rubbed the back of his head, not sure what to say. In this moment, he looked so young and open, something I didn't often see in him. "Um, well... yes."

It was true that I came across as uptight and a bit haughty, but that was just a facade. I liked to make jokes. I just didn't have my sidekick to join in my mischief anymore.

"Touché," I agreed, taking another sip. "You know, I wasn't always like this. I had to grow up very quickly when my brother fell ill, but I wasn't as serious and boring as I am now. I loved to make jokes, and to tell you the truth, my brother and I were a pretty hellish duo. My mother used to go crazy because of us. Sometimes we'd swap sugar and salt, or call strangers and try to sell them sex toys."

Wait a minute. Why am I telling him this? The whole point of coming here was to piss him off until he didn't want to see me anymore, not to tell him personal facts.

Alex sat down next to me, his eyes on the fountain. "I wish I could have met that part of you."

"People change, for better or for worse."

"I'll drink to that."

We toasted. It was weird, but for once, there was a kind of understanding between us. I just hoped it wouldn't become a habit.

CHAPTER 7

Alex

"How's my favourite redhead?"

As usual, Alex went into Elena's room to help with the lessons. Since the rehabilitation of her leg had begun, her presence at school had become irregular. Elena frowned when she saw Alex arrive. Despite the fact that he came several times a week, she still grumbled as soon as he arrived.

"I'm not a redhead! My hair is strawberry blonde. There's a difference."

Alex rolled his eyes. Was she ever going to be happy to see him? He decided to annoy her a bit more. "You're kidding, right? Your hair's orange. That means you're a redhead, honey."

Unlike what he expected, Elena placed her hands on her heart and pretended to be hurt. Alex smiled. Finally, she was playing along.

"Damn. Here you are, crushing my dreams. They say redheads don't have a soul."

"And you believe that?"

"No," she said in a detached tone.

"Then stop being so dramatic."

Alex took the textbooks out of his bag and sat down at the desk. She often grumbled about Alex's presence in her house, but she seemed to have understood that he would keep coming. At first, he'd come at her mother's request, but now he found himself intrigued by her. Sitting together in front of Elena's MacBook, Alex tried to load a search page. Nothing happened, and the progress cursor danced before their eyes.

Alex sighed. "I hate that coloured circle."

"Me too, dear."

He decided to be as dramatic as she was. "Look at that! We've got something in common. You'll see, we'll become friends because of the things we hate."

Elena raised an eyebrow. She tried to remain impassive, but the corners of her mouth lifted. Alex knew he was on the right track.

"I doubt we have anything in common."

Her attitude was a bit snobbish, but that was part of the deal. Alex understood her now. Beneath her cold, haughty demeanour, Elena hid a sensitive heart that had been wounded far too often. Her façade served as a shield. He had to keep up the momentum. Maybe he'd eventually find a crack in her defences.

"So, what do you hate?"

Elena blinked once before answering.

"I hate hypocrisy."

"Me too."

"And pity."

She wanted to send him a message; it was all too clear. Alex wasn't going to give up. He was so close. "Me too. See?

Lots of things in common."

Elena clicked her tongue. She'd hoped to find a flaw in Alex, but couldn't get through his good humour. He kind of liked this prickly side of her. She sighed and played along. In a voice lacking cheerfulness, she asked, "And what do you hate?"

Too many things.

"Cherry Coke and Vanilla Coke. It's disgusting."

"Are you kidding? Vanilla Coke is amazing!"

Alex couldn't help but wince, making her laugh. "I can't believe you like this crap. It tastes so chemical."

"And the taste of regular Coke isn't chemical?"

"Touché," he admitted with a sigh.

They turned their attention back to the screen, but the page still wouldn't load.

Alex closed the laptop and grabbed his notes. "Okay, it doesn't matter if the video doesn't load. I've already seen it, so I can explain. It's not that complicated."

"It explains radioactive radiation. What do you mean, it's not that complicated?" Elena frowned, her mouth set in a sceptical line. *Here's a crack.*

"You're having trouble with physics?"

"You don't?" she countered.

"No, I like it."

"Oh, you like science?"

Unlike many people, Alex liked anything to do with numbers. There were rules and logic, and anything with well-defined rules was predictable. And Alex liked predictable things. Logical things were easy to control. "Just physics and maths. Chemistry and biology are more abstract to me."

"For me, it's the opposite. I understand chemistry and

maths. The more I try to understand physics, the less I actually do."

Alex smiled at her and opened his notepad. He explained and helped her solve the exercises. As they studied, Alex understood how Elena had managed to be at the top of the class every year. She was a hard worker. Even when she didn't understand, she was stubborn and kept going until she got it right. Alex was impressed.

After a few hours, they finally stopped. Deserving a break, they went out for ice cream. He was surprised to see that Elena only took a scoop of vanilla ice cream and a bubble tea. It was a strangely basic choice of flavour for someone with such a grumpy disposition, but he decided not to comment. If he said anything, she'd probably smash her ice cream on his head.

They sat on a bench in the park to watch the ducks swim. Alex didn't quite understand why she enjoyed watching birds in a pond so much. After all, they did the same thing every day.

"Tell me about yourself."

Alex turned his head towards her, his palms getting sweaty. Her attention was still fixed on the water. It was the first time she'd shown any curiosity towards him. Now that Elena wanted to know more, he didn't know what to say. "What do you want to know?"

She shrugged. "Whatever you want. It feels like you know almost everything about me, even if I don't like that. But I don't know anything about you. Seems kind of unfair, don't you think?"

Elena turned back to him. Something in her blue eyes indicated that she had no intention of letting him off the hook. She was still struggling to hold his gaze, but she was trying.

Alex ran a hand through his hair, thinking. He'd wanted her to open up to him. Now she expected the same from him, and that wasn't part of the plan. What could he say that wasn't too personal, but personal enough for her to be satisfied with the answer? The only idea that came to him wasn't brilliant, not that he had a better option. Things had been so much simpler when she'd just ignored him.

"I had a massive crush on you in elementary school."

Elena choked on her bubble tea and quickly grabbed a tissue from her bag. She rubbed her nose, coughing. How such an elegant girl managed to get tea out of her nose was a mystery. Alex watched her, half disgusted and half amused. After a few seconds, she was back to her usual self. "I thought I wasn't your type."

"You were then."

A sardonic smile played on her lips. "You had shitty taste in girls, then."

"Why would you say that?"

"Of all the girls at school, I wasn't the prettiest or the most refined."

He couldn't contradict her. When they were in early elementary school, Elena was completely different from the person she was today. Her red hair was barely at shoulder length, and her eyes always sparkled with mischief. Back then, Alex thought she was so cool. Even if she looked more like a tomboy, her big, uneven-toothed smile had always charmed him. As a child, he'd been so shy, while she'd been a loud ray of sunshine. Times had changed, and they'd grown up. Now her teeth were perfectly aligned, but her warm smile was gone.

"True, but you were the coolest of them all. I was trying to impress you."

She giggled. "That's not how I remember it. One day you gave me a bracelet with shells, and the next you were throwing pencils at my face."

Alex laughed too. He'd been so clumsy with girls in elementary school. Several times he'd promised himself he'd confess his feelings to her, and each time he'd ended up chickening out. It was nice to think of those times when they'd been normal kids whom life hadn't destroyed yet, just like it was good to reconnect with someone he'd once cared so much about. Even if he had to keep his guard up. "I never claimed that my tactics to impress you would work."

She shook her head, but she was having fun. At least a little bit. "Thank you," she said, stuffing a spoonful of ice cream into her mouth. "I owe you."

"You don't owe me anything."

She pursed her lips. She really wanted to smash her ice cream on his head. He could see it in her eyes.

"You spent the whole afternoon explaining radiation to me and helping me solve the exercises for tomorrow's test, even though you didn't have to. I'm grateful."

"Then it's my pleasure."

Elena turned her attention back to the ducks. Sometimes he wondered what was going through her head. What was she thinking? How did she see the world? Elena looked back at him. Now that she'd woken up, she would keep digging.

"Why are you being so nice to me? From the start, I've been terrible towards you."

Alex smiled. She had been bitchy at times, which was a

breath of fresh air. Unlike a lot of people, Elena stood up to him. People tended to stay away from him, especially when they were wrong. Elena, even when she knew she was wrong, wouldn't budge. Was it ill will or stubbornness, Alex didn't know. If only she could look him in the eye when they argued. That was a worry for later.

"I'm not as nice as you think."

He wasn't going to pretend to be. There was a part of him he didn't want her to discover. A part of him was full of darkness. And if he could, he'd erase it from his memory forever. But under no circumstances could Elena know. It would taint the way she saw him, and he couldn't live with that. Elena looked at him as if she knew what he was thinking. It was impossible, yet the sincerity in her eyes gave him goosebumps. He could only hope she wouldn't figure him out.

"You are with me. Why?"

Because you're like me.

"Let's just say I think my presence can be good for you. I know you're going through a difficult time right now, and not so long ago, I went through some shit too. If I'd had a friend at my side, I think it would have been easier for me to get through it."

It might have helped him to take a better path than the one he had taken.

"You want to be my friend because you don't want me to be alone?"

"I also enjoy your company." Much more than he had expected.

"You really think so?"

Alex had managed to get through Elena's walls. He just

hoped she wouldn't get through his. She looked so vulnerable and hopeful. In this moment, she looked like the little girl he'd once adored, and Alex knew he was screwed. But what could he do when the fall was so easy?

"Of course. Let's be friends?"

Elena finally nodded. "I'd love to."

CHAPTER 8

Alex

The Fleureau house was unusually quiet. There was always noise coming from a TV or radio in one of the rooms. Today, there was nothing but absolute silence. Alex found Elena curled up on her bed. It was as if she were trying to make herself smaller, trying to disappear. Something bad must have happened. He put his hand on her shoulder, trying to get her attention. Elena startled and looked up at Alex, taking out her headphones. She hadn't heard him come in. Her cheeks were wet with tears. Alex had been right. Without thinking, he sat down beside her and took her in his arms. Elena burst into tears. He let her cry. It seemed that no one had been there for her for far too long.

"What happened?"

Elena clung to him like a lifeline. While Alex had promised himself not to get too attached to her, he was failing miserably. But none of his resolutions mattered when Elena was so close to him.

"Today marks three years since my brother died."

"I'm so sorry."

"Don't be. I should have died instead."

He felt his heart skip a beat. Alex knew Elena was struggling with her family situation and her accident, but she'd never talked about dying. He'd never realized how broken she was inside. Just like him.

"Don't say that. Your life is worth as much as anyone else's."

"Then why do I feel like I don't deserve to live?"

Her tears kept flowing. How could such a nice person feel so disposable? Alex tightened his embrace. If only he could make her understand how precious she was.

"Did your father tell you that?"

"I wonder if anyone would realize if I disappeared. No one would miss me."

"I'd miss you."

This new reality unnerved him. Alex mentally put the thought in a box—one he would open later.

"That's not true. There's nothing about me you could miss."

Alex didn't know what to do. Elena was desperate. When he'd been younger, Alex had found himself at the edge of the abyss, but his mother had been with him every step of the way. Between a father who didn't love her and a mother who never defended her, Elena was alone.

Alex stroked her hair. "You're my friend. Of course, I'd miss you. I know you can't believe this right now, but I'd be sad if anything happened to you."

Elena nestled her face in the crook of his neck, enveloping him in her sweet cherry blossom perfume. "They went to visit his grave. He didn't want me to come."

"You never had a chance to mourn his death. Your father never let you, did he?"

Elena had always taken the emotional and physical blows without ever having the chance to recover, believing she didn't deserve better. Alex couldn't imagine what it was like to be crushed relentlessly to the point of believing that his own life had no value whatsoever.

"Let's go."

Elena stepped back as if he'd just slapped her. "What?"

"Let's go and visit his grave."

Elena played with her hands, unsure what to do with herself. It was disturbing to see her like this. The girl who always looked so composed and stoic was a wreck. Alex wondered if it had been a mistake to suggest they go to the cemetery, but deep down, he knew it was what she needed. It was time she finally accepted her brother's passing. Otherwise, she'd never be able to move on.

"I'm not sure this is a good idea. He told me not to go."

"When are you going to start living for yourself?"

"You make it sound so easy."

"It's not easy."

Oh God, he knew. Alex hadn't had an easy time putting his life back together, but he was trying. Even if he struggled half the time. Life was a fucking mess, but it was necessary to move forward. He wanted her to move on and get better.

Elena looked up at him. For the first time, she was able to look him in the eye. She was ready. Alex stood up and handed her her jacket.

"I'm in my pyjamas."

"I'm not sure your brother would have minded. Let's go."

He expected her to find more excuses. She just rubbed her eyes before nodding. Alex ruffled her hair, and she swatted his hand away, a small smile on her lips.

Elena stayed silent on the drive there, twisting her fingers. When they arrived, Alex waited for her to react, but Elena was lost in her thoughts.

"Do you want me to wait here?"

Unlike what he had expected, she shook her head. In the distance, they could see Maura and Frank returning to their car. Once they were gone, Alex and Elena got out of the Polo. He put his hand on her back. She was trembling.

"Don't worry, princess, you're not alone."

***

Elena

Seeing my brother's grave had made me realize a few things. One, Mick was dead, and he would never come back to me. I had known this objectively, but seeing his grave three years later only confirmed what I'd been trying to ignore all this time. It made my sadness grow, something I'd thought impossible. Apparently, there's no limit to the amount of pain a human heart can feel. The only thing that changes is that you get used to it.

Two, I hadn't heard from my best friend in days. We'd never been the duo who sent messages to each other every day, but for the anniversary of my brother's death, I'd hoped for a little support from her. I hadn't heard from her in over a week. Yet she had seen my messages. Was this how our friendship was going to end? Ignoring each other? It sure looked that way.

Three, I didn't want to die. When I saw the grave, I had

prepared myself to feel even more guilty for having been the one who lived, but I hadn't. I was sure Alex's presence had a lot to do with it.

And four, I didn't want to lead the life I was leading now. But I was a coward. And so scared. My only ticket out had been taken away from me on the day of my accident. Now I was stuck in a life I didn't want, while being unable to get out of it. And that realization was the worst of all. The therapist was watching me, her lips pursed. I'd been sitting on her couch for half an hour without saying a word.

"Elena, I'm afraid you're shutting yourself off again. Please tell me how you feel?"

Sad? Distraught? Completely overwhelmed? So many options came to mind, but I didn't know which one to choose. I was so tired.

"What difference would it make if I stopped talking? It's not like my words have any value."

"That's where you're wrong. You're just as important as any other person."

I felt the emptiness in my chest deepen. Yes, I was as important as any other person, but no, my word wasn't worth shit. If someone could make my parents understand that, just like my brother (rest in peace), I, too, had a soul and feelings, and that I was worth as much as he was, I'd appreciate that. Except that nobody would do it. That was the reality I found myself stuck in.

"I don't feel like a person. I don't even feel human anymore. Just an indelible stain people are trying to get rid of at all costs. So what does it matter?"

Stacy smiled, tears shining in her eyes. I had just insinuated that my life was worthless and that I could probably disappear without anyone noticing my absence. Why did she look so relieved?

"This is the first time you've been honest in a session. You're finally ready to get better."

I didn't feel ready at all. As always, it felt like everything in my life was going wrong, and I couldn't keep my head above water. I was sinking, again and again. I was used to this sinking feeling by now. And I never hit bottom. That, too, had become familiar.

"I don't feel ready."

"But you are."

***

Kelsey walked into my room and plopped down on the couch. No hello, no kiss, nothing. She looked like she'd come here to talk business. She was usually so happy and bubbly, I hardly recognized her. I felt like I was facing a wall.

"Where have you been? I've been trying to reach you for over a week."

"I was busy." Her voice was cold. As if she'd just recited a text she'd learned by heart.

I frowned. What was wrong with her?

"Busy with what? What could be more important than the third anniversary of Mick's death?"

"Me," she replied without blinking.

"I'm not sure I understand."

"I needed time for myself."

"And I needed you!"

For three years, I'd kept my mouth shut; now I really

needed my best friend. Her gaze turned cold. She was going to leave me, too, wasn't she?

"You're not the only one who lost someone important that day, Lena. I needed some time for myself—I still do. I think it's for the best if we go our separate ways."

"What are you saying?"

"We're no good for each other. I don't think we should be friends anymore."

Kelsey left the room without looking back. My heart was heavy, but there were no more tears. I was too tired to cry.

***

Alex

Elena stopped in front of Alex, holding a bouquet of yellow tulips. She stood as straight as an arrow, determined. Alex raised an eyebrow. He closed his locker and gave her his full attention. The last time he'd seen her had been when they'd visited her brother's grave. That event had changed her. Something was different about her, but he couldn't put his finger on it.

"You got a secret admirer?"

Elena frowned, confused. "What? No, why would you think that?"

Alex pointed to the flowers with his chin. For some weird reason, she flushed. *Adorable.* Some students looked at them curiously before moving on. Granted. They formed a rather unusual duo.

"Oh, uhm... they're for you actually."

Alex chuckled. He'd clearly misheard. She frowned even more, clearly offended. Maybe he'd heard her right, after all. Elena threw the flowers at his face. She raised her head before heading off in the opposite direction. Alex had to do his best to catch up. She quickened her pace and exited the building.

"Elena, wait! Don't be mad."

"Forget it."

"Thanks for the flowers."

She turned back to him. So that was what had changed; Elena was getting bolder. She still had a long way to go, but she seemed to have decided not to let others walk over her so easily. "Is this a joke?"

"What? No!"

"You don't seem happy to receive flowers." She crossed her arms, lifting her chin.

God, she was infuriating, and yet he loved it.

"Why would you want to give me flowers?"

Her facade cracked. "They were pretty..."

"You... gave me flowers because you thought they were pretty."

Elena jumped from one foot to the other. She'd looked tough for a second; now she just looked like a cream puff. Alex felt like wrapping her in a blanket and feeding her ice cream. *Wait, that's weird.* He shook his head.

"Why are you being so nice to me? I don't deserve it."

"I like you, so get used to it."

She sat down on a bench in the park opposite the school. Kelsey walked past them without glancing in their direction. At first, he thought she hadn't seen them, but seeing Elena's face scrunch together, he knew something was up. Just as he turned back to her to ask the question, she spoke.

"Alex, do you think I'm a bad person?"

"No, I don't. Why would you think that?"

"You think I'm selfish?"

"You are. We all are. That's what makes us human."

"Am I too selfish?"

Where was this coming from? Sure, Elena could be difficult from time to time, and sure, it was hard to get through to her because she was stubborn and refused to let people in. But of all her flaws, selfishness was not a word that came to mind when he thought of her. Elena was always trying to please others to the point of not living for herself. Alex crossed his arms.

"Okay, what's going on?"

For a moment, she didn't speak. Alex waited; no sound came. He decided to push her a little. She was the kind of person who sometimes needed a push.

"Elena, talk to me."

She looked up at him and sighed. While she told him, Alex pinched the bridge of his nose. At first, he'd judged Kelsey while giving her the benefit of the doubt. In the end, he'd been right. She was a pest. Not having those kind of people in her life was the best thing that could happen to Elena, even if it hurt her.

"I think it's time for you to spend your life with people who care about you."

"I guess I'll always be alone, then."

"Nah, you got me."

Elena rested her head on his shoulder. "Poor you."

CHAPTER 9

Elena

I bundled up in my burgundy coat and mustard scarf and hurried outside to wait for Alex. After a few minutes, the Polo pulled up in front of the house. My friend raised an eyebrow when he found me outside. He was dressed in faded jeans and one of his eternal hoodies. This one was dark blue, like his car.

"You could have stayed inside. I wasn't going to forget you."

"What if we went to your place instead?"

I could see the hesitation in his eyes. Maybe I shouldn't have asked that.

"Why? This place is fine, too."

"I don't feel like staying here today," I admitted.

My parents had gotten into a fight just a few hours earlier, and I'd rather not be around when my father returned from God knows where.

On the other hand, seeing Alex's wary look, had I made a mistake by asking him to go to his house? Maybe he didn't want me to meet his family? That would be absurd. I already knew them. Maybe he'd prefer our friendship and the rest of his life to stay separated. But were we real friends then? As always, my thoughts spiralled out of control. One negative idea came after another. Alex put a hand on my shoulder, snapping me out of it.

"I know what you're thinking. Don't make that face. We'll go if you want."

I shook my head and took a step back. What had I been thinking? I shouldn't have left my room. "You don't want me in your house. I won't insist."

Alex rolled his eyes in exasperation. "Let's go."

I didn't know where he found all his patience. Sometimes it was crumbling. Still, Alex held out.

He headed for his car, then turned to make sure I was following him. Seeing that I hadn't moved, he sighed and ran a hand through his already tousled hair, making him look like Stiles Stilinski. "Do you know what you want?"

I frowned. "I know you don't want me to come to your home. Forget it, I won't ask again."

Alex stopped in front of me and put his face right up to mine. He looked annoyed. Unable to hold his gaze, I lowered my eyes.

"Either you get in the car of your own free will, or I'll put you in it."

I huffed. He wouldn't do it, would he? I was weak, and he knew it well enough. "You wouldn't dare."

"Wanna try?"

I hurried into the Polo and avoided looking in his direction. The landscape flashed before me as he drove, but I couldn't focus on what was in front of me. Maybe my biggest talent was screwing things up. Why did I always have to ruin everything? It was at times like these that I wondered if Alex regretted coming to visit me in the hospital. If he'd known I was like this, would he have insisted we become friends?

"Stop brooding like that."

His perceptiveness was terrifying.

"How do you know what I'm thinking?"

"You look sad. I didn't mean to make you feel unwelcome. I'm just not used to having people over."

He parked in front of his house and got out. I followed Alex into the house like a lost puppy. I couldn't even remember the last time I'd been here. We entered the kitchen and came face to face with Lexi, his mom. Her big green eyes widened as she realized I was here, right in front of her.

"Oh Lena, it's good to see you again!"

Lexi hugged me as she had done so many times before. For a few seconds, I hesitated to hug her back but finally gave in and returned the embrace. There was a time when I thought of her as an aunt, back when she came to us almost weekly. Things had changed since then. Her eyes were sad when she looked at me now. Since my brother had died, my mother had drowned herself in her work, and Lexi had stopped coming over. Was it because my mother had turned her back on her, or vice versa? I could read the pity she felt for me, as if I were a broken little thing she hadn't been able to put back together. She was right. In a way, I was disappointed with her for not coming to see me these last three years. But when I look back at how badly things turned out for my mother and me, maybe it was for the best.

"How beautiful you've become! A real woman."

She rubbed her wet eyes and smiled. I smiled back. Her presence made me strangely uncomfortable. It had been too long. I couldn't remember how I'd been with this woman before my life turned upside down. Out of the corner of my eye, I saw Alex watching us, eyebrows furrowed. It was strange to think that once, Lexi had been so close to us while Alex and I barely spoke, and now it was the other way around.

"Mom, have you seen my dance leggings?"

A teenager with dark brown hair like Alex's entered the room but stopped dead in her tracks when she noticed me. They both had trouble getting used to me being here. I silently watched the girl. I'd seen her before, but I couldn't put my finger on it.

"I can't believe you're here!" the girl yelled, jumping towards me. "I've been dreaming of meeting you for ages."

Wait, what?

"Do I know you?" I asked, uncomfortable.

"This is Audrey, my sister," Alex told me, twirling his car key on his finger.

I could usually remember the faces of people I met, but I couldn't remember hers. She'd grown so much.

"I was going to join your dance class, but since you've temporarily stopped..."

Audrey didn't finish her sentence, probably not wanting to make me feel any more uncomfortable. Her words gave me a twinge of sadness. Every day, I tried to occupy my mind as much as possible so as not to have to face the truth. I took a deep breath and forced myself to grin. Audrey quickly changed the subject.

"Are you as flexible as they say?"

I couldn't help laughing and nodding. Her carefree vibe was refreshing. "Want to see?"

The girl nodded back enthusiastically. Keeping my feet on the ground, I let my upper body move backward until I could touch the floor with my hands.

"She has no spine," Audrey exclaimed.

"I can't decide whether I'm disgusted or impressed," Alex added.

***

"Can you teach me a choreography?"

Before I had the time to reply, Alex was already reprimanding his sister. His gaze was stern. Being a big brother suited him like a glove. It made him endearing and even more attractive.

"Audrey, leave her alone. You know she's still recovering from her surgery."

"I don't mind," I reassured him, shrugging. It gave me a good excuse to dance, and it allowed me to make a fourteen-year-old happy.

The look on his face told me that he wanted to contradict me. Instead, Alex sighed but nodded. "Don't force it. Okay?"

"Okay!" Audrey gushed. "Teach me something badass!"

If only I could be as carefree as she was. My life had taken a wrong turn when I was her age. Everything that had happened before seemed like fragments of another life. Another me.

"What do you think of *The Feels* from Twice? It's not that complicated, but it's fun."

She nodded with so much enthusiasm that I feared she might lose her head.

God, it felt so good to be dancing again. My movements were not as precise as they used to be, but for the first time in months, I was dancing. Even if I could only do part of the steps, it was already more than I'd hoped for. Audrey and I spent over an hour going over the steps of the first verse and chorus.

Just as I was about to go on, Alex put his hand on my shoulder. "That's enough."

"But we aren't done yet!"

"You have all the time in the world to teach her the rest. You've done enough for today."

I crossed my arms over my chest, standing as straight as I could. I know I said the big brother image was great on him, but not when it was directed at me. "It's not for you to decide."

Alex and I stared at each other for a few seconds. His gaze was too strong, too intense. I lowered my eyes after a few interminable seconds. I really needed to learn to hold his gaze.

"True, but you know I'm right."

I wanted to fight back, just because I could, but Alex was right. Now that I was standing still, my knee was a little sore. Still, it was nothing to worry about. I nodded.

At suppertime, Lexi invited me to eat with them. I tried to back out, but when Alex and Audrey started to insist, I couldn't refuse. It was nice to eat with someone other than your reflection in the kitchen window. Lexi placed a large dish of pasta carbonara on the table, and it smelled divine. She grabbed my plate.

"Tell me when."

She began to fill the plate. Several times, she looked up at me until I signalled it was enough. Alex's brows went up.

"Are you going to eat all that?"

"You didn't really think I survived forty hours of dance a week by eating salad, did you?"

Alex laughed, and Audrey helped herself to more pasta. When the meal was over, I followed Alex upstairs. Once we were in his bedroom, Alex closed the door. I took the opportunity to look around, but noticed how sober it was. Even Mick's room seemed livelier, while no one had gone in there in years. The double bed was made without any crinkles like the ones made in the army. The room was perfectly tidy and had almost nothing that made it personal. The walls were a bland taupe colour, and a TV hung against the wall. Alex's room looked more like a guest room than the bedroom of a lively young man. The only thing that showed there was anyone living here was the PS4 plugged into the TV and an iPhone charger on one of the bedside tables. I sat on the edge of the bed, afraid to undo it.

"I didn't know what to expect, but it wasn't this," I confessed.

I'd expected a room like my big brother's: an unmade bed, dirty socks lying on the floor, and maybe a box of tissues on the nightstand. There was none of that here.

Alex sat next to me, smiling awkwardly. His cheeks had turned a pretty pink. "I know. My room's kind of lacklustre.

The silence in the room made me uncomfortable. Now that I was here, I didn't know what to say. How had an eighteen-year-old guy come to this?

Alex was the first to break the silence. "Tell me about your brother."

Alex was the first person apart from Stacey to ask me

about Mick. At first, I didn't know what to do; I didn't know what to say. I'd avoided talking about him for so long. Dealing with his passing was still something I had to learn. Alex sat down against the headboard of the bed, and I followed his movement. Mick...

"I don't know if you would have liked him," I admitted with a smile. "He was sweet, but very energetic. So outgoing that being around him was sometimes tiring."

Alex was much more at ease in groups than I was, but my brother had been a completely different kind of extrovert. He filled in every one of my shortcomings. When Mick was with me, I felt like a better version of myself—a prouder version. Now that he was gone, it was as if the best part of me had gone with him. Alex motioned for me to continue.

"He was funny, and he was my favourite person. You see, we always knew he was my father's favourite child, but Mick... he never let that hurt me. He always put me first, always stood by me, always made me feel loved, even with the parents we had."

Losing him was like losing my sun. My throat tightened. I took a deep breath and hugged one of the pillows to my chest. Alex's perfume clouded my mind, slightly easing the pain.

"Tell me something else."

Breaking the invisible barrier between us, Alex placed a warm palm on my arm.

"Mick always took me out for hamburgers, even though I wasn't allowed to eat them. Because of ballet, I had to watch my food intake very closely, which I don't do anymore, but it was very hard to be on a diet every day of my life. So he would secretly bring me hamburgers from time to time. And he'd bring chips back to my room when no one was looking."

"I'm sorry you lost him. Your brother seemed like an amazing person."

I bit my thumbnail as I looked out the window at the passing cars. The world around us seemed to move at an entirely different tempo. "He was, and I miss him terribly. I don't know if heaven exists, but believing he's somewhere up there helps me accept that he's gone."

Even though this room seemed empty, there was something about it that made me feel at ease. Sort of.

"Can I ask you a question?"

Alex beckoned me to speak. Now that I'd bared my heart to him, he didn't seem so intimidating anymore. Although he often hid it, Alex was a very empathetic person.

"Why did you hesitate when I asked you to come?"

"Uhm... I haven't brought anyone home in what must be seven years. Actually, I don't let anyone into my room when I'm here."

That explained why his mother and sister had been so shocked when we'd arrived. The more time I spent with Alex, the more mysterious he was. Yet, as a rule, it's supposed to be the other way around. With Alex, I felt that as soon as we tried to get closer to him, we were facing a wall. Not a wall made of cardboard—a real fortress wall, ready to take any attack from the outside. I couldn't help but wonder what was hidden behind those. After all, he already knew everything about me.

"Why?"

"I don't like it when people get too close to me. It makes me feel like I'm suffocating."

"Be honest. Does my presence here bother you?"

I was afraid of what he would say. Alex meant a lot to me,

even though I often felt I cared more about him than he did about me. Just the thought of being a burden to him made me want to vomit.

"No, it doesn't. I feel surprisingly calm." His face was more serene than usual.

"So you've never brought a girl here before?"

"Never," he said, shaking his head.

Impossible.

"What did you do then with your girlfriends? Didn't they ever wonder why they couldn't come to your place?"

Alex rubbed the back of his head, looking embarrassed. It was strangely adorable. I had to do my best not to pinch his cheeks. "This may surprise you, but I've never been in a relationship."

I was at a loss for words. Alex was known to be a fan favourite. The fact that he'd never been serious seemed implausible. Even playboys fall in love, right? I shook my head. "You're lying."

"I'm not. I've never been with anyone."

"How is this possible? I mean, you have a certain reputation, you know."

Alex raised an eyebrow, amused. He flicked me on the forehead. "Are you really asking me why I sleep around so much?"

Oh, well, that was a pretty straightforward way of putting it. His outspokenness never ceased to impress me.

"I guess so. You never met someone you liked?"

"Yes, but not enough to want more."

Though he smiled at me, there was a lot of doubt in his eyes. For the first time since we'd been hanging out, Alex was about to share a part of himself with me. I nodded in encouragement.

"I'm afraid of getting attached to someone, just as I'm afraid of losing my self-control in my relationship. If I'm alone, I can't hurt anyone, just as no one can hurt me. And even if I did find someone, that person would eventually leave once they got to know the real me."

My God, how I understood him.

CHAPTER 10

Elena

Unlike what I had planned, I spent my Friday evening at Alex's. I thought he'd want to avoid having me over, but he'd been the one inviting me to spend the evening with him.

Leaning against the counter, I watched Alex as he sliced a cucumber. He'd decided to make homemade hamburgers, something I never ate at home. Mom didn't like wasting much time cooking after work, so she just made quick and simple dishes. It was strangely domestic having Alex cooking for us.

"So not only are you smart and handsome, but you also know how to cook," I observed. "Assets truly aren't distributed equally at birth."

This man is too perfect. I was beginning to feel useless next to him. Apart from sports and studying, I had nothing to measure up. Alex raised an eyebrow.

"Instead of complaining, why don't you help me?"

"I can't cook."

Alex passed me a bamboo board, a knife, and some tomatoes.

"It's never too late to learn. Dice the tomatoes."

"Yes, sir."

I cut the first tomato as best I could and made a face at the result. Each piece of tomato had a different size and shape. Cutting the second tomato, I cut myself, like the clumsy idiot that I am. Alex looked up at me, surprised.

"Did you just manage to hurt yourself by cutting a tomato?"

"I told you I'm bad at cooking!" I exclaimed, pouting.

I sat on the countertop with my finger bandaged, leaving Alex in charge of the food. Whenever he wasn't looking, I pecked at the salad plate, stealing cucumber slices. At one point, Alex realized that the amount of vegetables was decreasing. He grabbed the salad bowl and put it out of my reach.

"If you don't cook, you don't peck."

I sighed. "I'd better find a man who knows how to cook, or I'll starve."

"Don't worry, I've got several recipes up my sleeve."

"What?"

His words caught me off guard. I couldn't answer anything coherently. He didn't mean what he'd just said, did he?

"You and I are annoying, so I don't think we'll find anyone who'll want us for a lifetime. Might as well stay together."

I knew he was joking, yet I couldn't help wondering if he meant what he said. Knowing Alex, he probably did.

"You think I'm annoying?"

"Yes. You think I'm annoying, too."

Those words were like a slap to the face. Of course, I knew I was annoying, but hearing him say it out loud hurt.

"Not really," I mumbled.

It was true that I didn't like the fact that he'd inserted himself into my daily life without giving me much of a choice. Yet I'd come to enjoy his company. When he wasn't making lame jokes, Alex was kind and thoughtful. I didn't like the fact that he found me annoying. As always, it made me feel like I wasn't good enough.

Alex put down his knife, focusing his attention on me. "I've upset you. Why?"

How could he not understand? "You think I'm a pain in the ass. Why?"

"Because you won't let me into your life."

I laced my fingers, looking into his eyes. He held my gaze with such force that I had to resist lowering my eyes. I had a bad feeling about the rest of the evening. But I had to know. "All right, let's be honest. If I tell you my most painful secrets, will you do the same?"

"I don't have secrets," he replied.

Too quick, too defensive. He was lying. I was stupid, but not *that* stupid.

"And you said you didn't like hypocrisy."

Alex clenched and unclenched his fist. I had gotten under his skin. Usually, nothing could disturb his cool; now cracks were becoming visible in his facade. I'd finally gotten a glimpse of the person behind the pretence, and I wasn't sure I liked what I was seeing.

Alex was a mess, just like me. But he and I had changed in different ways. Life had made me a scared, withdrawn girl. Alex seemed to have a feral beast locked inside him. And when it broke free of its chains… I didn't dare think about it. I'd heard many whispers in the school corridors that Alex had once again lost his temper and fought someone to a bloody pulp. They said that he became wild when anger overwhelmed him. The more time I spent with Alex, the more I realized how little I knew about him. The reasonable part of me whispered to let it go. Yet I couldn't listen to myself. How was I supposed to trust Alex and build a friendship with him if he wouldn't talk to me?

"What made you this way?"

Alex crossed his arms. "What way?"

"You know..." I began, twisting my fingers. "Slightly fucked up?"

"You think I'm fucked up?"

The air around us became heavier. More dangerous.

"Aren't we all a bit messed up inside?"

"You're probably right."

He went back to his vegetables, like I would give up.

"What happened to you?" I asked in a small voice.

That was the last straw. Alex turned to me, jaw clenched. "Does it matter?"

Alex was becoming aggressive. A dangerous gleam danced in his eyes, and my hands began to tremble. I'd seen that kind of look countless times; it had often been directed at me. I also knew how things could go wrong in the blink of an eye if I wasn't careful.

And yet, I couldn't help but say, "Yes, it does."

"Let it go!" he snapped, slamming his palm on the worktop.

Feeling my fear creep up on me, I decided to drop it and step back. Whatever he was hiding, it wasn't worth the risk.

"Do you think you could ever trust me enough to tell me about it?"

Staring into space, Alex lifted his chin. "It's not about trust. I don't want my past to influence your image of me."

CHAPTER 11

Elena

Alex: *I'm going to the basketball field. You coming?*
Elena: *Why not* ┐(͡° ͜ʖ ͡°)┌

I threw on a pair of grey jogger pants, a white sports top, and red Supra Skytops. What can I say? I just love sports. And now that I was finally allowed to move, I certainly wasn't going to waste the opportunity. Basketball wouldn't give me the same feeling of well-being as when I'd put on my pointe shoes, but I couldn't complain. Without wasting any time, I grabbed my keys and headed for the field.

The weather was strangely warm and sunny for an autumn day. After a twenty-minute walk, I spotted the basketball field. Several guys had already arrived. Mid-stretch, Alex waved and smiled at me. Not knowing his friends well, I positioned myself next to him, slightly behind. I wasn't as good at socializing as he was. I recognized Lucas and Yves. They were on the same soccer team as Alex. They smiled at me, although they were wondering why I was there.

"Where's Tiago? We haven't seen him in a while," Lucas asked.

"At Kelsey's," Alex replied, lacing up his shoes.

"Is our Wonder Boy finally getting serious?"

"Don't be ridiculous," Yves said. "He'll get bored, he always does. Especially when it's the girl who's chasing him."

I felt a little sick. Should I tell Kelsey? After all, she had been my friend for years. Then I remembered that I didn't owe her anything. She was a big girl. She'd do fine without me.

Yves shrugged. "Same for Alex. We all wonder how long he'll play before he tires of Elena."

Well, damn. Lucas gave me a panicked look, and Yves remembered that I was among them. He looked down. "Sorry."

"It's alright. I wonder the same thing."

Alex glared at me. I raised my hands in question. I'd been wondering for weeks when he'd get enough of me. I wasn't an interesting person.

"What?"

"Don't put yourself down like that."

Two other guys named John and Gauthier joined the group. If Gauthier was more or less ignoring me, John kept watching me with a mischievous gaze. His eyes lingered a little too long on my bare stomach and breasts before raising his head and smiling. He was quite handsome with his tanned skin and short, curly hair, but the way he looked at me as if I were nothing but a piece of meat was unsettling.

Yves created the teams: Yves, Gauthier, and I versus Alex, John, and Lucas. John stood next to me and put his hand on my lower back, where my skin was bare. *Just great.* The voice inside my head was screaming for him to let go. Not wanting to make a scene, I smiled.

"Do you want me to explain how to play?" he whispered in my ear.

"Don't get the wrong idea, I know how to play," I replied, stepping back slightly.

As soon as the game started, I pounced on the ball. God, it felt good to be moving again. My knee was still a little sore, but nothing crazy. Alex and John were leading the game, scoring the most goals. After several missed throws from my team, the winning team gave us a break that wasn't deserved.

Alex jogged over to me and patted my back with a smile. I hate to lose, but I didn't stand a chance against two guys who were nearly a hundred ninety centimetres. One of them grinned at me from across the field.

"I don't like the way John looks at me," I whispered.

He'd been giving me hungry eyes for a while. Was it because I was the only girl on the field or because he liked me? I couldn't tell. Either way, it made me feel uneasy. I couldn't help wishing he'd look away.

Alex glanced in his friend's direction and sighed. "I don't like it either."

I turned back to Alex, flashing my teeth. "Want to give me a hickey? Maybe he'll stop."

Alex rolled his eyes, exasperated. "Where do you get your crazy ideas?"

"I'm just saying, it could work."

My friend ruffled my hair before handing me a bottle of water, which I accepted gladly. "Don't tempt me."

My cheeks turned crimson. He was joking, right? Alex moved closer to me, and his breath tickled the skin of my neck. Oh dear, was he really going to do it? Seeing that I was speechless, Alex pinched my cheek, laughing.

"Adorable."

We started another game of basketball, and this time Alex and I were on the same team. Throughout the game, it was as if we were on the same wavelength. All it took was one look or nod to get our defence and offense on track. One score followed another.

"Alex and Lena are a power duo." Lucas laughed.

I couldn't argue with him. Alex and I were pretty strong together. John stuck to me to try and get the ball back. For a little while, I tried to get away from him so I could pass the ball to Alex. Until I felt a hand graze my butt. I dropped the ball and faced him. This time, I'd had enough. The hand on the small of my back wasn't great, but the hand grazing lower? No.

"Touch me one more time and I'll punch you."

The scumbag had the nerve to laugh, too. "Don't be so uptight."

My blood ran cold. I took the ball back and threw it against his face as hard as I could. John grunted in pain.

"It's called sexual touching," I said, crossing my arms. "When a woman says no, it's no, you dick."

"Come on, just look at you! Here you are playing all haughty, but you're just a tease."

Alex walked over. Now I understood why so many people were afraid of him. Not only was he taller than most people, but his gaze was also chilling. In this moment, it was clear that Alex would not hesitate to go for his throat. Although it wasn't me he was sizing up, I felt like running away.

"Let's rephrase that. Next time you touch her, *I* will punch you. That clearer?"

"Whatever. She's not worth it."

Without warning, John left the field. Yves, Lucas, and Gauthier gave us questioning looks, but didn't dare get any closer to Alex than necessary. I jumped from one foot to the other. So... Alex had defended me, which was kind of nice. Not many people did, so I was grateful for that. But he still seemed so upset, I didn't know what to do. After a few seconds, Alex turned to me. All traces of danger had disappeared.

"I'll take you home."

"All right, then. To the Batmobile!"

Alex sniffed. He was *so* judging me.

"What?"

"Oh... you prefer the Alexmobile?" I asked. "My bad."

"You are a strange one, aren't you?"

"Yep!"

He patted me on the head and headed for the parking lot. I followed him and climbed into the Polo. How was it possible that, even though I hardly knew him, I'd never felt more myself than when Alex was with me? I watched his profile as he drove. His skin was glowy, and a strange desire to stroke his cheek went through my mind. No wonder all the girls were falling for him. I felt like my hormones were boiling over when he was near.

"Thank you."

"What for?"

"For standing up for me, even though he's your friend."

"Hardly a friend. He's a jerk."

"Thank you anyway."

"You're welcome. It's my pleasure to help pretty damsels in distress."

I rolled my eyes and smiled. Damsel in distress. *My ass.*

"Don't exaggerate. I was doing fine. I'm a ninja!"

Alex laughed. The atmosphere between us was so light, like nothing had happened. It was a nice change to have a friend who had my back and participated in my stupid jokes. I hadn't had someone like that in my life for ages.

"Remind me never to make you angry."

Sugar by Maroon 5 was playing on the radio. Instinctively, I raised my hand to turn it up, then changed my mind. Out of the corner of my eye, I saw Alex smile. He turned the volume up.

"I didn't know you were a fan."

They'd been my favourite band for years. I knew the song by heart, but I kept from singing in front of Alex. We weren't that close yet.

"What can I say? I'm full of surprises."

"I can see that. A real Kinder Surprise."

I turned back to him, one hand on my heart, falsely offended. "Are you mocking me?"

"I don't know. You tell me."

I huffed. "Just to be clear: I'm smarter than you think."

"And pretty, and talented, and badass. I know you are. You're perfect."

Surprisingly, his voice wasn't dripping with sarcasm. He was good at talking shit.

"Again, I don't know if you're mocking me or not."

"Well, if you're as smart as you say you are, you'll figure it out for yourself.

I loved bickering with him. A carefree feeling came over me when we acted like children. With Alex, I rediscovered a version of myself I thought I'd lost for good.

"If I can interpret this the way I want to, I'd say you're

completely under my spell. It's better for my ego."

Instead of dropping me off in front of my house, Alex drove towards the Botanical Gardens.

"Where are we going?"

My friend flashed me a cheeky smile before pulling over. "To the Partea. I think we deserve a treat."

Was that little coffee shop becoming our place? Passing through the park's water jets, I ran my hand through the water, splashing Alex in the face.

"Are you serious?"

I did it again. Alex imitated my gesture, sending lots of water into my face. Without giving me time to retaliate, Alex lifted me up and went through the jets. In less than two seconds, we were soaked from head to toe. He set me down on the ground and winked. I pouted.

"That's not fair!"

I looked up at him. This was the first time we were standing so close, and now that Alex was within arm's length of me, I found myself unable to look away. Droplets glistened in his long eyelashes, and the late afternoon sun made the green of his irises warmer. His white T-shirt clung to his skin, leaving little imagination of what lay beneath that thin layer of fabric. Of course, I knew Alex was muscular. When he wasn't playing soccer or sparring in a boxing ring, he spent his time on a basketball court. Still, having him so close made me dizzy. I thought it was just me who felt this strange energy, but when I looked at Alex's eyes, I knew I wasn't the only one. His pupils were dilated, and his breathing was faster than usual. I put my hand on his cheek, and Alex intertwined his fingers with mine. We stood there for a moment, soaking up each other's presence. Was it normal to want to kiss your friend so badly? His gaze dropped to my chest, and he looked away.

"Let's go home."

"All right."

I couldn't help but feel a bit disappointed. The attraction between us had seemed almost palpable, so why was he pulling away so suddenly? Alex pulled a black sweater from his trunk and handed it to me.

"I'm not cold," I said.

"Please, put it on."

"But why?"

He still didn't look my way. What was he thinking? I thought we'd had a moment. Maybe I'd been the only one who felt it.

"Your top has become see-through."

Oh...

"Don't look then."

Alex fixed his eyes on mine, avoiding at all costs looking any lower. His intense gaze made me feel vulnerable and desired at the same time. I swallowed. Alex was my friend. I had to keep that in mind.

"Princess, I'm still a guy."

"You find me attractive?"

Alex nodded, which was surprising. I thought that since I was in the friendzone, my appearance would have no impact on him.

"Every guy with eyes is attracted to you."

"I thought I wasn't your type?"

A small smirk appeared on his lips. "That was a lie, of course."

"So you *are* under my spell."

I liked to annoy him. That was why his next words caught me off guard.

"Obviously."

This revelation made me feel strangely euphoric. I'd never really cared what boys thought of me. Still, it mattered to me what Alex thought. A lot. I grabbed his sweater. There was no way I was admitting this to him. I lifted my head. "Glad we got that straight.

"Shut up."

CHAPTER 12

Elena

Several weeks had passed, and I found myself more and more often at the Niessens' house. It was still strange to be in a house where people talked to each other, but it was a kind of strangeness I was beginning to associate with my everyday life. A daily routine that I cherished far more than I dared admit. If only I had known how fragile this new normal was.

I was scrolling on Alex's phone, looking for movie ideas on his Disney+ account, when a message from Tiago popped up. I tried to swipe away the message, ending up opening the inbox unintentionally.

"Oh shit!"

I wanted to close the messages, but the content caught my eye.

> Tiago: *There's a party, are you coming tonight?*
> Alex: *Some other time*
> Tiago: *I convinced Melissa to come*
> Alex: *Okay, just let me cancel my plans*
> Tiago: *See you*

Disappointment washed over me. What an idiot I'd been to think Alex wanted to spend time with me for real. As if he, Alex Niessen, the flirt and the heartthrob, wanted us to be friends. I'd fallen for it like the fool I was. I should have learned my lesson, that it was too good to be true. I was never anyone's first choice. I wasn't even a second choice—I was just needlessly filling space. *What an idiot!* I felt my eyes prickle, tears about to escape. It seemed my heart was just made to be broken, over and over again, never giving me time to pick up the pieces. I grabbed my things and got up to leave the room when Alex walked in.

"Where are you going?" asked the stranger in front of me.

Because deep down, that was all he was. I lowered my eyes. I wasn't going to give him the satisfaction of seeing me cry. He didn't need to know I was broken. Hell, he didn't need to know he was the one who had broken me this time.

"I'm going home. Where else would I go?"

My tone was more biting than I'd intended. I could no longer keep my emotions in check. I had to get out of here before I collapsed.

"We were going to work on our physics project."

"I'll send you my part."

"You suck at physics."

"I'll manage."

Every time I moved towards the door, Alex blocked my path. "Why are you suddenly trying to run away from me?"

I hoped he would let me go, and that I'd never have to see him again. "You were going to find a way to get rid of me tonight anyway, so I'd better go."

"How do you know that?"

So he wasn't even trying to deny it. That hurt. I took a

breath, trying to keep the tears at bay, and lifted my head toward him. I handed him back his phone and knew I was in for a rough time if I didn't leave now.

A dangerous gleam danced in Alex's eyes. "You really can't stop digging, even when I tell you not to."

His voice was deeper than usual, his tone more than accusatory. As much as I wanted to be as far away from him as possible, I couldn't let him walk all over me. All my life, people had stepped on me, forgetting that I was a human being like any other. I'd had enough.

"It was an accident. I didn't want to see the message."

"Stop lying!"

He was accusing me of lying when he had intended to abandon me with a lame excuse? I felt like murder. Except I wasn't the only one about to explode.

"You're a hypocrite, Elena. You always pretend to be understanding, but the truth is you're just like everyone else. You don't respect other people's privacy."

Without realizing what I was doing, I slapped him across the face. Alex was unable to react, caught off guard. My palm throbbed, but I ignored it.

"And when did you ever respect mine?" I burst into tears. "You never gave me a choice; you never asked me for anything. You're an asshole and a liar, and I never want to see you again!"

This wasn't fair. Why was I just an object to everyone? For the first time, I was finally seeing Alex's true face, and I hated it. I had to leave.

"Fucking hell!" shouted Alex.

Cold fear made my body turn to stone. More than ever, I hoped to disappear for good.

Alex

"Fucking hell!" shouted Alex, beside himself.

In a fit of rage, he struck the wall. Alex felt the pain in his hand but ignored it. He turned back to Elena to tell her a piece of his mind. His heart sank when he saw her petrified. Her eyes wide open, Elena was frozen in fear. His anger went up in smoke, and guilt took over. She wasn't like the others. Elena had a history of violence in her own home. Without thinking, Alex had become the kind of person who had traumatized her all these years.

"Hey, it's just me."

He took a step towards her, waking her from her torpor. Elena took a few steps back, putting as much distance between herself and him as possible. Alex felt sadness wash over him. How could he have lost his temper with her? Elena's back hit the wall. Realizing she was trapped, she slid to the floor and hid her face. Her whole body trembled as if it already knew what was going to happen. Alex slowly approached and sat down opposite her. He put his hand on Elena's arm, only for her body to shake harder. Not knowing what to do, Alex removed her arms from her eyes so he could see her face.

"Lena, please, look at me."

Elena tugged at her arms, trying to pull away from Alex, but he didn't let go. He'd be unable to live with himself if she hated him.

"Please," he implored.

Elena looked up. Her cheeks were streaked with tears, her

gaze panicked. "Please don't hurt me."

His heart broke as he heard her speak. "I could never hurt you." Alex wiped her cheeks, trying to be as delicate as possible. He moved beside her and beckoned her closer. Elena hesitated, and Alex found himself begging her with his eyes. He wouldn't be able to watch himself in a mirror if she started seeing him as a monster. *Please, not you.*

Elena finally moved closer and accepted his embrace.

"I'm sorry I scared you. I know you may not believe me, but I would never lay a hand on you."

He had hoped that touching her would calm her down, but her body kept shaking. Because of him. What had he done?

"I'm scared, Alex."

"I know. I won't do it again."

"You don't want to hit me?"

"I was never going to hit you."

Elena pursed her lips, unconvinced.

"I've never hit a woman, and I never will. I have a certain code, you know."

Elena smiled at him, even though her lip was still wobbling, and Alex felt as though he could breathe again. At least a little.

"Your hand is bleeding."

"Shit."

CHAPTER 13

Alex

A few days later, Alex dropped by Elena's to work on the project. She had said everything was fine, still her gaze was unfocused. Since Alex had lost his temper, it had become impossible to talk to her. Once he'd calmed down, Elena went home. Even though she had put on a small smile, he understood that she needed some distance. Few people wanted to keep Alex around once they'd seen that part of him. He just hoped that, unlike the others, Elena would still want him around.

"Do you need help with your part?"

"I'm done."

"The weather is nice. Shall we go get ice cream?"

"No, you can go," she replied, her voice distant.

"How much longer are you going to stay mad?"

Her eyebrows furrowed, her gaze turning icy. Alex had been used to her cold stares, but this was different. She no longer trusted him; he could no longer reach her. If she'd put walls around her heart in the past, this time she was prepared, and Alex wouldn't be able to get through them. He knew he'd screwed up. He'd thought he'd made things right the last time, but now that Elena was thinking clearly, she didn't seem to want him anymore. He hadn't expected her rejection to sting so much, but it did. She was too lovely, and if he'd promised himself he wouldn't let her get too close, she'd found a way into his life. Now that she was leaving, he didn't want her to. He had to make it up to her. Alex left the Fleureau house with a heavy heart. Although Elena was a pain in the ass, he'd come to care about her and enjoy spending time together. Now that it might be over, he felt empty and alone. Maybe he should have been honest with her and with himself. Alex had tried so hard to be her friend, but he'd never let her get close enough for her to become his. That had been a mistake. And he was going to fix it. He just hoped that now that she'd seen what was under his mask, she wouldn't let him go.

***

"Are you sure this is what she needs?"

"You don't like it?" asked Alex, looking at his sister, then at the stuffed toy.

Audrey raised an eyebrow, unconvinced by Alex's choice. He was holding a white unicorn with a pink and purple holographic mane. When he pressed its stomach, it played a little country tune. It was ridiculous; it was exactly what Elena needed. When they were in elementary school, she'd loved horses. Alex hoped that by playing the sentimental, nostalgic card, she'd be less reluctant to see him again.

"Are you certain you're trying to make amends here?"

"Who knows?"

Alex had spent the week looking for a gift that would please her, even if what he'd planned had cost him an arm and a leg. He had to prove to her that he cared.

Arriving at Elena's house, he knocked on her door, hiding the stuffed toy behind him. Elena looked up from her book, surprised to see him. She immediately noticed that he was hiding something.

Elena raised her eyebrows. "You didn't tell me you were coming." Her voice was deeper than usual.

Alex shrugged. "I like to improvise."

Elena didn't flinch. She waited for Alex to say what he had to say, then for him to leave. He saw it on her face. She had no desire to be in the same room as him. It hurt, but Alex carried on. He couldn't afford to screw up now if he wanted to reclaim his place in her heart.

"I brought you a present."

Without giving her time to reply, he handed her the unicorn with its large, glittering eyes.

Elena took the plushie with a wary grimace. "Is there a bomb inside?"

Alex rolled his eyes. She was as dramatic as usual, which was a good sign. At least, he hoped it was.

"Thanks, I guess."

Alex took two tickets out of his pocket and handed them to her.

Elena hesitated for a moment. "What is it?"

"Two tickets for the *Nutcracker* ballet at Bozar."

She stared at the tickets without answering. She wanted to take the tickets, but resisted the temptation. Elena finally shook her head. "That's kind, but I can't accept a gift like that."

Not from you was what she meant. He decided to change tactics. Maybe trying to convince wouldn't work.

"The show is this Friday, and starts at six. Be ready at five. I'll pick you up."

Without waiting for her reply, he left the room and returned to his car. Once settled in the Polo, he let his head fall back with a sigh. The whole forgiveness thing was a lot harder than he'd anticipated, but Alex wasn't going to give up. He wasn't going to let her go, not if there was still a chance she could forgive him. Alex clung to that small hope.

***

Against all the odds, Elena was ready when he came to pick her up. Surrounded by soft makeup, her blue eyes were even more intense. She waited for him on the porch of her house. All the way there, she remained silent. Out of the corner of his eye, Alex could see her playing nervously with her fingers. She was still afraid of him. He wanted to take her hands and tell her everything would be all right, that she'd never have to see that part of him again, but Alex couldn't make such a promise. He'd started spiralling too soon; he didn't know how to be normal anymore. Alex tried to talk about anything and everything, but just like a few days ago, he was facing a wall.

During the show, her eyes sparkled. She watched each dance move with great attention. When the show was over, Elena finally turned to him. She still wasn't looking him in the eye, but it was a start. And it was everything he'd hoped for.

"Thank you for tonight. It was lovely."

Elena smiled at him for the first time in days. Even if her smile was merely polite, Alex considered it a victory. He just had to persevere.

"Are you hungry? We can grab a bite."

"I'm not hungry." As she spoke, her stomach rumbled. Elena rolled her eyes. It was almost convincing.

Alex chuckled.

"Well, obviously I'm hungry. But I'll eat when I get home."

She really wanted to get away from him as soon as possible. She continued to be stubborn, so Alex decided to take the bull by the horns. It seemed to work best. He grabbed her hand and headed for the shopping street. At least she wasn't protesting. Maybe Alex was being too insistent, but he had to talk to her. He had to apologize. If, after that, she still didn't want him back, he'd accept her choice. Only then.

"Do you like fast food?"

"It's all right."

They entered a Burger King. Waiting for their order to arrive, they sat down in a corner of the restaurant. Alex tried to lighten the mood.

"I'm sorry, but I can't afford to take you to a five-star restaurant."

Unlike what he expected, she smiled, and this time, it was genuine. "You should have told me. I could have paid for the food."

"The whole purpose of this day was to make amends. Letting you pay for anything is out of the question."

"So you're trying to buy my forgiveness."

Elena crossed her arms, her eyes now stern. It was as if she had a switch that could turn her heart to ice in less than a second. Was this a typical girl thing? Or was it an Elena thing? Despite her looking like an angry puppy, her quick wit and touchiness kept him on his toes. One wrong move and the puppy would turn into a rabid dog.

"Yes. No!"

Alex ran a hand through his hair, sighing. He seemed to do everything wrong when it came to her. Why did she always see evil everywhere? Alex took the grunt. If he wanted her to let him back in, he needed to work hard. Her jaw clenched. Any trace of good humour, fragile as it was, was gone.

"Why does my forgiveness mean so much to you?"

"I don't want to leave things the way they are since..." He gestured nervously with his hands, not knowing what to call it. Everything that could go wrong that day had gone wrong.

"I'm not a charity case," she said harshly. "You don't have to try so hard to clear your conscience. I'll get over it. You can go back to your little life."

Elena was ready to move on, which disempowered him. Alex had become used to knowing she didn't find it easy to move on. Yet, since she'd started working on herself during therapy, she no longer hesitated to sort things out in her life. Including him. Alex hadn't been as honest about the whole friendship thing as he should have been, and seeing her ready to move on so quickly stung more than he cared to admit.

"You really don't understand, do you?"

She kept her eyes on her cup while she fiddled with the wrapper of her straw. He couldn't work out what she was thinking. Everything so clear to him was an enigma to her. But that was partly his fault. If he hadn't tried to stop her from seeing who he really was, things might have ended differently.

"If I'm trying to make amends, it's not to have a clear conscience. I want to be able to spend time with you again without your hands trembling every time I come near you. Lena, I'm truly sorry for the way I've behaved towards you."

She finally looked up. Her blue eyes shone with unshed tears. "Why would you want to spend your time with me?"

"I like your company, that's all."

Because of all the emotional abuse, Elena was the kind of person who needed regular reassurance. On top of that, now that she'd made up her mind to get on with her life, Alex was going to have to hang on if he wanted her to keep him around. Alex didn't know if he'd be up to the task, but he wanted to try. When they were on the same wavelength, there was something that made their friendship special. He missed those carefree moments with her. When they were together, they weren't that angry guy and that traumatized girl, just Elena and Alex. And he blamed himself for shattering that.

"So, do you forgive me?"

She pretended to think. "That depends. Can I keep Neighomi?"

"Who?"

"The unicorn."

"Of course. It was a gift."

CHAPTER 14

Alex

"That was amazing."

Melissa let herself fall back, sighing with satisfaction. Her breaths were still rapid. Alex lay back and watched the ceiling in silence, coming to his senses. He hoped to get some sleep. He was tired, but felt restless for some reason. As long as she didn't start talking. Or worse. Being clingy. The rules were simple: just sex, nothing else. And yet, some of them started unpacking their whole lives after their orgasm. Others needed affection. As he had predicted, Melissa began to chat. Fortunately, her chatter was unimportant, so he pretended to listen. The moment she placed her hand on his bare chest to caress him, Alex tensed. *Damn it.* He jerked away.

"Can I use your shower?"

Her eyes widened before she nodded. Without giving her time to say something, Alex grabbed his clothes and disappeared into the bathroom. His heart was pounding and his hands were trembling. Why did they always have to touch him? Feeling his self-loathing turn to nausea, Alex reached the toilet just in time before vomiting his guts out.

The blonde had caught his eye on a drunken night out, and Alex had lusted after her for weeks. Now that he was here, he had to leave. Spending time with Melissa had only made him feel worse, unlike what he had hoped for. A quick shower later, he found himself in his car. He'd tried to smoke a cigarette before setting off. No success there either. His hands were still trembling, and he couldn't shake the uneasy feeling.

Every time a girl touched him affectionately after sex, he felt ashamed. Dirty. Each time, he thought it would be the last time, and yet he returned to his bad habits without ever being able to stop. A therapist had once said that Alex had self-destructive tendencies. If only she knew how right she'd been.

Alex reached for his phone, and Elena's name appeared on the screen. He opened the picture of her and Neighomi watching *The Lord of the Rings*. It was as if she was smiling at him and not at the camera. The message under the picture said: *We're getting ready for the marathon!* Alex smiled before replying.

Alex: *You're watching Lord of the Rings without me? You wound me*

By the time he went to put his phone back, she had already answered.

Elena: *You can still join me to see the rest \(★ω★)/*
Alex: *Pause it. I'm on my way*

Without wasting any time, he started the car. Alex didn't

know why he wanted to see Elena when the presence of the others was putting him on edge. Yet he felt the need to see her. Arriving at Elena's, she observed him as he removed his jacket.

"You look terrible."

"I'm tired, is all."

Needless to say, he hadn't slept in two nights, and instead of finding sleep at Melissa's, he'd found anxiety and remorse. Elena wouldn't understand. She smiled at him, and he felt some of his unease lift. It was strange how her mere presence managed to soothe him.

"Are you sure you can survive a marathon?"

"Is that a challenge?"

"Maybe."

Alex dropped onto the bed with a sigh. Elena placed a cool hand on his forehead, concern appearing on her delicate face. Unlike with Melissa, her touch didn't freeze him.

"You look feverish. Are you sure you're alright?"

With you by my side? Absolutely. Alex bit his tongue to keep from saying that out loud. He didn't know when she'd become his safe haven, but now that he did, his anxiety subdued. Panic always seemed to have less of a hold on him when Elena stood beside him. Seeing that she was waiting for a reaction, he nodded. Elena left the room in a hurry. When she was there, he didn't feel the need to destroy himself to forget. His mind was at peace. Alex wondered when she'd begun to play such an important role in his life. Maybe he'd simply forgotten that she'd been there for years, ever since the day she'd reached out to help him get up when they were children.

Elena returned, a steaming mug and a bottle of Coke in

hand.

"I'd make you a bowl of soup, but you know my culinary skills. You'll have to survive on tea." She grabbed a large pink blanket and wrapped Alex in it as if he were a child.

He couldn't keep from laughing, but let her do her thing. He wasn't used to someone taking care of him. And strangely enough, it was pleasant. Because it was her.

"Better?"

"I appreciate your efforts, but I'm not sick."

Suddenly, Elena's gaze turned sad. "That's what my brother always said. Until they told him he was dying."

That explained why she was always so worried whenever Alex did anything more than sneeze.

"I promise I'm fine. If I'm not better by tomorrow, I'll go see a doctor. Okay?"

Elena nodded then smiled, her worry dissipating. She lay down next to him and wrapped herself in the same blanket. She gave him a conspiratorial grin. "Ready?"

"Fuck yeah."

***

Something poked his cheek, waking Alex from a deep sleep. He had to blink a few times and found Elena just two centimetres from him. She was in his personal space, and still, he felt calm. She flashed him a wide grin.

"See? You didn't make it to the end of the marathon."

Alex stretched, yawning. He'd really tried to stay awake, but he had been too exhausted. Normally, Alex had to test his limits to clear his head and get some sleep. Next to her, sleep had found him fast.

"I made it halfway through the second film. For someone who hasn't slept in two days, that wasn't too bad."

Elena rested her head on her pillow, all smiles. Unlike what he was used to from her, she looked Alex in the eye. She was radiant; her gaze open. No wonder he felt so at home with her. Her kindness and the way she cared for him were able to relax him in a way no one else had managed before.

"Did you manage to get some rest?"

"Yeah. I could definitely get used to falling asleep when you're with me."

"Are you implying that I'm drowsy and that I am like a sleeping pill?"

She pretended to pout, and Alex smiled back.

"Don't be ridiculous. I don't know how you do it, but I feel serene when you're around."

"Then close your eyes and take a nap."

She stroked his hair, and Alex sighed with pleasure. Elena seemed to be the only one who could touch him without an anxiety attack shaking him. Her presence really did make him feel more at ease. He didn't know how she did it, but for once, he stopped worrying and enjoyed the moment.

"Sorry. I ruined your marathon."

"Don't worry. I like taking care of you."

***

Alex was a bit nervous. His coach had insisted he take part in the kickboxing tournament, but Alex wasn't feeling it. Overly competitive by nature, Alex only participated when he knew victory was assured. In other words, there was enough rage inside him to punch whoever was standing in the ring. Today was no such day. A few years earlier, he had picked up kickboxing because he had so much bottled-up anger. That violence had never left him, but now that he needed it, he felt empty. And as luck would have it, today he had to fight Robbe, a guy who had even more self-control problems than Alex. *Just great.*

"Are you ready?"

Matthew, his coach, put a hand on his shoulder. Alex shrugged. This time, he was going to have to rely on his skills and technique rather than his determination to crush someone.

"I guess," he said, jumping from one foot to the other.

"You look nervous. That's unusual."

"I usually know in advance that I'm going to win."

His phone buzzed. The coach gave him a disapproving look. No phones before a tournament. He quickly glanced down.

Elena: *Good luck with your tournament! If you win, I'll treat you to ice cream and a massage* ٩(●‿●)۶

Alex: *I'm looking forward to it.*

Matthew clicked his tongue.

"Alex, put that phone away and focus!"

Knowing that his coach wasn't going to do him any favours, he put his phone in his bag.

"Why are you grinning like an idiot?"

"I just got the motivation I needed."

The coach hesitated to answer and finally ignored him.

They headed for the ring, and Alex took a deep breath. On the other side of the room, he spotted his opponent already watching him. Robbe had come to win. This wasn't going to be fun.

***

"A new round of drinks!"

The club members raised their glasses, shouting at the top of their lungs. The coach returned to Alex and patted him on the back with a smile. He'd won. For most of the fight, Robbe had had the upper hand. Alex had started to tire towards the end, but not enough for his opponent. Robbe's punches became more violent and uncontrolled, eventually disqualifying him and making Alex the winner. If Robbe hadn't lost it at the last moment, Alex would have been knocked out. It wasn't a victory to be proud of, but he didn't care when it was finally over.

He left the bar for a cigarette. Alex closed his eyes and enjoyed the quiet. All the club members stayed inside and continued to celebrate. The only thing Alex wanted to do now was to get what he'd been promised and to see Elena.

"If that isn't the star of the show."

Alex stood face to face with the person he no longer wished to see. He tried to put on a polite smile. It was best not to look for trouble. The fight had exhausted him.

"Hi, Robbe. You did well."

"Save your stupid ass comments. It was my win. The referee clearly showed favouritism."

Alex raised his palms. He really didn't want to get

involved in another fight.

"Dude, calm down, it was just a friendly tournament. It doesn't mean a thing."

"You have no idea how much money we've lost because of you."

Bets? This made the situation even trickier. Alex had already bet a few coins on certain fighters as a joke. But he'd never noticed that there were bigger bets in their circle. Two more guys emerged from the shadows. Alex wasn't going to make it out of here like nothing had happened. He put out his cigarette. *This is going to hurt.*

***

"Alex, what happened?"

Alex struggled to open his eyes. Xavier, the bar owner, was crouching down opposite him, his face taut with worry. Alex must have lost consciousness at some point because Robbe and his buddies had disappeared. His whole body ached. He tried to stand up, without success. Xavier put his hand on his shoulder and forced him to remain seated.

"I'll tell Matthew to take you to a doctor."

No way. Alex shook his head. He wanted to protest and say he'd manage. He always did. But every breath he took was painful.

"At least let me call someone to come get you."

Alex handed him his phone before letting his head fall back against the wall. He wouldn't make it home alone.

Someone touched his cheek. He'd probably been unconscious again. He blinked to find Elena in front of him.

She looked sad. Alex tried to smile to reassure her, but ended up grimacing. His lower lip was split.

"Bring him to my car," an unfamiliar voice commanded.

Alex wanted to retaliate. He didn't want to leave with a stranger.

Elena silently pleaded with him. "Please, let us help you."

Finally, he nodded. Two men helped him up and into a car that smelled of new leather. Alex tried to see who the driver was, but he was getting dizzy. It had been a long time since he'd been in this state. He had hoped to keep Elena away from this part of his life. Now it was too late. He didn't want her to think he'd thrown himself headlong into a fight when he was trying to do better. Alex didn't understand why he cared so much about what she thought. She turned back to him, her blue eyes filled with worry.

"How are you?"

"I've been better."

Elena and a pretty woman who must have been in her late twenties took him out of the car and into his room. He heard his mother panic, but the blonde woman seemed to know how to reassure her. Once Alex was lying on his bed, she came and sat beside him. Elena followed her like a puppy. There was a strange resemblance between them.

"Hey, Alex, I'm Jade. I'm a doctor. May I look at your wounds?"

Alex glanced at Elena. She had called a doctor. Elena beckoned him to accept. Alex merely nodded. He was too tired.

"Don't worry, his wounds are superficial. Alex, I'd advise you to stay in bed for a few days."

Once the treatments were over, Jade kissed Elena and Lexi goodbye. *Who is she?*

***

Rays of sunlight illuminated the room, waking Alex from his sleep. His whole body was numb with pain. It would take weeks to fully heal. He turned his head to find himself face to face with Elena again. The dancer was sleeping peacefully. Her head rested on her arms, and Alex felt warmth spread through his chest. She'd been watching over him all night. How she had managed to fall asleep while sitting on the floor was a mystery. Before giving himself time to think, Alex stroked her cheek. Elena startled awake. The moment she caught sight of Alex, her face broke into a broad smile. He smiled back. She stretched and yawned, revealing a piece of skin that looked so soft. He already knew she was beautiful and hot, but the more time they spent together, the more Elena seemed to become his type again. Who was he trying to fool? She was totally his type; she always had been.

"How are you feeling?"

The question snapped Alex out of his thoughts. He shook his head. Alex had to stop himself from staring at her like a hungry animal. "A little sore, but fine."

If Elena knew he was lying, she made no comment. She reached for the first-aid kit on the bedside table. "I'll take care of your wounds, okay? Jade said they had to be cleaned the first few days."

"Who's Jade? You seem to trust her." Alex began to understand her way of thinking. Elena didn't easily trust others. The people she did trust had to be exceptional.

"Jade is my mother's younger sister. She's actually a gynaecologist, but she's a good doctor."

Elena looked at her hands for a second. She seemed to

want to add something, so Alex gave her time to organize her thoughts.

Elena shook her head and took the sanitiser out of the kit. "You know, I was really scared when we found you all bloody and panting."

Alex frowned. His pulse quickened. "I don't want to talk about it."

"I'm not asking you to. I just need you to know how I feel."

She began to clean the cuts on his face. As usual, Elena showed him gentleness and kindness he didn't deserve. He couldn't help but wince when she placed the alcohol-soaked cotton on his lip.

"Sorry," she mumbled.

When she was done tending to his face, she helped him sit up to remove his shirt. In other circumstances, having Elena undress him would have been much more pleasant. And Alex would be lying if he said he didn't want it to happen in this particular other context. There was no reason to lie; she was gorgeous. In fact, Elena had set the bar so high that no one else could match her. But Alex couldn't say such a thing to her. Their friendship was complicated and fragile enough as it was.

Elena sat down beside him, making him feel as if she'd just punched him in the stomach with her sad eyes. Alex could hardly swallow. He hated those looks. They were the same ones his mother and friends had given him for years: sadness, compassion, pity. Alex felt something inside him break. Of all the people in the world, he didn't want Elena to look at him like that. He didn't want her to see him as weak and vulnerable. Anger and shame bubbled in his chest.

Elena continued to look after him in a heavy silence. Why did everything always have to be so complicated between them? Her gaze lingered on Alex's wounds for a few seconds too long. Elena reached for his face, and Alex snapped. It was too hard. His anger boiled in his veins.

"Don't touch me!"

Don't look at me like I'm broken. He turned his gaze to the ceiling and tried to master his breathing. It was a lost cause. Why was he so weak? As his thoughts spiralled out of control, his panic grew by the minute. He just wanted it to stop. He gasped when Elena put her hand on his shoulder. Alex tried to pull away, but couldn't. He turned to Elena. Her hands trembled slightly. She was still afraid, but this time, Elena wasn't trying to get away from him. Her gaze was resolute.

"Don't push me away."

Was he ever going to stop screwing things up when she was around? His eyes burned. Elena took him in her arms and he burst into tears. How had he managed to sink so low? Shame left a bitter taste on his tongue.

"You're okay. I'm with you."

Her heartbeat was strong and calm. Despite the pain in his limbs, Alex clung to her. He followed the rhythm of her breathing and waited for the panic to dissipate. Elena stroked his hair, softer than ever. Maybe when she was around, he didn't have to pretend to be okay.

"One day, my father was more violent than usual and pushed my mother," she confessed. "Mom couldn't get up. I don't know if you've heard, but at the time I couldn't speak. I was freaked out, so I called Jade to come and help us. I wasn't sure if a sound would come out of my throat when I called her, but my voice came back. Since then, it's always

Jade who looks after us whenever anything happens."

Alex moved away slightly so he could look her in the face. Elena smiled at him. She must have been an angel in another life.

Today, more than ever, he was grateful to Maura for putting him back on Elena's path. "Why are you telling me this?"

"Maybe you'll feel better in my presence if I'm more open with you?"

Maybe he needed to open his heart, too. There was no way someone as perfect as her would put up with his bullshit without knowing why. But Alex was terrified. He hadn't opened his heart to anyone since...

"Don't feel you have to tell me anything just because I shared a piece of my life. That's not how it works." Elena dabbed his cheeks and eyes with a tissue, avoiding any wounds.

"But you want to know what happened."

"True, but just because I want to know doesn't mean I have to know."

Since when was she so docile? Unless he'd misjudged her? "Since when are you so understanding?"

She laughed. He was relieved she wasn't taking it the wrong way.

She continued to run her fingers through his hair. "In truth, I'm not the type to meddle in other people's affairs."

Alex raised an eyebrow and immediately regretted it. It hurt. Elena, who didn't want to meddle in other people's lives? Yeah right. "Are you sure we're talking about you here?"

"I know I insisted a lot with you, but that was only because you know everything about me, and I know nothing about you. I just wanted the situation to be more balanced, but insisting wasn't right."

"You wanted to know more about me simply out of principle, not because you were curious?"

Elena rubbed the back of her head. It was a habit of Alex's that she had taken over. *Adorable*.

"I guess? I'm interested in your life, but it's not in my nature to stick my nose in someone else's business. I'm sorry I pushed you."

"And I'm sorry I called you a hypocrite."

"Maybe it's time we learned to trust each other if we want this friendship to work, don't you think?"

Alex nodded. It was time he accepted that Elena had managed to worm her way into his heart and make a place for herself there. As if she understood what he was thinking, she tightened her arms around him.

"Thank you for helping."

"Always."

CHAPTER 15

Alex

A strange feeling of unease roused Alex from his slumber. He ached all over, but that wasn't what had woken him up. It was the pretty brunette standing just inches from him. The stranger gazed at him with her big blue eyes, a shade Alex felt he'd seen many times before. His head was spinning, and he could hardly keep his eyes open. Panic was not far away. Who was she? Alex didn't let anyone into his room, so how had she ended up here?

"Ella, give him time to wake up."

The teenager stepped back, and Alex glanced towards the door, where Jade and his mother were standing. Jade's smile reassured him. She had the same calm aura as Elena. Ella, on the other hand, seemed to be a live wire.

"Hey, Alex, I've come to see how your wounds are. Can I come in?"

Alex nodded. She gave the young girl a heavy look before coming to sit on the edge of the bed.

"This is Ella, my goddaughter. She's going to help me clean your wounds, if that's alright."

"I don't mean to be rude, but why would I accept this?"

His mother was about to protest, but Jade waved her off. "I'm training her in first aid. Don't worry, she knows what to do. If at some point you want her to stop, I'll do it."

Alex hesitated. This kid had waltzed into the one place where he felt he was in control. And now she was going to treat him, even though she looked younger than he was. Seeing Ella's hopeful gaze, Alex felt himself accept. Something was endearing about her that made her look like an overexcited puppy. She smiled and came to stand beside him. Ella cleaned his wounds and re-bandaged him. Jade was right. The kid knew what she was doing.

Elena knocked on the door. The room seemed brighter now that she was there. She stopped dead in her tracks when she saw Ella. The moment the brunette became aware of Elena's presence, her grip on his shoulder tightened, and Alex groaned in pain. This girl had the strength of a bull.

Ella let go, covering her mouth. "Sorry..."

Ella kept fidgeting like a hyperactive child, and Jade beckoned her to leave. She ran to Elena and jumped into her arms. His friend was taken aback, but returned her embrace. Tears glistened in her eyes.

"What a coincidence!" Jade mused, all smiles.

Alex knew from the look on the doctor's face that she'd planned the whole thing. He just didn't know why. After Ella released Elena, she never let her out of her sight. Elena rubbed her eyes, a shy smile on her lips. She sat down on the edge of the bed, and Ella leaned against her. The three of them watched Alex with the same piercing blue gaze. They all had very distinct faces, but their eyes were a family heirloom. Elena and Jade had thin faces and high cheekbones, and Ella had well-defined eyebrows and a full mouth. But where Elena's nose was thin and straight, Jade and Ella's were small and round.

"How do you feel?" she asked.

"Alive."

Jade cleared her throat before turning back to her niece. She had something planned. "Lena, this weekend we're celebrating the wedding anniversary of Grandma Louise and Grandpa François. Did you know?"

All traces of colour in her face vanished, giving way to sadness. She shook her head. Alex took her hand to comfort her. She in turn squeezed it. Elena hadn't seen her family since her brother's funeral, three years earlier. Her mother hadn't let her.

"You should come. They miss you so much. I'm sure it would be a nice surprise."

Jade was good at playing on people's heartstrings. This caught Ella's attention. She begged Elena with her eyes. "Please come! We have so much to talk about."

Elena wasn't going to resist her for long.

Alex was surprised to hear that her voice was deeper than that of her aunt and cousin. More mature. "I don't know if this is a good idea."

"I think you should go," Alex said.

He knew how much she missed them. Elena turned to him, questioning him with her eyes. She was asking for his opinion. He nodded to reassure her.

"Too bad you can't come with me."

Alex smiled at her. She'd be okay. Elena was a fighter, she just had to realize it.

Elena

I was nervous, and by nervous, I didn't just mean a racing pulse, but also nausea, sweaty palms, and being unable to hold still for more than two seconds. How was I going to tell my mother I was going to see my family this weekend? She'd never explicitly forbidden me to see them, but she'd clearly told me to avoid Jade and my grandparents whenever possible. Why? I didn't know. All my life, I'd been very close to my grandfather and aunt. After my brother's funeral, everything had changed. Now that I was about to see them again, I didn't know if it was a good idea. After all, I hadn't heard from them in three years, and the Christmas and birthday cards had stopped coming.

"Stop pacing like that. You're like a caged lion."

Except that I felt more like the lamb that would be thrown to the lion once I left the Niessen home. Alex got up and stopped in front of me. He was grimacing from the pain.

"You should lie down."

Alex ignored my words and placed his palms on my cheeks. His gaze was calm and benevolent, and a small part of my unease dissipated. How he did it was a mystery.

"It's time for you to think about yourself and what *you* want in life. Your mother made her choices, but she can't make yours. Do you want to go to this family party?"

I'd wanted to see them for years, although I'd never dared. I hadn't dared go against my mother, and I hadn't dared tell my family how out of control my father had become. Alex was right. It was time for me to think about myself. I nodded, unable to answer.

"Then go."

"What if they don't want me?"

"Jade and Ella want you. If your family is as caring as they are, you'll be fine."

I hugged him without thinking. He winced but hugged me back.

"Sorry..."

"You Fleureau ladies are all brutes."

If only he could come with me. I had become far too dependent on his support. I really had to learn to cope on my own, but I felt invincible when Alex was with me. The doorbell rang and my pulse quickened even more. I knew I was going to disappoint my mother, and I didn't feel ready to do so.

"Don't worry, I'm with you."

***

When I walked into my grandparents' kitchen, all eyes were on me. My grandfather frowned, and one of my aunts shook her head disapprovingly. I felt like a deer caught in the headlights. Coming here had been a mistake. Why had I thought this would be a good idea?

"What are you doing here?" an uncle asked.

I shouldn't be surprised. It was delusional to think they'd all be happy to see me; of course, they wouldn't be delighted at my sudden presence. I was a stranger to them now. The anguish that had settled in my chest was starting to suffocate me, and my head was spinning. For a brief moment, I hesitated to call Alex. I had to get out of here.

"Stop tormenting her!"

I looked up at the person who'd just spoken. Grandma Louise. Tears shone in her eyes. Without hesitating, she hugged me, her peony perfume tickling my nose. She smelled just like I remembered. My eyes stung. God, how I'd missed her.

"My little girl, I'm so happy to see you."

She let go of me and looked at me from every angle. Out of the corner of my eye, I noticed Aunt Laurene and her husband watching us warily, but I decided to ignore them.

"Maura finally let you see us again?"

So she knew... I shook my head. To be honest, Mom had tried to forbid me from coming. Alex had stood beside me despite the pain he was currently in, a reassuring hand on my back. His warmth had given me courage when I'd finally said, "It's my family and I want to go and see them. So either you let me go, or I'll jump out the window and go anyway." For many long seconds, she stared at me in silence, then gave Alex a confused look. My friend didn't flinch. Unlike me, Alex wasn't intimidated by my mother. And if it hadn't been for him, I'd probably have chickened out without saying these things.

"No, she didn't want me to come."

Grandma's face showed her disappointment, but she maintained her smile. "I shouldn't be surprised," Grandma admitted, pinching my cheek affectionately. "Ever since Jade and I tried to get you out of there, she's held a terrible grudge against us."

I frowned. "You wanted to take me in?"

"My dear, we all know that Frank and Maura weren't

good enough for you."

For years, I'd thought my mother was afraid someone would find out about my father. When what she really wanted was to keep me close? This revelation baffled me. If only they'd been able to get me out of there. Grandma beckoned me to follow her. We sat down at the kitchen table, and at no point did she let go of my hand.

She changed the subject. "You've become a beautiful young woman."

"I'm just trying to look like you, Grandma."

Her laughter sounded like a melody. One that I had missed terribly. "Look at that, what a charmer."

My grandfather mumbled something incomprehensible before leaving the room. If only I hadn't been such a coward, I could have visited him sooner. I rubbed my eyes with my sleeve. Mick had always been the smooth talker in the family. Finding myself here at our grandparents' house without him was strange, but I didn't want to live without them anymore.

"Do you think Grandpa will forgive me?"

"Of course, he will. You've always been his darling little girl. He just needs some time."

Of all their seven grandchildren, Ella and I were the only girls. This had always meant that our grandparents pampered us a little more than the boys. It had also been in our favour when we got into trouble. The boys had always received the most persistent punishments, whereas Ella and I usually got away with anything. And when Grandma or one of our parents scolded us, Grandpa always gave us sweets on the sly. He was disappointed that I hadn't come to see him when we'd been so close.

Ella and Jade entered the kitchen, Tupperware and pie

boxes in hand. My cousin jumped into my arms, then left to greet the others. Aunt Laurene turned up her nose. Ella still wore her riding outfit.

"Ella, you smell like horses."

"That's not nice," Ella countered, making a sad puppy face.

Aunt Laurene always had a knack for hurling barbs. I hadn't missed that part of the family. Jade ruffled her goddaughter's curly hair.

"Ella, wash up quickly," Grandma said, kissing her cheek. "Then we'll eat."

A few minutes later, my cousin came out of the bathroom, wearing a long Hard Rock Café T-shirt and black leggings. She came to stand beside me, and some of my anxiety vanished. With Grandma, Jade, and Ella by my side, I felt a little more at home. If only Alex could be here. I took my iPhone out of my pocket and saw his message.

Alex: *How's the family party?*
Elena: *I expected worse* (=^·ω·^=) *as always*
Alex: ╲(￣▽￣)╱

It was the first time he used an emoji in his messages. Was I rubbing off on him? I grinned despite myself. The fact that he cared, even though he wasn't there, made me feel better. This boy made me feel so much. In fact, Alex had just made me feel again. As if the day he'd walked into my life, I'd started to live once more. Ella hovered her head over my shoulder before turning back to me with a mischievous smirk. *Oh no...*

"Is Alex your boyfriend?"

"What?" I squeaked. "No, he isn't! Why would you think that?"

Alex and I together? It seemed pretty unlikely. After all, he'd never want someone as boring and weak as me. And at that moment, I didn't have the strength to give my heart to anyone. So why did the idea of him not wanting me make my heart clench?

Ella pulled me out of my thoughts. "You seemed very close when we were over."

"We're just friends," I replied, keeping my eyes glued to my hands.

"Do you want him to be your boyfriend?"

I wanted to tell her no, but no sound came out when I opened my mouth. Why couldn't I answer? It was a simple question. Of course, Ella noticed. Barely a year younger than I was, her round cheeks and enthusiastic reactions made her look more childish than she was. Underneath this first impression, however, was an intelligent and extremely perceptive young girl. Too perceptive.

"What are you talking about?" Jade asked as she passed us by.

"Lena's future boyfriend."

My cheeks flushed. I'd forgotten this part of family gatherings. There was always a time to get embarrassed. Ella gave me a smug smile before changing the subject.

"Remember when you jumped off the swing and broke your wrist?"

I crossed my arms over my chest and smiled. "Remember when you pushed me too hard and I lost my balance before jumping and breaking my wrist?"

Ella pouted. "Shhhh! We agreed we wouldn't talk about

that detail anymore. Besides, it was your idea."

"Touché."

At the far end of the room, Grandma and Grandpa smiled as they watched us. Disobedience wasn't something I'd seen in the cards for myself. Yet here I was. Going against my mother had been a good idea. I hadn't felt this free in far too long.

***

Back at my parents' house a few hours later, I bumped into my mother in the hallway. She was the last person I wanted to see at that moment.

"How was the party?"

"Great."

I tried not to say too much. The vaguer I could be, the better. With what I'd just learned, I didn't know where I stood. I was disappointed and angry. Two feelings that didn't mix well, and yet they often went hand in hand.

"What did you talk about?"

Mom was trying to play it cool, but this was an interrogation. I was well aware of it. An inquisition I had no desire to take part in. I ignored her and went up the stairs. Mom's footsteps echoed behind me.

"Elena, I asked you a question," she said harshly.

It wasn't often she spoke to me like that. The audacity! I turned back to her, angrier than ever. This was the last straw.

"You forbade me to see my family for years, while all they wanted to do was get me out of this wretched place. You deliberately left me here when I had a chance to get out! And you want me to talk to you like nothing happened?"

Mom's eyes widened at my sudden outburst. All these years, I'd lived day and night with fear in my stomach, not knowing if the next time I would be the one found unconscious on the floor. And what for? Mom took a step towards me, and I stepped back.

"Elena, calm down. I can explain."

I clenched my jaw. I planted myself in front of her and put my face level with hers. My mother had never looked so small before.

"Can you explain why you left me here, knowing it was dangerous? So tell me why you never stood up for me to Dad. Explain why you kept me from being safe."

She opened her mouth without uttering a sound. Just when I thought I'd hit rock bottom countless times, I realized there simply was no bottom. Just as there was no escape for me as long as I lived here. How could my own mother have knowingly put me in such a situation? Sensing that she was unable to answer, or even to meet my gaze, I simply told her:

"When I'm eighteen, I'll go and live with Grandma and Grandpa."

Without giving her time to react, I slammed the door and locked myself in the dark.

CHAPTER 16

Elena

Since last time's fiasco, Alex wouldn't let me near any sharp objects. Instead, I was allowed to simply observe him. I sat on the worktop and watched while he took a board from the cupboard. Now he knew better than I where to find what he needed. Alex probably knew better than my mother where the utensils were kept. And we lived here.

It was those quiet, cosy days we spent together that I enjoyed the most. Maybe that made me an unadventurous person, but I liked having Alex all to myself. When we were alone, he showed sides of himself he tended to hide when other people were around. The Alex who is kind, funny, and caring is my favourite. Boiling oil splashed, and a few drops splashed onto his face.

"Damn it!"

He removed the pan from the heat before rubbing his jaw. A red spot was already forming on his skin. I took an ice cube out of the freezer and wrapped it in a paper towel. I got back on my perch and pulled Alex towards me. It wouldn't be a big burn, but it still looked painful. He tried to take the ice cube out of my hand as I placed it against his chin.

"It's okay, I can do it."

"You don't have the patience to take care of yourself," I said, pushing his hand away. "Let me do it."

I expected him to retaliate. Alex wasn't one to like being taken care of, yet he stayed. When I lifted my eyes to his, they were fixed on my lips. Although we were always together, being this close physically was different. His breath caressed my cheek. I had to admit it, his closeness made me feel all kinds of things. His lips were pure temptation, and I often wondered what they tasted like. Something I wouldn't admit out loud. We were friends. Was it normal to be that attracted to your friend? *Oh, God.* Who was I trying to fool? I had the biggest crush on Alex, and if he was attracted to me even a little, that would be amazing. This wasn't how I'd planned things to go when I'd let him into my life. Now it was too late. Alex was everything I loved. Sweet, charming, and, if I did say so myself, just my type. Despite his flaws, Alex was everything I wanted in one single person. Deep down, I was afraid this crush could become something more, because I wasn't ready for that. But falling for him was easy, I knew that. I cleared my throat, which snapped Alex out of his daze. I removed the ice cube from his chin to find the redness already fading.

"If we apply a little ointment, the redness will be gone in a few hours."

His irises weighed on me. Without warning, Alex placed his lips on mine. My body reacted on instinct, and I kissed him back. His lips were soft, and I couldn't tear myself away from the kiss, even if I'd wanted to (which I didn't). Alex placed a hand on the small of my back to pull me closer. I spread my legs slightly, and he pressed himself against me.

The tip of his tongue caressed mine. It was intoxicating. Our bubble burst when Alex stepped back in one swift movement. It took me a few seconds to realize what had just happened, my mind too clouded.

"I'm sorry, I don't know what came over me." Alex took another step back, trying to put as much distance between us as possible. If his breathing hadn't been so rapid, I would have taken his reaction as an insult.

"I'm not sorry."

It was a kiss. So, how had he managed to take my breath away like that? It was a good thing I was already sitting because I wouldn't have been able to stand on my own. Alex seemed nervous. Was he as affected by our kiss as I was, or was he regretting it? I had to try and lighten the mood.

"Wow, you really are a good kisser, huh?"

It worked. Alex finally looked back at me, and he was smiling. I'd never kissed anyone like that, and sharing this experience with Alex had never crossed my mind before. Wasn't it ironic that my first kiss, and by that I mean the passionate sort where you don't feel butterflies in your stomach but a flock of thunderbirds, was with the guy who absolutely wanted me to be his friend?

"Thanks, you're pretty good yourself."

I got down from the worktop and patted his arm. I couldn't show him how much I'd loved it. It would only freak him out.

"I'll get the ointment. Try not to set my kitchen on fire in the meantime."

***

Coming out of a slumber, I realized that I must have fallen asleep for a few hours. The sun was shining outside, whereas earlier it had been grey. On my bedside table stood a thermos and a bottle of water. Had I dozed off so long that my mother was back from her flower shop already? I turned my head and saw Alex sitting on the couch, reading a science textbook. How long had he been there? Unable to stop myself from yawning, I stretched. God, everything hurt. Alex looked up.

"Ah, you're finally awake."

I rubbed my eyes. Despite the nap, I would have gladly slept a bit longer. "What time is it?"

"About half past three."

Alex abandoned his book and sat down next to me on the bed. The last time I'd seen him, we'd kissed. Was this going to influence the way we behaved towards each other? For several days, I'd been racking my brain. I'd thought about it way too much, wondering if I was going to lose the only friend I had left, all because of a stupid kiss. A kiss I'd enjoyed far more than I should have, and a kiss I'd dreamed of for the last few nights, but still... Why did the only kiss that made me feel anything have to be with him? Sure, Alex was my friend and someone I'd come to care about immensely. But that kiss... I couldn't get it out of my head. Never, ever had anyone been able to make my head spin the way Alex had. And never had I felt so desired and cherished at the same time. My cheeks turned red. Of course, it wasn't lost on him. Alex placed his hand, which felt oddly cool, on my forehead, and his gaze was worried.

"What's wrong? When I saw you weren't in class today and didn't answer my messages, I knew something was up."

My cheeks heated up even more. This kind of

conversation was pretty awkward to have. Just as I was about to answer, my cramps started up again, and I rolled into a ball. Sometimes it sucks to be a woman.

"Elena, are you okay?"

His voice was tense. I gave a thumbs-up to show I was fine. It may hurt like hell, but I wasn't sick. No need to worry him any further. Alex bent down to my level. His green eyes were full of concern, as I'd expected. I sighed.

"I'm just on my period. I'm used to it."

His eyes widened slightly, but he remained silent. Alex lay down beside me and patted his chest. Without hesitating, I lay my head on him and listened to his heartbeat. It was calm and steady, just like him. He ran his hand through my hair, and I winced. In other circumstances, it would have been cute.

"Sorry if my hair is a bit greasy. I didn't have the courage to wash it today."

"It's fine. I don't mind." Alex continued to run his fingers through my hair.

I felt like a cat about to purr. I looked up at him. "I never knew you were such a tactile person," I teased.

"Me neither," Alex admitted with a smile. "I discover a lot of new sides of myself when you're around."

CHAPTER 17

Elena

A too-sweet show was on TV, but neither Alex nor I had the courage to change it. Alex sighed.

"These cliché movies are ridiculous. And let's not even talk about the stupid nicknames they give each other."

"Some of them are cute."

It was true that some couples' nicknames were really ridiculous. Those like "my love" or "darling", I found rather endearing. Alex gave me a sidelong glance. He was *so* judging me.

"I can call you my little Snuggle Bug if you like."

I laughed. Sometimes I wondered where he got his weird ideas from, no matter how entertaining they were. "Are you serious?"

"Perhaps you prefer *Moon of my life?*"

I watched him in silence. It was indeed a nickname I'd prefer to "honey bunny" or some other vomit-inducing nonsense.

Alex frowned at my lack of response. "You don't have the reference..."

For a brief moment, I wondered. Did I really want to

come across as such a nerd? This was Alex. As much as I wanted to impress him, he already knew me too well. So I decided to play along. Even though I was going to look like the biggest geek of all time. To hell with my dignity. "*Shekh ma shieraki anni.*"

Alex let out a cry of victory. I burst out laughing, seeing him so proud. It was only a *Game of Thrones* line, but his eyes sparkled with pleasure.

"I knew it. You are the woman of my life!"

My mouth fell agape. Someone had to tell him not to play with my heartstrings like that. Alex rolled his eyes at the look on my face, a childish smile on his lips.

"Don't take it so seriously. I was only joking."

If only you really meant it... Instead of continuing to watch the show that was on, Alex put on the first season of *Game of Thrones*. After a few episodes, my eyelids grew heavy. I rested my head against his chest and inhaled his perfume. His scent had become so familiar that it enveloped me in a cocoon. Alex put his arms around my shoulders to pull me closer. At times like this, I felt like I was right where I belonged. The show long forgotten, I closed my eyes and drifted off.

Suddenly, Alex's heartbeat spiked, and he tensed up like a bow. I moved back to see what was happening, but Alex was already standing up. His gaze resembled that of a wild animal, making my own heart rate climb.

What was happening to him? "Are you okay?"

Staring into space, he didn't hear me. The moment I touched his arm, he snapped out of his trance and took a step back, putting as much distance between us as possible.

"Alex, what's wrong?"

"I just remembered I have something urgent to do. I'll call you later."

Without giving me time to answer, Alex grabbed his coat and in the blink of an eye, he was gone.

***

In full panic mode, I spent my time pacing back and forth in my room. Why was it that every time things were going well between us, Alex slipped through my fingers? Did I expect too much from him? Maybe our kiss had scared him off? Maybe he thought I was too clingy? Too dependent? The more I thought about it, the more I was overwhelmed by scenarios, each more negative than the last. And Alex hadn't returned my calls since he'd left that afternoon, which only added to my poor mental state. I couldn't stand being in the dark any longer, so I called his sister.

"Hello?"

"Hi, it's Lena. Can you do me a favour?"

"Sure?"

"Tell your brother to answer my calls, or I'll gut him."

The silence at the other end of the line made my palms sweaty.

"Isn't Alex at your place?"

Realizing what was happening, I tried to save the situation the best I could. I couldn't worry his family until I was sure.

"Oh! He must have gone to the convenience store."

I hung up and started pacing again. My fear only increased. What had happened to make Alex leave like that? He was avoiding me, and I couldn't help feeling guilty, though I had no idea why. Had I said or done something to upset him? Why would he run away like that?

***

It was past eleven when the ringing of my phone pulled me out of the negative whirlwind my thoughts had become. Alex's name appeared on the screen, and my pulse quickened. My nerves were eating me up.

"Lenaaaa," Alex sang on the other end of the line.

"Damn it, Alex! Where the *hell* are you?"

"I miss you."

My breath caught in my throat. I recognized that way of articulating. Frank often spoke with such a heavy tongue. "Are you drunk?"

"Just a little."

Alex was completely wasted. I just didn't know if it was only alcohol or worse. What had happened?

"Don't you miss me?"

"Alex, where are you?" I asked impatiently.

"At a party. I'll come back to your place."

I leapt to my feet and grabbed my shoes and bag. There was no way I was letting him hit the road while he had booze in his system. I wouldn't be able to forgive myself if anything happened. "Don't. I'll come and get you. Give me the address."

"Okay."

The bus ride seemed to take forever. What was he doing on the other side of town at such an hour? Actually, I knew. I just couldn't figure out why. I thought everything was fine between us, but apparently, I had been the only one. Just like a few months earlier, Alex had been about to leave me to party elsewhere too. I felt torn between sadness and anger. I'd been really stupid to believe he cared about me, and that he'd changed. Just when I'd thought we'd made some progress, here we were back at square one. Again.

A girl named Melissa opened the door. If I took into account the disgust my presence evoked in her, I wasn't exactly welcome here.

"I'm here for Alex."

"Why?"

"Because he asked me to."

For some reason, she didn't feel like letting me through, so I pushed her aside and went into the house. I really wasn't in the mood, and if I had to hit her with a vase to get her to move, then so be it.

Alex was slumped on the sofa in a position that couldn't be comfortable. He opened his bloodshot eyes and grinned, floating on a cloud of artificial bliss. Alex had never been this happy to see me while sober. I wasn't too sure what that meant. I followed him as he staggered to the door. *If he falls, I won't pick him up.*

"Give me your keys. I'll drive."

Despite the alcohol clouding his senses, Alex shook his head. "You don't have your license yet."

As he approached, the smell of weed tickled my nostrils, and I winced. *Great.* Our relationship really had taken ten steps backward.

"And you're high and drunk. So you're not driving either."

Without giving him time to react, I took the keys out of his hand. I prayed we wouldn't run into any cops on the road, or we'd both be in serious trouble. I helped Alex put on his seatbelt, and for a second, I considered strangling him with it. I started the Polo. Alex rested his head against the window.

"You're driving too harsh," my friend muttered.

"If you hadn't drunk so much, I wouldn't have even needed to drive at all!"

Feeling that I was about to explode, I decided to concentrate on the road and ignore him. I was so angry with him that I would have rammed him.

"You're angry."

Wow, how perceptive.

"I'm not angry."

"Yes, you are."

"I'm not. I'm absolutely furious! What you did was selfish and stupid."

I glared at him, and Alex lowered his eyes. *That's right, be ashamed.* It wasn't in his nature to be so docile.

He remained silent for the rest of the journey. I parked Alex's car in front of his house before getting out. Audrey opened the front door, surprised to see me get out of her brother's car. She was already in her pyjamas. Alex staggered out of the car.

Still ready to commit murder, I pushed him inside.

"What happened?"

"Your brother's an idiot! That's what happened."

Alex stumbled down the stairs while I was seething on the inside. My already limited patience seemed to have completely disappeared. "Drunk people piss me off," I said, pinching the bridge of my nose.

At least, unlike my asshole of a father, Alex was just in a good mood when he'd had too much to drink. He didn't turn into an aggressive jerk who wanted to punch everything that moved, which was an improvement compared to when he was sober. Maybe that's why he always drank so much at parties. Audrey and I followed him back to his room. Alex dropped onto his bed, and his sister gave me a worried look.

"I'll explain when I'm done with him."

The girl nodded. Poor kid. Hopefully, this didn't happen too often.

"Are you staying over?"

I glanced at my watch. It was already past one in the morning. No more buses were running at this hour, so I nodded. The only thing I'd wanted was to spend a quiet day, and it had turned into a total disaster.

"Okay, you can sleep with me."

Audrey left the room, closing the door behind her. I turned back to Alex, whose eyes were shut. I poked his leg with my foot to get his attention.

"Oi, Alex, you're not going to sleep just yet."

He gave me a smile. If he had the slightest idea of what I was thinking, he'd swallow his smile down. I helped him take off his jacket and noticed a purple mark decorating his neck. My heart clenched, nausea roiling in my stomach. Had Alex really run away from me to drink and fuck around? Was it Melissa? I didn't expect our kiss to mean much to him, but I'd hoped for a bit more respect than this. Was I really worth so little to him? My eyes burned. With a jerk, I took off his shoes and threw them on the floor. I wanted to scream or cry, whichever came first.

"You're super hot when you're angry."

And now he's rambling.

"Want to see something sexier?"

"What?"

"My fist in your face!"

"There's no point. He's even more stupid when he's

drunk." Audrey was back with a glass of water and a bucket. She was right.

I was getting carried away for nothing. Alex wasn't lucid; there was no point in getting upset now. I rubbed my eyes hard when the tears threatened to fall.

"See those pretty Greek statues?" Alex asked, staring at me.

"Yes?"

I silently questioned his sister, not sure of what he was getting at. She didn't understand either.

"Well, you don't look like them at all."

Okay, not only had he left me hanging, but now he was insulting me. *Great*. Could this get even better? *Breathe, Lena. Hitting a person who's high would be unfair.* "He's really asking for me to kill him."

"You've got a much better ass. And you're sweeter, too." Alex laughed at his own joke.

I decided to ignore his comment about my butt for now. He was digging his own grave just fine.

"Are you icing?" Alex continued. "Because I want to put you on top and lick every part of you."

I should have known better than to listen to words drenched in alcohol, but that didn't stop Alex's words from piquing my curiosity or making me blush. His sister coughed.

"I think he's trying to give you a compliment."

"At least he's nice when he's drunk."

I grabbed one of his old T-shirts before heading for the bathroom. Now that I was alone, I allowed myself to breathe. This day had turned into total chaos, and I was exhausted, both physically and emotionally. I hurried to wash my face and put on Alex's T-shirt. It was large and arrived just below my butt. I decided to check on Alex one last time, no matter how angry I still was with him, and tiptoed into his room. Alex seemed to be asleep, but turned his head towards me when I approached. He still had that little smile on his face. I sat down beside him.

"How are you feeling?"

"So far, so good. You?"

"I could be better," I admitted, biting my thumbnail. "Alex?" I hated the way my voice trembled.

"Hmmm?"

"Why did you leave?"

"I needed to be away from you."

That hurt. So I'd been right; he'd run away from me. "Did I do something wrong?"

"No, you were perfect as always," he replied, his gaze on the ceiling.

Was that a compliment or a reproach? I took advantage of the situation. When Alex was sober, he avoided my questions, but when he was drunk, he seemed open to sharing his feelings. Deep down I knew it was wrong of me to take advantage of him when he wasn't really aware of his actions. That was a problem for another time. He wouldn't answer me if I asked him a few hours later.

"So why?"

"I had to check something."

"Check what?"

"You're asking a lot of questions."

Hopefully he doesn't notice...

"Please. I won't be able to feel better if you don't tell me what's going on."

A sigh left his lips, and a heavy silence settled between us.

Was he going to answer? The only sign that he hadn't fallen asleep was his fingers tapping on his stomach. "I realized I'm in love with you. I freaked out."

All the air in my lungs escaped, leaving me panting. "Is that why you ran away?"

Alex nodded. I had to bite my lip to keep from bursting into tears. Was it so wrong to love me? It seemed that no matter what he said, I was going to cry anyway.

"I tried to sleep with someone at the party, but it only made me feel worse. I couldn't get you out of my head, even when she touched me. And that made me realize that I want to be with you, no matter what we do or who we are. No matter how terrified I am."

Tears rolled down my cheeks. My mind was a mess, and I couldn't figure out what I was supposed to feel. I was still angry and stressed, but my heart had started to beat faster. A strange cocktail of happiness and panic made my head spin. Would Alex still feel the same when sober?

"Why are you so afraid to love me?"

He gave me a sad smile. It was unsettling to see him show his vulnerable side. For the first time since I knew him, he was finally going to be honest with me—*really* honest. "Because I'm giving you all the keys to hurt me."

"Are you sure you're not sober?" I squinted.

"Nope, as drunk as a skunk."

Was he making fun of me or not? Too tired, I got out of bed.

Alex grabbed my leg and pulled me towards him. Trying not to crush him, I had to straddle his lap. "Your skin is so soft."

Alex stroked my thighs, and I raised an eyebrow.

"Don't touch, buddy," I said, pushing his hand away. "Drunk people don't turn me on."

A silent laugh shook his body. "You don't know what you're missing."

"Oh, but I do. You'll either puke on me or fall asleep before we're done. I'll pass."

Alex pouted, and I couldn't help but smile, some of my unease finally dissipating. This man really had a way of getting on my nerves just as much as his presence could make me feel better in seconds. He didn't know it, but he already had the keys to hurt me too; he'd had them for a while now. Alex returned my smile. I placed a kiss on his forehead before heading for the door.

"I'm going to miss you tonight."

"Good night, Alex."

"Good night, Lena."

***

I tiptoed into Audrey's room, but she looked up from her book, still awake. She beckoned me closer. I lay down beside her.

"How is he?"

"He's alright, we've talked. I just don't know if what he said is true."

"Alex is honest when he's drunk. What did he say?"

Should I tell Audrey what had happened? I wasn't sure Alex would agree with me sharing what he'd just said. On the other hand, maybe talking it over with her would help.

"He said he fell in love with me and freaked out."

Her eyebrows went up in shock. "So he's relapsing."

"What do you mean?"

"My brother is an ostrich. When he feels strong emotions, he runs."

That sounded familiar enough. Audrey let her head fall back into the pillow with a sigh. Apparently, Alex's behaviour had affected them all. How had he become like this?

"For a while, Alex took drugs. Mom tried to help him by sending him to a therapist, but he resisted. When you force Alex to do something, he gets stubborn and refuses to see reason."

"What did you do then?"

"We had no choice but to trust him. It worked out because Alex calmed down. When he goes out now, all he does is drink or smoke weed. But he stopped going out months ago, so I don't know what got into him."

I bit my thumbnail. All the answers I was looking for were there. Would I finally know? "What made him like that?"

Audrey pursed her lips. "I can't tell you. First, because I'm not sure he wants you to know, but also because I was never told the full story. I was six when he suffered a trauma. He's been spiralling ever since.

He suffered a trauma and has been spiralling ever since...

***

Audrey and I were having breakfast when Alex came into the kitchen. The way he was frowning and pushing against his temples, it was impossible to ignore how hungover he was. Alex sat down next to me without speaking. Did he remember what had happened that night? I gave him a glass of water and paracetamol. Although I was still angry with him, I also felt sorry for him. Audrey and I continued talking, leaving Alex to sober up.

"I can't figure out if you're being nice or letting me stew."

I took a bite of my toast. A big part of me wanted to let him stew, another part wanted to stay away from him. Because let's be honest, his confession had turned my world upside down. In a good way. But no, it wasn't enough to completely dissipate my anger, let alone my pain. The anguish I'd felt the day before had been too much. His little sister looked like a small animal facing danger. With our temperaments, things could get out of hand very quickly.

"It depends. Are you going to tell me why you left me to go to a party?"

Alex hadn't expected me to go on the offensive immediately. Given the day and night I'd just had, I wasn't going to go easy on him. Despite our discussion the night before, I wanted to see what his response would be now that he was sober. He wasn't going to admit he was in love with me now that he'd come to his senses, was he? Alex was far too secretive about his feelings to admit it while being lucid.

He shrugged as if he didn't care. "I needed to get out."

I expected him to elaborate a bit, but Alex kept his gaze fixed on his sister. Audrey stood up.

"Leave her alone. She was worried sick yesterday when you disappeared."

Alex changed the subject. "How did I get home?"

"I brought you back."

His face contorted into a reproachful grimace. As if things could have turned out differently. "You don't have a license."

My blood boiled over. "What was I supposed to do then? You didn't really think I'd let you drive after you'd been drinking and smoking, did you? Do you have any idea how worried we've been?"

Alex rubbed his temples like I was giving him a splitting headache. *Well, babe, buckle up then.* Alex glared at me. A few months earlier, I would have been petrified. Now I knew he wouldn't hurt me. Not physically, at least.

"Why are you giving me a hard time?" he asked in a biting tone. "As far as I know, you're not my mother or my girlfriend."

His words felt like a slap to my face, but I swallowed them down. The look on his face told me he already regretted those words, not that he intended to take them back. But he was right, I suppose.

I took a deep breath and regained my usual composure. All right, then. If he wanted to be an asshole, I wasn't going to insist. So I did what I did best: I turned my pain into cold, calm anger. "You're right, I'm not. I've got better things to do than waste my time on you."

My cruel words hurt him, but I was so angry. How was it possible to be this happy and furious at the same time? I reached for my bag. Audrey gave me a sad look. She walked me to the front door, and I kissed her cheek. Alex followed, staying behind. Audrey disappeared, not wanting to see the shitshow between me and her brother come to life. I left the house and turned back to him. I'd told myself I wasn't going to insist, but I wasn't done yet. Alex clenched his jaw; he knew the storm was about to break.

"You know, Alex, I'm well aware I'm not your girlfriend or your mom, but I thought we were friends."

"We *are* friends."

"You don't treat your friends the way you treated me."

Just like the day before, he lowered his eyes. His guilt must be killing him if he couldn't hold *my* gaze. Maybe I should have gone easier on him. It was too late now. The machine was already in motion.

"I don't think you realize how worried I was about you. What you did really hurt me. You ditched me to go to a party, leaving me in the dark. I felt guilty for hours, thinking I'd done something wrong. And then you call me when you're wasted, like nothing happened!"

For half a second, Alex looked like a fragile, wounded child. A second later, his face was once more a stoic mask. I took a deep breath and ran a hand through my hair. Damn it. He really didn't understand how stupid he'd been.

"I broke the law for you. Did you think for one moment how your family would have felt if you'd driven that night and gotten in a car accident? Their lives would have been shattered. Next time you want to do things on your own, at least think about those who care about you for a second."

Finally done, I descended the steps of his porch. I felt like an overcharged battery. Alex took a step towards me, and I stepped back.

"Do you want me to drop you off?"

"I'll walk."

He took another step. "It's a long walk."

"I'll walk for hours if it gets me away from you."

Every time I opened my mouth, I kept hurling boiling acid at his heart. Every word I said hurt him, and even though I was furious, he didn't deserve this. His eyes reflected his pain.

"I'm sorry. I just need to be away from you for a while.

I'm really disappointed in you."

"I understand."

"Bye, Alex." Without looking back, I left. I could hear his voice crack.

"Bye, Lena."

CHAPTER 18

Elena

Slumped on my desk, I was staring out the window, ignoring my physics assignment. I'd been working on it for hours, and still, I didn't understand a thing. Of all the subjects, this one was useless to me. Someone knocked on my door, snapping me out of my thoughts. Or rather, the absence of thought. Seeing Alex standing a few feet away, my heart sank. I'd avoided him in the school halls for days after I'd told him I needed to be away from him. That was just over a week ago, but it had felt like a lifetime. Alex entered my room, leaving enough distance between us, as if he feared I would bite his face off. I spun around in my desk chair so I could face him. Dark circles bruised the skin under his eyes, and his features were drawn, proof that the last few days had been tough.

"Hey."

"What are you doing here?" I asked instead of greeting him.

"You didn't answer my messages or calls, so I decided to drop by."

That little pang of guilt that was never far away these days stirred again. It was true, I had ignored him. Truth be told, I was scared out of my wits and didn't know what to say. "Hey, Alex! You ran away from me to get drunk. When you were high, you told me you loved me, and I'd like to know if you feel the same now that you're sober?" Yeah, that didn't sound like a good idea.

At first, I'd been angry, but now I felt restless. If Alex had run away from me like this, there was a reason behind it. I really wanted to know if he felt the same now, but it terrified me too. If he didn't love me, it would crush me. But if he did love me, what would happen to us?

Seeing that Alex was still waiting for a reaction, I cleared my throat. What a mess. Wasn't falling in love supposed to be wonderful? "Uhm, yeah. Sorry about that."

I had no excuse. No need to pretend like I had one. Alex handed me a small white box, and I raised an eyebrow. Since when did my presence make him nervous?

"What is that?"

"A token of reconciliation."

I opened the box only to find a cupcake with candy-pink frosting and lots of little sugar butterflies. I closed the box. "I don't like sweets."

Alex ran a hand over his face, inhaling sharply. I could tell by the way he clenched his jaw that he wanted to strangle me. Or jump out the window. After all, I wasn't making it easy for him. Making him work for it a little was satisfying. Me sadistic? Absolutely.

"You've really decided to make me pay, haven't you?

I smiled. I really appreciated that he'd gone out of his way to get me a cupcake and had come all the way to my house. No one else would have done it. Not for me. "Well, since you made an effort to get to the bakery, I'll make an effort to eat it."

His gaze softened when he realized I was pulling his leg. He breathed out a sigh of relief. "I really thought that you were going to give me a hard time."

"Honestly, I did think about it, but I can see you've beaten yourself up enough already."

"I'm truly sorry, Lena. I didn't mean to do this to you." He ran a hand through his hair, all his self-confidence gone.

Had the last few days been as horrible for him as they had been for me? Not having Alex in my life for a week had been torture, and I couldn't help wondering if he'd felt the same.

"Do you think you can forgive me?"

"It depends. Will you do something like this again?"

I cared about him, but I couldn't go through that kind of anguish again. Nor that kind of disappointment. He'd already done it twice. I couldn't afford to get my hopes up. My heart couldn't bear being crushed again, not by Alex.

"Of course not. I don't want to lose our friendship."

I stood in front of him, and Alex took me in his arms. He squeezed hard, like he was afraid I'd push him away or disappear. I tried to swallow back my tears, to no avail. Missing him so much was frightening. I pushed the thought out of my mind to enjoy the moment.

"I don't want to be like this anymore," my friend whispered against my neck.

"How?"

"Fucked up."

If only things could be simple.

"Why are you here?"

"I needed to see you." His sudden honesty caught me off

guard.

I rolled my eyes to hide the effect his words had on me. "You make it sound like it's vital."

Alex ruffled my hair, laughing. "You're my best friend. Obviously, I need to see you."

I placed both hands over my heart and let myself fall back onto my bed. "Ouch! I just got friendzoned."

"What?"

"What?" I repeated.

"What did you just say?"

I shook my head and continued to deny everything. I could see by the look on his face that Alex was getting confused. "Nothing."

"But you..." my friend tried.

"Nope."

Alex and I burst out laughing. It was nice to be able to tease each other again. He sat down next to me. I hesitated. Should I pretend nothing had happened, or should I try and get the truth out of him? Finding out the truth was scary, but not knowing made me sick. I could still feel my panicked heart pounding in my throat. I had to at least try.

"Are you going to tell me why you ran away?"

I had to know how Alex felt about me.

A small smirk played on his lips. "You're not going to give up, are you?"

"I'd like to understand."

"I'm not ready to talk about it. Can you accept that?"

I should have known. Alex hadn't said what I'd hoped for. Yet, without him even realizing it, he'd given me the answer. I bit my lip. It was hard to keep my composure, especially in the face of this truth. But this time, I had to be the stronger one. Alex needed that. I could keep his secret and pretend nothing had happened until he was ready. "Okay, I won't insist."

His face relaxed instantly. "Thank you."

That didn't mean I couldn't tease him a little. After all, humour was part of my survival mechanism. "Do you remember that night?"

Alex leaned back, worried. "Not really, no. I vaguely remember seeing you arrive at the party. And you putting me to bed."

I tried to keep my expression as neutral as possible. "You really don't remember anything else?"

"Why are you insisting? What did I do?"

I smiled, feeling that I was going to have a marvellous time. I rubbed my hands together, impatient to tell him.

"The question should be: what did I say?"

"What did I say?" Alex asked with a sigh.

I told him about his monologue on Greek statues, and how he thought I had a nice ass. Not to mention the icing-licking part.

His cheeks turned red. My friend ran his hands over his face, cursing. "I didn't say that."

"Oh, yes, you did. In front of Audrey."

"Shit..." The pretty colour on his cheeks spread to his ears and neck.

"There's more," I continued, looking at my pastel pink nails.

Alex looked up at me, expecting the worst. He wasn't ready.

"You tried to convince me to have sex with you.

Alex dropped his head into his hands.

I patted his head, savouring the moment. "You're super hot when you're angry," I said, imitating drunk Alex.

Alex rolled his eyes so much that I was afraid his eyes would disappear. He let himself fall back into the pillows. "You're enjoying this, huh?"

"You have no idea."

"I'm ashamed."

"Even I was ashamed for you."

I put on a movie and sat back next to Alex. He let his head rest on my thighs.

"Can you even see the screen like this?" I asked, sceptical.

"Of course."

I had my doubts, but didn't comment. If he wanted to rest, I wasn't going to force him to watch with me. I played with a few silky locks of his dark hair. It took him only a few minutes to drift. I'd chosen the movie, and yet I couldn't concentrate on what was happening on the screen. Alex had come back. And he loved me, but he didn't want me to know because... because what? He'd said that being in love with me frightened him because he was afraid I'd hurt him. But how could I? Alex was a wonderful person, and above all, he was my best friend. I loved him too. God, I loved him so much. And if he was afraid of me finding out, I'd just have to prove to him how much he meant to me. I didn't necessarily believe in fate, but someone had put Alex in my path, and I didn't want to live without him anymore. We were both fucked up, sure, but we were stronger together.

CHAPTER 19

Elena

The sound of a plate smashing against the floor woke me up. It was soon followed by Frank screaming in the kitchen. My heart pounded in my throat, keeping me from swallowing. Mom's voice was getting louder, too. Now it was only a matter of minutes before he would come to my room. Why was she playing his game? We both knew how bad it could get. For her and for me. Leaving nothing to chance, I grabbed my phone and coat. The kitchen was closed. I took the opportunity to put on my boots before slipping out the front door.

Once outside, I ran as fast as I could. I had to get away from that house. Blood was rushing to my ears; I couldn't hear anything other than my panicked heartbeat. The soreness in my knee flared up, and I had to stop running. When I finally reached the bus stop, I dropped onto the bench. It was only two in the morning. What now? Where was I supposed to go? My breath came out in little white puffs. *Great*. I was out of my father's reach, but I was on the verge of hypothermia. Without thinking, I called Alex.

After a few seconds, he picked up. "Hello?"

His sleepy voice instantly made me feel guilty. Except that I had nowhere else to go.

"It's me. Can you come and get me?" My voice was shaky. I expected him to tell me to go back to bed.

A door closed in the background. "Where are you?"

"At the bus stop on the corner of my street."

"I'll be there in twenty."

"Okay."

After what seemed an eternity, but was only fifteen minutes, the Polo stopped in front of me. I jumped inside the car under Alex's silent gaze. He tried to read me, but was too tired. I could feel my guilt for waking him up increase. He had better things to do than come looking for me in the middle of the night. And yet, now that he was here, I felt safe again.

"I'm sorry I called you. I didn't know where else to go."

Alex put his hand on my forehead and turned up the heat. "You're freezing. Couldn't you wait inside?"

I lowered my eyes. Had I been in danger? I wasn't sure, but just the thought of waiting in that house made me nauseous. It felt like I was going to puke my guts and my heart out from fear. Feeling my hands trembling, I hid them under my coat.

"I'm glad you called me."

"You don't mind?"

"If you're scared, I want you to call me. I'd rather be woken up in the middle of the night than find out later something's happened to you."

Throughout the drive, my heart continued to beat wildly. I couldn't shake the restlessness. My mother was still there, and I could only pray that nothing would happen to her during the night. I followed Alex inside his house, trying to make as little noise as possible. Once in his room, I finally allowed myself to take a deep breath.

"Wanna talk about it?" Alex asked, snapping me out of my thoughts.

I shook my head. It was late, and Alex was exhausted. I couldn't keep cutting his night short. And to say what? That I'd been afraid my father would lay a hand on me? That conversation could wait a few more hours.

"Maybe tomorrow."

"Cute pyjamas," he observed with a wry smile.

I looked down at my fluffy Pusheen pyjamas. These weren't the outfit I had in mind for my first night at Alex's house. Had I known, I would have planned something lighter and shorter, but that would be for another time. Right then, I didn't care.

"Let's go to bed. I'm beat."

"Where do I sleep?"

"Here."

"I'm not going to sleep with you."

Alex exhaled loudly through his nose, getting irritated. "Elena, it's late. Don't be difficult."

Well done, Lena...

Seeing my face, his gaze softened. "I'm sorry, I'm just tired."

Before I could reply, Alex wrapped his arms around my shoulders. I inhaled his scent and tried to calm down. I really needed to relax. Everything was fine now. Nobody could hurt me here.

"You must have been scared if you decided to call me."

I hugged Alex back. When my friend let go of me, he

motioned for me to lie down. I lay down without complaining when I heard Alex laugh.

"Relax, I'm not going to eat you."

He lay down, leaving enough space between us. I was grateful.

"I know. I have faith in you. I just don't want to invade your privacy too much."

Each time, I felt like I was imposing myself. That every time he held out his hand, I took his whole arm. It wasn't fair to him; I also didn't know how to stop. Alex had become like my centre of gravity, and each and every time, I was drawn to him like a moth to a flame.

"It's a bit late for that, don't you think?" Yet there was no reproach in his tone.

"I'm sorry. I really didn't... I really didn't mean to impose on you like that."

"I don't mind. I like your company."

I knew that. He was in love with me after all. A knowledge that made my heart dance to crazy rhythms. I just hoped that he'd be able to tell me one day. "If I ever ask too much, promise you'll tell me?"

"I will."

Alex fell asleep in a heartbeat. I silently thanked the heavens for placing him in my path.

***

I awoke from a deep, dreamless sleep to the sound of an alarm going off. My mind still foggy, I sensed that something was different. I just couldn't figure out what. My brain felt like teddy bear stuffing. Whatever it was, I liked it, and I didn't want it to stop.

The alarm clock continued to sing. I opened my eyes to find myself face to face with Alex's torso. His arms were wrapped around me. I didn't remember us ending up in this position, but it felt good. Alex was still fast asleep and didn't hear the alarm. When I touched his cheek, he mumbled something incomprehensible. If he was surprised to find me in his arms, he didn't let go.

"Hi."

"Hi," I repeated, smiling.

His eyelids closed again. I continued to poke his cheek, but instead of standing up, Alex tightened his grip around me.

"We have to get up."

I made a face as I watched myself in the mirror. I wasn't one to flatter myself often, but usually my dress style was quite elegant. Now, I looked ridiculous, and not just a little. Since I'd left the house in a panic, I hadn't thought to take any clothes with me. To avoid waking his family, Alex grabbed some clean clothes from the dryer. That was how I ended up wearing his mom's psychedelic jeans and a fuchsia T-shirt with silver stars that belonged to Audrey. With my long burgundy coat and camel boots, I looked like I had walked straight out of a laundry. When I came out of the bathroom, Alex put his hand over his mouth to keep from laughing, and failed miserably.

"My darling, you look magnificent!" my friend exclaimed, bringing his hands together.

"Shut up."

"Let's go, fashion disaster."

When Alex stopped the car in the parking lot, I unbuckled my seatbelt. Here was to hope that no one would say anything about my outfit.

"See you later," I said.

"Where are you going?"

Confused, I pointed to the school building with my thumb. Where else was I supposed to go? "Well, to school."

"Wait for me then."

"But don't you want to join your friends?"

"Yes, but you can come with me. You're on your own, anyway."

His words rubbed me the wrong way. What did he mean by that? "I'm not a charity case. Just because I'm alone doesn't mean you have to keep me company."

I ruminated as I got out of the car. *He's got nerve.* All right, I owed him after what he'd done for me last night, and I was probably getting a little carried away. But still. Couldn't a girl be alone anymore without others feeling sorry for her?

"Elena, wait!"

Alex had to run to catch up, but I kept moving towards the entrance.

"You know damn well that's not what I meant."

I stopped dead in my tracks and held his gaze. "And yet that's exactly what you said."

"I know, I'm sorry. I didn't mean to vex you."

I crossed my arms, waiting for his explanation. Alex ran a hand over his face. I was wearing out his patience. His self-control was admirable. Some students gave us funny looks before moving on. Was it because I was dressed like a clown, or because I was standing up to Alex? Or worse, both?

"I just wanted to spend more time with you. Since you're

alone most of the time, I didn't think you'd mind staying with me."

A pang of guilt formed in my chest. Deep down, I knew Alex only wanted what was best for me. Yet the thought of him wanting to spend time with me because I was alone made my skin prickle. I didn't want him to see me as pathetic. "So it's not because you feel sorry for me?"

Alex rolled his eyes. "I know that if you're alone, it's your choice. I'm not that stupid."

Sometimes, well, most of the time, I wondered how he could stand me. I was annoying, and I'd ruined the morning. And it had started so well. I bit my thumbnail. Maybe it was time I learned to control my shitty temper. "I'm sorry. I just... I got carried away."

"Oh really," he said, arms crossed.

"I mean it."

"Don't go for my throat like that next time. I know you better than you think."

There was nothing I could say. He was right. Alex turned towards the entrance and motioned for me to follow. Glad that he still wanted me around even when I was unbearable, I followed in silence. We joined Lucas and Yves in the hall. They greeted each other, then his two friends turned to me.

"Hi, Lena! It's good to see you again. Did you come together?"

Once a shy girl, always a shy girl, so I simply nodded. The boys continued chatting while I began to get distracted. I startled when Alex dropped his forehead onto my shoulder. I patted his head.

"Tired?"

"Knackered."

He already had trouble sleeping. Now I'd cut another one of his nights short. Alex put an arm around my waist. It was such a simple gesture, and yet it made me melt.

"Sorry. I'll try not to wake you up at night anymore."

Alex's two friends fell silent, their eyes fixed on us, and my cheeks turned crimson. My words had been interpreted in a different way than I'd intended.

My friend chuckled into my neck. His breath on my skin made me shiver. "I didn't know you were naughty," Alex whispered. "Was I wrong?"

Oh no, he was flirting with me, wasn't he? My cheeks heated up. I shook my head. I had to save what little dignity I had left. "Gotta go!"

Without giving him time to tease me any further, I fled to my first class. Oh God, this morning was a roller coaster of feelings.

***

"Yo!"

I looked up from my exercise when Nina, a classmate, slid into the chair next to me. She's a pretty girl with a bob cut of brown hair, and slightly taller than me. As someone who's a hundred and seventy-three centimetres, it was rather surprising. I was used to always being the tallest.

"Hi."

For a while, we worked in silence, but I could feel her glancing at me every now and then. She watched me with her big brown eyes. For some strange reason, she seemed genuinely curious about me. Which was odd. No one in this school had ever considered me interesting enough. Not that I'd ever cared about that before. Since I used to spend all my time at the dance academy, I'd never had enough time to worry about what my classmates thought. Unless it was the outfit that intrigued her? I hated that I looked like a clown, no matter how shallow that made me. Her stare made me uncomfortable.

"Is there a problem?"

"Are you and Alex dating?" she asked without hesitation.

Of course. Alex, the famous heartbreaker. I should have known people would ask questions. It was inevitable. "Why?"

"I thought you were."

"Would it change anything for you if we were?"

Nina laughed, which drew the teacher's attention. We quickly looked down to avoid trouble. She moved closer to me to whisper, "Oh no, not anymore."

"Are you... close to Alex?"

Was I going to have to fight for him? The idea seemed a little absurd, but we were talking about high school. Anything was possible here. She looked up at the clock above the blackboard. The bell rang in the corridors, indicating recess. Nina cocked her head to one side.

"We have a past."

"Please don't tell me you're a jealous ex who wants to see me suffer," I joked.

"When I said a past, I meant a purely physical one."

Ah... She was one of his former sex friends. That made the whole thing a bit awkward. Nina shrugged as if she'd just told me what the weather was like outside. Her excessive honesty was disconcerting.

Seeing my face, she smiled. "Sorry, you probably don't

want to know about all this. We're friends now. It's just that I've noticed Alex is different with you."

Nina had piqued my curiosity. It was strange to talk about Alex with someone I hardly knew; it also allowed me to know a bit more about Alex. No matter how close we'd become in recent months, there was still a part of him that he tried to keep hidden.

"What do you mean?"

"He used to hate touching people, and it always felt like I hit a wall whenever the conversation got too personal. But now he's laughing and following you like an enamoured puppy. It's a good change."

Her words puzzled me. The Alex she knew seemed different from the one I knew. Sure, he's a little taciturn and moody, but Alex is genuinely sweet. And funny.

"Alex is really nice, but it's true that he's very distant when he's suspicious."

"I wish you happiness," she said, one hand on my forearm.

"We're not together."

Nina raised an eyebrow, a small smirk on her lips. Of course, she didn't believe me. "I only wish you happiness. It's up to you whether it's platonic or more."

***

Alex

When Alex headed for the park at lunchtime, he was surprised to find Elena and Nina eating together. Nina was part of his past. Elena was part of his present and, he hoped, his future. Seeing them together was like mixing two parts of him that weren't meant to coexist. Elena turned to him, smiling. It was the first time she was at ease with others. Alex sat down on the grass beside her and listened to the girls talk, without ever taking part in the conversation. Once Nina was gone, Alex's skin prickled from the nerves.

"Does it bother you that I've..."

"That you...?" she repeated.

For once, Alex was at a loss for words, which amused her. He ran a hand through his hair. No matter how much he wanted to become better for her, she already knew his reputation. A reputation he wanted to erase, but couldn't.

"That you had sex with Nina?"

Elena's voice was calm. Too calm, even.

"With Nina and many others."

"Why would it bother me?"

Alex smiled to hide his disappointment. He didn't want Elena to judge his bad old habits. Still, he was hoping for a little possessiveness from her. Alex had stopped going to parties, had stopped the one-night stands, the drinking... He'd stopped it all because he loved her. Did she really not care? Elena must've noticed his internal turmoil, given how her gaze softened.

"Let's say I'd mind if you still did it now."

***

As he got home, Alex spotted his mother sitting at the kitchen table. He quickly tried to turn back until she beckoned him to come closer. Did she know about Elena? Despite all the mistakes he'd made, he'd never snuck a girl in.

"Are you going to explain why Elena was here last night?"

Shit. Alex sat down next to her, knowing he couldn't escape the conversation. "There was trouble at her place. She panicked, and I picked her up."

Lexi wasn't satisfied with his answer. No one would believe such a lame excuse in any other context. "Did you..."

"No," he retorted.

Everyone believed something was going on between them. Now that he'd accepted his feelings, Alex understood why. He looked like a puppy in love. Gosh, he felt like a puppy in love. Lexi tucked a blonde lock behind his ear—a gene neither he nor Audrey had inherited.

"Alex, you should watch out with Elena. I know she's kind, but I think she's taking advantage of your kindness."

Alex frowned. He knew her. He knew she'd rather suffer in silence than ask for help. If she called him, she must've been desperate. "I want her to use my kindness."

Lexi's eyes widened at his honesty. "You can't save her, Alex."

"But she needs me."

"What she needs is professional help. You can't feel responsible for something that's none of your business."

Deep down, Alex knew that his mother was right. He couldn't help wanting to be with Elena. He wanted to help her, just as he'd wanted someone to help him, years ago.

When he didn't answer, Lexi frowned as something must have clicked in her mind. "You're in love with her."

There was no point in denying it. Anyone who took the time to look at him would have noticed. Alex was so transparent that maybe even Elena could see it. He prayed that she couldn't. Alex had no idea what to do if one day she realized he loved her, and that she was incapable of loving him back.

"Sweetheart, in a relationship, it's important that both parties can be happy on their own. You've spent years picking up the pieces of your heart. Don't give away what's left of it."

She was right, once again. He knew his heart was damaged and fragile, but Elena was worth it. He'd given her the power to break it again with a snap of her fingers. "Like I had a chance with her."

Elena was too good for him. That didn't stop him from wanting her just the same. She was kind and funny and smart, and every time they were together, he couldn't help but hope she would love him too.

"What?"

Alex lifted his gaze. "Mom, look at me. I don't stand a chance. I'm a wreck. The day she realizes what she's worth, she won't want a reject."

"Alexander, I forbid you to say such a thing. You don't know what you're worth either."

"She's too good for me, and you know it. You know how broken I am."

Elena had seen him lose it once; that day had thrown a big chill into their friendship. Alex lost control when he got angry, but seeing the terror in Elena's eyes had the effect of a cold shower. She had seen how destructive his behaviour was. He didn't want to be that person anymore. Elena deserved better. Maybe he did, too.

"If that's what you really think, why don't you become a better person for her?"

CHAPTER 20

Elena

"Ouch!"

I dropped my hockey stick to the floor in shock. Blood was already beading on my finger, where her stick had hit my hand. Sophie, my opponent, left her goal and ran towards me.

"I'm sorry!"

"I'm fine," I assured her.

"Time out. Elena, are you okay?"

The gym teacher led me into the locker room to tend to my wound. At least, there was no pain. Injuring myself during gym hours seemed to be becoming a theme.

"That's a nasty cut you've got there, but it won't leave a scar."

"It's okay, I'm not worried."

"Elena, I'm so sorry..."

Sophie, the petite, curvy blonde with the doe eyes, stayed by our side. I'd never really talked to her, but I knew she was a friend of Nina's. Although she'd just injured me and made me stop playing in the middle of a match (something I hated), I couldn't blame her for a scratch. She already felt bad enough. I tried to reassure her as best I could.

"Don't worry. Accidents happen."

Sophie gave me a grateful smile. Returning to the gym hall, the teacher motioned for me to stay on the bench while the rest of the group resumed the game. Sophie sat down next to me and we chatted for a while. Too bad I'd never talked to her before, she was pretty cool.

"Lena!" Alex jogged over to us. He placed his hands on my cheeks to check up on me, a worried frown on his face. "Are you alright? They told me you got hurt." His attention fell on my bandaged hand. He furiously turned to Sophie. "Couldn't you be more careful?"

His tone was so aggressive that Sophie shrank back. Several people came to stand around us when they saw Alex getting angry.

I needed to calm him down before he went completely berserk, and I elbowed him in the ribs. "Alex, stop," I hissed. "I'm fine. It's just a scratch."

His nostrils twitched. "It could have been worse."

"But it's not, so don't be angry with her. It was an accident." I nodded towards her for him to apologize.

We held each other's gaze until he reluctantly surrendered.

Alex turned back to Sophie with a scowl on his face. "Sorry."

It was a lie—we all knew that. Alex was making an effort, much to everyone's surprise, so I couldn't complain. The famously taciturn bad boy wasn't actually half as bad.

"Alex, would you do us the honour of returning to the field?" His gym teacher approached us, his patience wearing thin.

Alex ignored him, his attention still on me. "Are you going to be okay?"

I rolled my eyes. *What a mother hen!* "Yeah. Now go!"

Alex returned to the game, and Nina sauntered over to us, applauding. "Wow! You tamed our beast." Nina patted me on the shoulder, amused by what had just happened.

I turned back to Sophie, who looked like she'd been through a rollercoaster. "I'm sorry for his behaviour. Alex isn't a bad guy, but when it comes to me, he tends to be overprotective."

"Cute."

I bit my lip. With Alex, it was all or nothing. But that was just how he was, and I wouldn't change a thing. "He thinks I'm made of glass."

"Obviously," Nina said. "He's mad about you."

"He is."

Though he always thought that I was more fragile than I really was, I appreciated this overprotective side that would pop up as soon as he thought I was in danger.

Nina raised an eyebrow. "You're not even trying to deny it?"

"I know how he feels, so I won't pretend otherwise."

I just had to find a way to make Alex understand how I felt. Telling him I loved him wasn't enough. He wouldn't believe me.

***

"You okay, Soso? Not too traumatized by Alex?" Nina asked, grabbing her gym bag.

We left the changing rooms and headed for the park for our lunch break. It was strange to follow this duo like a lost duckling. Something about them drew me in like a magnet. Sophie shivered as she thought back to the morning's misadventure.

"I really thought he was going to hit me or something."

"Same, and yet I've known him since elementary school."

Nina sighed dramatically. Alex had this aggressive, bad-boy image that stuck to him. Too bad nobody could see beyond the illusion. Sophie and Nina looked back at me.

"And you?" asked Sophie.

"What about me?"

"Did you ever feel like you were going to get struck by lightning by Alex?"

"Oh, yes. I almost peed myself," I admitted, laughing.

One had to tread carefully when Alex was involved. Seeing all the anger he had in him had petrified me once. Now I knew who hid behind that anger: someone in pain, who was afraid of getting hurt again.

"How did a nice girl like you end up dating Alex?" Sophie asked, taking a sip of water.

Nina cackled. Sophie didn't know our situation. What seemed like "in a relationship" to others was actually "it's complicated" for us.

"Actually, we're not dating..."

Sophie's eyes widened. She didn't believe me. "Yeah, right."

"No, I'm serious, we're not together."

"Oh, good. Your duo is that of the big bad wolf and the sweet, innocent lamb."

"Alex is nice when he wants to be," Nina replied. "He's

not always so cold."

"He always seems so distant," Sophie stammered, confused. "It's as if everything bothers him."

I couldn't contradict her. This was indeed the image Alex displayed. I had to break this distorted image. "It's a facade. Alex is a very sensitive and thoughtful person, but he hides it under an air of apathy."

This piqued Nina's curiosity. "Tell us more."

Goodbye, bad boy; hello, sweet pea. Alex was going to hate me for what I was about to say, but they had to know. I beckoned them closer. The girls played along, leaning in.

"When I'm in pain because of my period, he makes sure that my hot-water bottle is always filled, that I always have enough water, and he strokes my hair. He also brings me bubble tea to cheer me up."

"Are you sure we're talking about Alex?" Sophie asked suspiciously.

"Don't be jealous."

"Damn. I should have dated Alex when I had the chance," Nina complained in fake disappointment.

"Too late. He's mine now."

Not yet, that was. He would be, and once he was mine, I wouldn't share. Me possessive? Never. I wanted to cherish him and show him every day how great he was. There's no way I'd let him go as long as he wanted me to. But before that, I needed to work on myself so I could measure up.

Nina elbowed me in the ribs. "See why I tell you that everyone thinks you're dating?"

"So you're really not?"

"Not yet."

"I don't understand..."

"Nobody understands but them." Nina shrugged.

Yes, Alex was crazy about me. And yes, I was just as crazy about him. It would have to wait a bit longer. Nina gave me a knowing look. Perceptive as she was, she knew where my mind was at.

"How do you feel about him?"

I didn't know what made me open up to them, but something about these two girls inspired my trust. So I answered, "The same as he does."

"Does he know?"

"He will."

Someone grabbed me by my waist to lift me up. I recognized Alex's scent and let him spin me around like a rag doll. I'd never admit it out loud, but his showing me affection in public made my heart beat a little faster, and that warmth I felt in my chest when Alex was with me spread a little further every day. When he set me down, he didn't let go. Alex rested his head on my shoulder, and I stroked his hair. It was still damp from the shower.

"How was your morning?"

"Hmmm. How's your wound?"

"It's fine, it doesn't hurt."

Alex noticed that Nina and Sophie were watching. Nina was intrigued. Sophie, on the other hand, was uncomfortable. The poor girl was probably expecting Alex to shout at her again. He quickly looked away, as if struggling to face her.

"You feel guilty, don't you?" I asked in a low voice.

Alex let go of me, smiling apologetically. "I exaggerated, didn't I?"

"Oh yes, you made her feel guilty for nothing."

Even though he'd overreacted and attacked someone who didn't deserve that, I wasn't angry with him. Alex just wanted to protect me; I couldn't blame him for that. If anything, it made me love him even more, and I didn't know that was still possible.

"Maybe you should clear things up with Sophie now you've cooled down."

"You're right." Alex approached Sophie, rubbing the back of his head. I put my hand on his back to encourage him. "Uhm, I wanted to apologize for getting angry with you earlier."

She gave him a sceptical look before turning back to me, waiting for my reaction. I nodded. If only the others could see him the way I did.

"Okay, I accept your apology."

Alex let out a long breath, relieved she no longer resented him. Nina put her arms around Sophie's shoulders.

"Don't worry, Alex," she reassured him with a smile. "We know that when it comes to Elena, you're not thinking straight."

His cheeks flushed pink. "Touché."

Nina laid out a blanket on the ground for a picnic. This time, Alex joined in our conversations and opened up a little more to them.

"Lena, Sophie and I are going shopping on Saturday. Wanna come?"

I hesitated. I couldn't remember the last time I went shopping with other girls. As tempting as their invitation was, I couldn't accept. Sophie and Nina had been best friends since kindergarten, and I was an intruder. Their kindness was precious to me, but I couldn't encroach on their friendship.

"No thanks, but I appreciate it."

"Why not?" Nina insisted.

Sophie pouted. Alex bumped his shoulder against mine, nodding toward Nina and Sophie. Of course, he understood what I was thinking.

"They want to spend time with you. Don't be afraid to accept."

"Are you afraid of us?"

Now being the centre of attention, I lowered my eyes. I could feel what little self-confidence I had crumbling away, my old insecurities taking over again. I'd always tried to stay out of other people's way, knowing that I couldn't be what they expected me to be. And yet, I really wanted them to like me.

Alex put his arm around my waist. "She's afraid of being a burden to you," Alex explained, answering for me. "Elena finds it hard to understand that some of us want to spend time with her because we like her."

As always, Alex had read me like an open book and pinpointed what I was feeling. *Sometimes I hate his insight.*

Nina threw herself at me, pushing Alex away while Sophie patted my shoulder.

"If we ask you to come with us, it's because we want you to be there," Sophie said.

"You don't think I'm intruding on your friendship?"

Sophie shook her head, her gaze benevolent. "No way! You'd be a perfect addition to our duo."

"You'd be the icing on our cake!" Nina added, still half draped over me.

I laughed as Alex choked on his saliva.

"What do you say? Are you coming with us?"

They hadn't just invited me for a day's shopping. For the first time in ages, I realized that some people *actually* wanted me. Me, Elena, the shy girl with the shitty life. Nina and Sophie were opening their hearts, waiting for me to walk in, and I was grateful.

"I'd love to."

CHAPTER 21

Elena

Nina returned with our drinks, and I sipped my iced tea, exhausted. I'd forgotten that shopping could be so tiring. Because of my dance training, I'd never had time to do much else, and when I had any free time outside dance and classes, I preferred to sleep. Not being able to dance daily and at the level I'd reached was something that always stuck in my craw. And yet, shopping like normal girls was a nice change. Nina rested her head in her hand, giving me a mischievous smile.

"So, what's the most exciting thing you've done with Alex?"

"If you're talking about sex, I'm afraid I'm going to have to disappoint you. We're not there yet."

At least, I hoped we were at the "not yet" stage, and not the "not at all" one. Nina pouted. Would it be a good idea to ask her what Alex liked, or would that be too weird? Sophie snapped me out of my head.

"Are you waiting for a special occasion?" she asked, taking a sip of her too-sweet-looking Frappuccino.

"Everyone thinks that."

I guess I had a sign on my head that said *innocence*. I might as well have it tattooed on my forehead. I wasn't complaining, but this wasn't me either. Did Alex see me this way, too? I'd never thought about it before, but now I wanted to know. If he thought I was a virgin, would that scare him?

"You aren't?"

I shrugged. I wasn't particularly proud or pleased with the way I'd lost my virginity. When I looked back, the only thing I could say was: my first time had been on New Year's Eve while I was completely wasted. With a guy who'd come out of the closet a few weeks later, no less. Ever since then, I hadn't dared to go much further while being sober.

"I didn't wait for Alex, so I won't wait for anything special."

"Does Alex know?" Nina asked, now serious.

"I never told him, no. Do you think I should?"

After all, he'd had his fill of sex with others. Did I really have to tell him about this misadventure? It was embarrassing. Besides, why was I even thinking about it? Alex didn't even know how I felt about him. My mind was skipping steps.

"I think it would be good for you both to know where you stand," Sophie said, ever the voice of wisdom. "Maybe Alex won't be afraid to go there with you if he knows it's not your first time."

Her words confirmed what I was thinking. "I suppose you're right. But seriously, why does everyone think I'm a virgin?"

And why did it matter in other people's opinions? I let my forehead rest against the table with a sigh as Sophie placed her hand on my head.

"You look like an angel."

"Damn."

Nina's face changed in the blink of an eye. From the girl bubblier than a Golden Retriever, she now sported a serious, menacing air. But her attention wasn't on us. Her stern attitude made me uneasy. The Nina in front of me looked dangerous. She reminded me of Alex. No wonder they were friends. I was about to turn back to what she'd seen when Sophie shook her head. Piqued by curiosity, I turned around despite Sophie's warning. Kelsey stood at the other end of the coffee shop. My throat tightened. We'd managed not to bump into each other. Seeing her again gave me a strange feeling. This girl had been my best friend, and yet we'd parted like strangers. It was as if the last fifteen years had never happened.

Nina crossed her arms. Kelsey grabbed her order and left the shop without giving us a last glance, her head held high. If I'd been in her shoes, I'd have run away from Dark Nina, too. She was someone I didn't want to be around. Once my former best friend had left, Nina smiled again, her bad mood long gone.

Sensing my confusion, Sophie smiled. "Nina protects her family."

The girl tapped her heart twice with her fist. "I'm a guard dog."

We spent the rest of the afternoon at Nina's. Her house wasn't the biggest, but it was so welcoming. Her house was the complete opposite of mine. Nina gave us both fluffy pyjamas and warm socks. I glanced at Sophie.

"It's more comfortable. You don't have to change."

Once the three of us had changed, we dropped onto the bed with bottles of Coke and chips. For a homebody like me, this was my favourite part of the day. Being able to chat about anything and everything with my friends while lounging was something I particularly relished.

Nina turned back to me. I knew she was going to ask me a personal question, so I took a chip to give me courage. "Can I ask you something?"

"Sure."

"Why were you afraid to become friends with us? It's okay if you don't want to answer."

I took another chip, giving myself time to clear my head. Nina didn't beat around the bush. It was a quality I greatly appreciated. She was also good at stressing me out. So I let go. "Let's just say that some people made me believe for a long time that I was worthless and unworthy of love. I ended up believing it, I guess.

"Who would do such a thing?" Sophie asked, frowning. "No one close to you, I hope?"

"My father."

There it was. The secret I'd tried to keep from the world for so long was now out in the open. I thought sharing this part of me would be wrong, but against all odds, I felt calm.

"What a dick," Nina spat.

I hesitated to elaborate. I was the biggest coward when it came to opening up to others. Their kind looks encouraged me without making me feel like I had to talk. *Breathe in. Breathe out.*

"When my brother died, my father never recovered. All his joy of life and love for others disappeared. Now he's a bitter drunk."

A heavy silence settled over the room. They were both hesitating how to react to the chaos that was my life. Nina was the first to react.

"Your brother's gone?" she repeated, her voice soft and calm.

"Yes, he passed away three years ago."

It was strange to talk about my brother like that, in past tense. It made the fact that he was never coming back a little more real, but I no longer felt the guilt that crushed my chest whenever I thought of him. I missed Mick. I'd always miss him. That didn't stop me from needing to get better. Without him.

"I'm sorry," Sophie murmured. "Now I understand why you're afraid to get attached to others."

She brought me closer like a mother would. Nina threw herself on top of us to hug us. Tears welled up in my eyes. Without hesitation, I hugged them back.

CHAPTER 22

Elena

On a bright day when I was locked in my room with Derek Hale, Alex waltzed inside and closed my computer in one swift motion. What had gotten him in such a good mood? Alex opened my curtains and dropped onto my bed. The sunlight was blinding.

"Let's go out for a drink! I need to get out. It's been too long."

Eyes still squinting, I tilted my head to one side. It was at times like this that I remembered how different we were. Where I was the introvert who never left the house, Alex liked crowded places.

"You go out all the time. How is that possible?"

Alex flicked me on the forehead. "Because I spend all my time with you."

He hardly ever saw his friends anymore because of me. "Sorry."

Alex grabbed my face with a smile, then touched the tip of my nose with his. "If I spend my time with you, it's because I want to. Now go get dressed, love. We're off."

A shower later, we were downtown, heading for, and I

quote, "a very nice little place with great mocktails". Alex knew I wasn't tempted by alcohol. At first, we talked about everything and nothing. Then something in the air changed. I didn't understand what it was, but it had an impact on my friend, Alex became silent. Something was bothering him. I acted as if nothing had happened, knowing full well that he didn't like to be rushed when he was in his own world.

By the time I saw the terrace of the café, Alex had stopped following me. He was livid, like an animal caught in the headlights.

"Alex, are you okay?"

I put my hand on his arm, and immediately withdrew it when he tensed under my fingertips.

"Hello, Alexander. It's been a while."

A man in his mid-twenties stopped in front of us. He waited for an answer from Alex that never came. He was petrified. The man took a step in our direction, and, without thinking, I stepped in between them. I didn't know what was going on that had Alex in such a state, but something inside me was screaming not to let this guy get any closer. The intruder raised his eyebrows, surprised by my intervention.

"And you are?" he asked, full of disdain.

"His girlfriend."

Okay, total lie. My instinct told me to keep him away from Alex. The stranger held out his hand. His smile was insincere, giving me a strange feeling. *Don't show weakness, Lena.* I shook his hand with my most convincing smile. This snapped Alex out of his torpor. In one movement, he pushed the man's hand away from mine as if he were contagious. I gathered my courage; I had to react before Alex did. A cornered animal was as unpredictable as it could be dangerous.

"I think it's for the best if you leave," I suggested in a voice I wanted to sound calm and controlled.

If my intervention displeased him, he didn't object. There were too many people around us.

"See you soon, Alexander."

He also gave me a small nod before disappearing into the crowd. It took Alex a few heartbeats to come to his senses. It was as if he'd seen a ghost in this person's eyes. "Are you alright?"

His fear broke my heart. I nodded. He watched me from head to toe to make sure I was unscathed. Who was this man? And what had he done to Alex to petrify him like that? I tried to give him a reassuring smile.

"Are you?"

"I'll be fine."

"Shall we go to your place instead?"

Alex nodded. I didn't know what to expect when he spoke, but I certainly didn't expect this:

"So you're my girlfriend, huh?"

He heard that? My cheeks flushed. *Damn!* Alex, on the other hand, sported a smug expression. This was how his defence mechanism worked. Alex had to pretend nothing had happened, or he'd collapse. I cleared my throat and tried to look confident. "Yeah, I thought he might leave us alone if I said we were together..."

Alex nodded with a hum. Was he mad at me for saying that? I headed for the car so I wouldn't have to look at him. It was best to move on.

"Would you like to be my girlfriend for the day?"

The shock his words gave me stopped me in my tracks. "Why would you want that?"

"Please?"

How could I refuse when he smiled so sweetly? Everyone knew I was at his mercy. I couldn't help grinning back. "Okay."

In this moment, I was a way for him to forget what had just happened. I could be a diversion if that's what he needed. Alex intertwined our fingers. Unsure of what to do, I let him take the lead and followed him. I had no idea how to behave in a relationship. I'd never dared to be with a boy before because of my emotional baggage.

Ever the gentleman, he opened the Polo's door for me. On the way home, the silence was heavy, and I didn't know how to break it. Something serious had happened between them. Now that the truth was at hand, I didn't dare ask. Alex was the first to speak.

"You want to know what happened, don't you?" His eyes never left the road.

"Of course, I want to know."

"Then why aren't you asking?"

"Because you have to decide if you want me to know."

I knew all too well what it was like to carry wounds from your past, and how difficult it was to talk about them. Often, the pain we feel can be suffocating, and the mere idea of having to say out loud what's destroying us seems unbearable. I couldn't push Alex.

Alex knew what was going on in my life; he'd been in the wrong place at the wrong time. If things hadn't gone the way they did, I'm not sure I would've ever told him. It was too hard. Alex put his hand on my thigh.

"I want you to know."

"Okay." My pulse quickened. I'd been trying to find out

what had happened to him for months, but now that I'd seen his pain, I wasn't so sure anymore.

At his house, we passed Audrey and their mother. I barely had time to greet them before Alex dragged me to his room.

"Gosh, you must really want to spend time alone with me," I quipped as I entered his room.

"So? You got a problem with that?" Alex raised a mocking eyebrow. Every trace of tension in him seemed to have disappeared.

It was a delusion, so I pretended nothing had happened. "Nope, not at all."

Without warning, Alex placed a quick kiss on my lips. Before I could kiss him back, he was already backing away. "You can't say no today."

A part of me wanted to protest, but seeing his playful, childlike expression, I smiled like an idiot despite myself. After all, I was his girlfriend for twenty-four hours. *This should get interesting.* Alex brought his face closer, and my eyelids closed, waiting for him to kiss me again. Nothing happened. Had I misinterpreted his intention? I opened my eyes, finding Alex just two centimetres from my face. My cheeks heated under his piercing gaze. From here, I could count the few freckles dotting his nose and cheeks. His tender eyes took my breath away. No one had ever looked at me like that. Unlike the others, Alex looked at me as if I meant everything to him. He was able to make me feel loved without even saying it. Deep down, I hoped he'd tell me anyway. Then I could tell him how I felt about him without him running away.

"I never realized how much you look like a doll," he observed, taking my face in his palm.

That was rather unexpected and, if I may say so, a little

anticlimactic. Maybe I should be brave for once in my life and tell him how I feel. Would he be ready to accept my feelings? The words were on the tip of my tongue, but when I opened my mouth, no sound came out. Why was it so hard? I pushed his hand away.

"Are you trying to tell me I'm pretty or artificial?"

Alex pretended to think, as if the question was really worth asking. "Good question. I'm not sure."

I gave him a little tap on the shoulder. "You're ruining the moment! Shouldn't you be kissing me now that you finally have the chance?"

Alex burst out laughing. Where did this courage come from? "Oh, I see. You find me irresistible and you want to kiss me desperately, but you don't know how to ask."

Touché. My cheeks flushed hotter. He'd hit the bull's-eye, as always. I shrugged nonchalantly, trying not to lose face, but it was all in vain. Alex knew me too well. Of course he was aware that I had an urge to kiss him. *Fuck it!* Leaving him no time to tease me or time for me to chicken out, I put my lips on his. And it was a failure—I'd gone too hard. It wasn't the first time we'd kissed, but it was the first time I'd been the one initiating it. Alex chuckled against my mouth.

"Sorry..."

"Don't be."

"I'm not a good kisser."

"Sure you are. You just put too much pressure on yourself, that's all."

He drew invisible shapes on my cheeks without ever moving away from me. His scent made my head spin. Alex ran his fingers over my arms, sending shivers down my spine. He kissed me again, gently. Not wanting to spoil the moment,

I hesitated before kissing him back. His kisses were so soft and patient, and every time he touched me, I wanted more.

He pulled away from me, grinning. "See? You're a good kisser."

"You're just saying that to make me feel better."

Alex rubbed the back of his head. His cheeks reddened slightly. "I've been dying to kiss you again ever since that time in your kitchen."

"Really?"

"You have no idea how addicted I am to you, now do you?"

Before I could say anything, Alex pulled me closer. This time, his lips were hungry, and the pressure I'd felt before evaporated. When he was this close to me, my body went on autopilot. I couldn't tell how long we'd been there, or how we'd ended up on his bed, but it felt like time had slowed down. Like, there was no one here but us. Kissing him was addictive; every kiss made me feel drunk in the best possible way.

Just as his hands ventured to my chest, an alarm bell rang in my head. I recoiled. My vision was unfocused, and my head felt foggy. Being near him was dangerous. Loving Alex was so easy, and being with him made me forget that we weren't really a couple. The lines blurred when we were together. Even though I knew I couldn't let myself go completely, my heart struggled to understand. Alex was my better half, and it was impossible to fight it.

"Please, don't. I'm not ready."

Alex's eyes widened, taken aback. He raised both hands to signal that he wouldn't do anything. I must've looked indecisive.

"I didn't ask you to be with me today to sleep with you."

"I know," I mumbled, running my hands through my hair. "That's not what I meant."

The confusion on his face made my panic increase. How could I make him understand what I was feeling when my mind was turned upside down? The words poured out of my mouth like a tsunami. "It's not that I don't want to have sex with you, because trust me, I really do. Just not right now."

Realizing what I just said, my cheeks and neck burned crimson. I hid my face in my hands. I really had a talent for making a fool of myself. Alex laughed, and I felt even more stupid. What on earth had possessed me to speak without thinking?

"I appreciate your honesty," he quipped.

I wanted to disappear underground with my shame. "Stop laughing, it's not funny."

"You're right. It is *very* funny." His arms slipped around my waist, and I lowered my hands slightly to see his face, expecting a mocking look. Alex smiled at me, his gaze open.

How could I have doubted him for even a second? Alex was aloof and angry at times, but above all, he was kind and thoughtful. And deep down, I knew I didn't deserve him. "I'm sorry."

"What for?"

"I ruined the moment because I panicked."

Alex took my hands in his. He drew new little circles on my skin, and instantly my nerves calmed. "We have all the time in the world."

When did life start being so good to me? I hoped our lives weren't just meant to intersect but to travel a long road together. Alex placed his lips on the hollow of my neck. There was a certain pressure against my skin. By the time I realized what he was doing, it was too late. My eyes widened. He looked up, laughing.

"What the hell?"

"You're the one who asked me to give you a hickey, not that long ago. There you have it. Now get off my lap, I'm hungry."

Without giving me time to move, Alex pushed me off, and my face landed on the pillows. I glared at him, which didn't intimidate him one bit.

At supper, Lexi and Audrey were talking about something I couldn't focus on. Alex's hand was on my knee, making it impossible to think of anything but the warmth of his touch. If my life felt like an eternal winter, Alex was the fire that warmed my days. As if he could read my mind, my friend gave me a knowing smile I gave back.

"You two seem closer than usual," Lexi observed. "Are you finally dating?"

"No," I replied.

"Yes," Alex said at the same time.

Audrey grimaced. Lexi just laughed. Her green eyes lingered on my neck before quickly focusing on her glass of wine. Alex chuckled while I felt like disappearing underground, never to come up again. How was I going to get out of this situation alive? I wanted his mother and sister to like me and consider me good enough. Right now, I looked like the girl who came here to fuck. I let my head fall between my arms.

"It's not what you think." Alex sighed. "I only did it to annoy her."

Unlike what I'd feared, Lexi shrugged, not caring that

much. "You're grown-ups, you can do what you want. Just don't be too loud."

His mother put a hand on my arm when she noticed my mortified expression. Lexi was so much more chill than my mom would ever be. If she saw me come home with a hickey, she'd go ballistic.

"Don't worry, my dear, you can hide it with concealer."

***

After getting ready for bed, I returned to the bedroom and hid under the blanket, keeping a certain distance from Alex. Even though he'd had his tongue in my mouth a few hours earlier, which still felt weird, I couldn't figure out how or if I should initiate contact. I wanted to touch him. I just didn't know how to. This whole boyfriend/girlfriend thing was new. It was ironic, wasn't it? I hadn't cared about my first time, but initiating contact with him scared me. I'd skipped steps and gone straight to "drunk sex" without having learned to love first, and without having learned to show my feelings to the person I loved.

Alex lay on his side, and I held my breath. As always, I was unnecessarily worrying; I couldn't help it. He watched me in silence. I could almost hear the cogwheels in his head as he was thinking. Alex hesitated.

"Would you like to be my girlfriend, but for real?"

His question caught me off guard. It shouldn't have—he'd already confessed his feelings. And yet, despite all his efforts, I still couldn't get used to the idea that someone like Alex could be interested in someone like me. Except for a broken heart, I had nothing to offer. He knew that.

"I'd love to."

"I feel like a 'but' is coming."

This man was reading me like an open book, to the point where it was unsettling. I shuddered.

"I just don't think it's the right time," I admitted in a low voice.

"You never think it's the right time."

I felt the need to explain myself. I didn't want there to be a misunderstanding between us simply because I couldn't express my feelings properly. I wanted to be with him, more than anything, but first I wanted to become worthy of him.

"Alex, how am I supposed to love you right if I can't love myself? I want to be with you. When you're with me, I feel like I can overcome anything. I feel like I'm worth something. But I need to understand that I'm just as worthy when you're not around."

"What are you going to do?" he asked, holding his breath.

A huge shadow hovered over my head; it had been there for a while. I simply couldn't ignore it anymore. Alex sounded so hopeful that it was difficult to swallow. It was time for me to face the truth. I had to get on with my life and finally move on.

"I think it's time I braved my problems, don't you?"

Alex remained silent, but nodded. I was a coward.

"I know it's selfish of me to ask, but do you think you could wait for me?"

"No."

I didn't know which hurt more: his neutral face or his decisive tone. I was aware I was asking too much—I *always* asked too much—and yet I hadn't expected Alex to reject my question so fast. I swallowed.

"Okay."

"I'm not going to stand here like an idiot while you deal with your problems. I'll be with you every step of the way."

Tears welled up in my eyes. Alex's face lost all its colour. Why was he looking so worried? All I wanted was to kiss him until we were breathless.

"Why are you crying? What did I do wrong?"

"You didn't do anything wrong," I stammered, crying like a baby. "Thank you."

CHAPTER 23

Elena

Alex had been looking outside for over an hour, lost in thought, and I didn't know whether to get him out of it or not. Ever since I told him that I wanted to confront my demons the day before, he had been in some kind of trance, seemingly fighting an inner battle. When I got up to go to the kitchen, he snapped out of his torpor. All I wanted to do was run and hug him, and tell him everything would be all right. Seeing him so sad was like a punch in the gut. But I didn't. Right now, he was too fragile for me to rush over to him. This time, Alex would have to decide when or if he wanted to come to me.

"Are you leaving?"

"No, I was just going to grab a snack. Do you want me to leave?"

Perhaps this wasn't the best time to talk. Alex was still shaken. Who was that man? And what had happened to put Alex in such a state of distress?

"Why would I want you to leave?" he asked.

"Maybe you need time to collect your thoughts?"

Alex tapped his finger against the window, the only sign

of his anxiety. "I don't need to. I guess I need to stop trying to figure out what to say and just talk."

"You sure you're ready to talk?"

Because I wasn't. I was touched by the fact that he wanted me to know. But was it supposed to go like this? It felt like Alex was forcing himself to open up, and I wasn't convinced that this was the best thing for him to do. He rubbed his palms over his face.

"I don't think I'll ever be ready. Lena, I can't do this anymore."

"Do what?"

"Keep that part of me away from you. You're one of the people I care about most, and not being honest with you feels too heavy."

So this was the moment of truth. I sat back on his bed.

"That person we ran into hurt you, didn't he?"

"He destroyed me."

Faced with my worried look, Alex smiled. It wasn't genuine, though. He was just trying to reassure me, as always. I had to pull myself together and be strong. He needed it.

"I'm fine now, don't worry."

He was lying through his teeth. The pretence was over, he couldn't fool me anymore. Either Alex turned his pain into uncontrollable anger, or he drowned it with alcohol and drugs.

"I don't think you're doing as well as you want me to believe. You wouldn't have your temper not attraction to drugs if you were."

I expected him to retort and tell me how broken I was.

Instead, he nodded. "You're right, but I'm working on it. I know it may not seem like it, but I've been to therapy for years. I've also been in talking groups. I'm really trying. I guess I just… struggle to get there." Alex sat down on the bed and hugged a pillow. In this moment, he didn't look like an adult, but like a terrified, lost child. The child I'd once known. I'd never seen him so shaken before.

It hit me then that I knew almost nothing about him when he wasn't with me. Alex rarely talked about himself, and when he did, he only shared small anecdotes. Yet his life was just as complicated as mine was, if not more so. His hands trembled slightly. I moved towards him, but Alex moved his hands away to stay out of my reach. Without hesitation, I grabbed his wrists. Alex tried to pull away, so I tightened my grip. He looked up at me, and I held his gaze. I couldn't let him sink into his distress. And if I couldn't keep him out of it, I'd go down with him.

"You're safe. It's just me."

"I don't know where to start."

"You don't have to tell me anything. You know that, right?"

Alex nodded, his eyes focused on our entwined hands. "I just hope your image of me doesn't change."

"If it changes, it will only make you more human to me."

He took a deep breath. For the first time, Alex was unable to hold my gaze. My thumbs traced little circles on his palms, trying to comfort him.

"When I was a kid, I was in a swimming club. I didn't particularly like it at first, but as I was good at sports, my parents enrolled me in several clubs, including swimming, tennis, and soccer. Because I was smaller than others my age, they often teased me. I was also one of the best on the team, and the coach's favourite, so most of my clubmates didn't like me that much. I thought it was because I trained and did my best that our coach appreciated me so much, but I was wrong."

My blood ran cold, my heart pounding in my temples. This couldn't be true. *Please, let me be wrong.*

Alex smiled sadly. "You get it, don't you?"

I swallowed.

"He abused you."

"One day, after winning a competition, I was cornered by some of the team members. They started hitting and kicking me. I was alone and unable to defend myself. The coach heard that something was going on and intervened. He gave me first aid before taking me to the doctor. For several days, I was unable to leave the house because of injuries, but he came to see me every day to make sure I recovered quickly. My mom was so grateful to him. After all, he didn't *have* to look after me so much. At first, nobody understood what was really going on. When I went back to the club, things had changed. None of the other kids dared say anything mean to me anymore. They were trying to be nice. The coach's behaviour changed too. He spent more time training me personally to become better for our competitions. He gave me chocolate when my training went well. Vincent had become my best friend. One day, I don't know exactly what happened, but I found his behaviour too kind and clingy. I was uncomfortable, but I didn't understand why. It went on for a while. A smile here, a hand on the shoulder there. It was as if he expected the same of me."

Nausea made my head spin. How anyone could touch a defenceless child was beyond me.

"You were the victim of a sexual predator. Did he…"

My voice cracked. How was I supposed to finish that question? The answer frightened me. Alex shook his head, still smiling. Why was he trying to be strong, even at a time like this?

"I wasn't raped, if that's what you meant. I was found in time. My story isn't as bad as other people's."

Something snapped inside me. This wasn't right. "Stop."

"Elena, I'm fine. It happened eight years ago."

"Don't you dare say that. Even if he didn't actually rape you, this person manipulated you, took advantage of your naivete to abuse your trust, and *touched* you. If he'd had more time, he would have. So don't say that what you suffered wasn't that bad. You have as much right to suffer as anyone else."

I'd hit home. His breaths quickened, his eyes unable to focus. Without thinking, I hugged him closer to my heart. I could feel his pain, and it was making me sick. If I could take some of that pain away from him, I would. Alex clung to me like a lifeline, and my heart cracked. I stroked his hair, waiting for him to recover. After a while, Alex lay on his back and put his head on my thighs to look at me. His eyes glistened with unshed tears.

"You're right, I'm not fine at all. I thought I was doing okay, but seeing him again made me realize that it was an illusion I forced myself to believe in. Sometimes I can't help wondering what would've happened if they'd found me ten minutes later. I can't even imagine how much it would screw someone up when you see how much this destroyed me."

His voice croaked. Alex took my hand and placed it over his heart. It was beating so fast that I feared it would fly out of his chest.

"You see, Vincent was a person I admired and considered one of my closest friends. What he did... he was turning me into his personal slave, an object to satisfy his messed-up desires. I wasn't hurt physically, but that doesn't take away the fear and emotional pain. Though it's been years, I still wake up some nights because I'm terrified. It's a stain I can't erase, and sometimes I feel like it's going to suffocate me."

What could I possibly say? I couldn't make his trauma go away. I just hoped I could help him as he had helped me, and I prayed he could overcome his past and be happy. For real this time.

"I'm so sorry you had to go through all this... But he can't hurt you anymore."

Alex raised an eyebrow. "Why's that? Are you going to protect me?"

Would I be able to? One thing was certain: I would do everything within my power. "Of course!" I exclaimed, tensing my arm muscles. "Look at my biceps. Aren't you impressed by my physique?"

For the first time since he'd opened his heart to me, his smile was sincere, and I could breathe again.

"Yes, I feel so safe now."

I rolled my eyes, but deep down I felt reassured. If he could make jokes, that was a good sign. "What I mean is, he hurt you then, but you're a man now. A physically very strong person. No one can hurt you like that. And even if he tries, I won't let him get anywhere near you."

"You're adorable."

Not the answer I was expecting. I pouted. "I'm trying to be strong and confident here..."

Alex placed a kiss on my fingers. "You are. But you're also

adorable, and I love how protective you are."

"You know I'd move heaven and earth for you, don't you?"

I hoped he understood that I was sincere. I loved him so much. At this point, I would do anything for him.

"I know."

***

Ever since Alex had told me about his past, he had acted like a different person. Okay, this might be a slight exaggeration, but things had changed. We'd become even closer, something I'd thought impossible. There was no longer that wall around his heart. Now that I belonged there, he didn't want me to leave. It was nice to be accepted and loved, especially by someone I loved just as much.

"Do you really have to go back to that house? I don't like leaving you alone here." Alex looked at my house as if the devil himself were there.

Maybe he wasn't wrong.

"I don't have another option. Where would I go?"

"You could stay at my place."

I liked the idea, no matter how unrealistic it really was. "I can't stay at your place forever."

"Why not? My mother adores you."

"I can't take advantage of you like that. It wouldn't be right."

They had already been so good to me. I couldn't keep relying on them indefinitely. Besides, deep down, I knew that Lexi's affection for me had shifted as our friendship had evolved. Alex wanted to retort, but thought better of it.

"Call me if anything happens, okay? I don't care what time it is or why. If anything happens, I'll come get you."

"I mean, look at you. You'll be a perfect boyfriend," I joked to lighten the situation.

This time, it didn't work. He was more serious than ever. "Promise me!" he insisted.

"I promise."

As I entered the house, I tried to make my way to my room on silent feet to avoid Frank. Luck was not on my side; he was already in the corridor. He seemed particularly sober, which lulled me into a fake sense of safety. My father raised an eyebrow when he spotted me, but didn't show more interest than that. My body froze, unsure of what would happen. When he was sober, he wasn't physically violent. His words became his weapons: sharp and made to wound a person to a bloody pulp.

"Where have you been?"

Like you give a shit.

"At a friend's house."

His gaze fell on the bruise on my neck, and I swallowed. I should have followed Lexi's advice and hidden that hickey with concealer.

"Friends, you say. Looks like you got fucked instead."

How was I ever going to stand up to him? His words had the same effect as his fists. My breath caught in my throat. I lowered my eyes and hurried to my room. I wouldn't break in front of him. Not this time.

CHAPTER 24

Alex

"What do you want to watch?"

Elena looked at the DVDs they had. Alex didn't know what style of film she would choose. He feared something romantic and clichéd. Even if they usually had the same tastes, sooner or later she would force him to watch something like *Titanic*, wouldn't she? Elena pulled out *Knights of the Zodiac*. Oof.

"I didn't expect that."

Elena smiled gently, observing the disc case.

"When we were little, my brother and I used to watch *Knights of the Zodiac* as we ate our breakfast before leaving for school."

"I feared you'd choose a romantic movie. I'm relieved."

Elena patted the top of his head before heading back to the bedroom. She moved around the house as if she were at home—a sight that made him so happy.

"Just because I'm a girl doesn't mean I like romantic movies by default. I don't particularly like mushy stuff. You should know that by now."

Fair enough. Alex turned on the anime before turning back to Elena. Seeing her lying on his bed was becoming a habit, and it was putting Alex in a tizzy. He loved her so much, it was almost comical. Alex took a deep breath and sat down on the bed as well. While Elena's eyes were glued to the TV, Alex couldn't help but look at her. At first, he'd been afraid their friendship would suffer once the truth about his past came out. Everyone who had learned what had happened looked at him with sad eyes. Elena had stayed the same. She didn't act like nothing had happened, but she also didn't treat him as if he was going to collapse as soon as anyone got near. With her, he wasn't a victim or a reject. He was just Alex. After a moment, she turned her head towards him, raising an eyebrow.

"Is there a reason you're staring at me like that?"

Without saying a word, Alex pressed his lips to hers. Realizing he'd just kissed her when she'd told him she wanted to wait, he expected her to push him away. Alex abruptly pulled back. By acting without thinking, he'd taken advantage of the situation and become the kind of guy he despised.

"I'm sorry. I shouldn't have done that."

Elena gave him a mischievous smile.

"I know I'm irresistible, but warn me next time."

"You're not mad?"

She turned fully towards him, ignoring what was happening on the screen. Elena put her hand on the back of Alex's neck and kissed him. Gently at first, she became more confident as he kissed her back. Elena lay on her back and drew Alex to her. Lost in their own world, time had stopped.

Although they were friends first, kissing her made him feel like he belonged with her. As if they were made for each other. *What a cliché.* And yet, this strange girl had become his home, and being with her was as natural as breathing.

"Please close the door when you're going to do something dirty."

Audrey gave them a nasty look while Elena laughed into his neck. They got up to face her.

"My bad. Sorry."

He'd better close his door next time if they want peace. Unlike him, Elena didn't seem annoyed or uncomfortable.

"No, it's my fault. I let myself be tempted by the devil. It won't happen again."

"Did you just insinuate I'm a demon?"

"A beautiful demon. I want that to be clear."

"So you really only like me for my looks, huh?"

Elena gave him a sidelong glance. "Surely you didn't think I'd be interested in something as trivial as your personality?"

Alex placed his hands on his heart, pretending to be hurt. He was becoming as dramatic as she was. Audrey's face contorted in disgust at their banter, and she closed the door.

"We should close this door more often if you're going to kiss me again," she said, combing back her hair.

How could she be so calm when he was so nervous? Alex decided to lay his cards on the table. He needed to be honest. Elena was a drug.

"I'm selfish. Until you say stop, I'll take whatever I can get."

Elena stared at him with her blue eyes, taking her time to think. She was hesitating whether or not to tell the truth.

"It's hard to resist when it's you. I want you."

That familiar bad feeling bubbled to the surface again. Elena noticed his confusion.

"Alex, what's wrong?"

"I keep thinking something bad will happen. I'm afraid you'll pull away from me."

"Why would you think that?"

Alex closed his eyes. Why was he so anxious? He didn't know where this fear was coming from, only that the closer he became to Elena, the more he felt they'd never be together, and the thought made him nauseous. His heart was loud in his temples. He gasped when Elena climbed onto his lap. She placed her palms on his face. Every touch made him even more addicted to her, and she had no idea how much power she wielded over him.

"Alex, talk to me."

He ran his hands through his hair. *Breathe*. She needed to know how he felt. He couldn't hide it from her anymore, even if she might not share his feelings. Alex just hoped his feelings wouldn't push her away. It didn't matter if she loved him or not; he didn't want to live without her anymore.

"I love you, and it terrifies me."

Elena smiled so brightly that her eyes turned into crescent moons. Alex couldn't help smiling back, seeing her so happy. She rested her forehead against his.

"I wasn't going to tell you this now or like this, but it doesn't matter. I love you, too, Alex."

His heart continued to beat wildly. She placed a kiss on his cheek, still beaming. How could someone as good as her love someone like him? His eyes burned. He wanted to cry happy tears. Alex knew how much he loved her; he'd known it for a while. And he'd accepted the fact that this love would only be one-sided because she was with him, and that was enough. But to be loved by the person he cherished most seemed unreal. Yet he couldn't deny it now that he knew. Elena's eyes were filled with love and affection. Love and affection for *him*. How had he never realized it before? His fears vanished like snow in the sun. Elena gently wiped away the tears that escaped. He felt ridiculous crying in front of her, but couldn't stop the tears from falling.

"I wanted to do something cute to tell you."

She was adorable. Knowing her, Elena would probably have given him flowers and a little card with a teddy bear on it. "See, you're a romantic!"

Elena pouted, her gaze playful. "Just because I don't like romance movies doesn't mean I'm not romantic."

"Why me?"

He had to know. Elena took Alex's arms and placed them around her waist. It was kind of exciting when she was the one in charge.

"What?" she asked, taken aback.

"Why would you want to be with me and not someone else?"

"I don't know. It's... It's just you. My heart decided it would be you."

A laugh left his lips. "That's cheesy, even for you."

"I know. I'm ashamed of saying it out loud." She hid her face in the crook of his neck, giggling.

"What if I'm not good enough?"

Elena became serious again. He knew he was going too fast. They weren't even together yet. Being the angel she was, Elena remained patient and reassured him.

"You know, Alex, it's never been about whether we're

good enough for each other. It's about making efforts. I want to be the best version of myself so I can be with you, maybe you should try to do the same. And we'll work out the rest together."

She lay down and beckoned him to join her. There was nothing he could refuse her, so he followed, watching her.

"You really think I can become better?"

"Yeah. You're already getting better every day. I just don't understand how you never realized I was crazy about you? We've been dancing around each other for months."

Easy. Alex had always thought that no one could care about him that way. After his trauma, he'd lost himself to the point of believing he was no longer worthy. And yet, Elena loved him despite knowing everything about him.

"There's a difference between being interested and loving someone," he simply said. "I thought you were just interested."

"Believe me, I'm way past that stage. I'm totally, completely, madly, deeply in love with you. But don't worry, I don't mind reminding you every day."

Had she always been so cheesy and corny? This was a new side of Elena he couldn't help but adore. Elena was so calm. For once, Alex didn't hesitate and let her take the lead. He, the control freak, was letting her take control of them, of him. It was confusing, and it was frightening. But he trusted her. Elena tried to read him.

"Does it bother you that I'm taking so long?" she asked, less confident. "Be honest."

Alex pondered over the question. He'd never been in a relationship before. With Elena, it was different. He felt excited about finally learning to be in a relationship. As long as she was there, there was no rush. Every moment together was worth it. Knowing she felt the same was more than he could have hoped for.

"Why would it?"

"You don't feel like I'm messing with your head, do you?"

"Love, take all the time you need. As long as I know you're as serious about us as I am, I can wait."

Elena snuggled into his arms like a kitten. Her warmth enveloped him like a blanket.

"You're the best."

"I know."

***

Elena

"Elena, how are you?"

Alex's mother entered the kitchen, still dressed in her pyjamas.

"Good. You?"

No matter how many hours I spent in this house, I never felt at ease when Lexi was around. Yet she'd known me since I was born. Something about her presence always made me want to look down. When I was alone, she always seemed happier to see me than when I was with Alex.

"Good."

Lexi sat opposite me, watching me in silence. This was getting uncomfortable. "Can I ask you something?"

I tried to hold her gaze, but it was hard. Anxiety gnawed at my inner peace. I shook my head and swallowed. Oh God, what had I done now?

"You and Alex can do what you want, you're old enough. But don't shock my youngest daughter."

Oh no. My cheeks flushed. This was a misunderstanding, and I wanted to put things right. I didn't want my future mother-in-law to think I was spending my time at her place just to sleep with her son. Sure, we'd kissed, but that was all it had been.

"It's not what you think. We haven't…"

Lexi raised an eyebrow as she waited for me to finish my sentence.

I cleared my throat and resumed, "It's a misunderstanding. We haven't done anything. We kissed, but we don't intend to go further than that. Alex and I talked about it."

Alex had just confessed his feelings. With both our pasts, taking our time was the right thing to do. We were both insecure, and we both had trouble accepting someone else's affection. I wanted us to build a relationship full of trust and patience. Yes, sure, I also wanted amazing sex. I was just a girl with hormones, like everyone else. But that would have to wait a little longer. The first thing I had to do was pick up the pieces of my life and move on so I could get better.

"I'm just going to ask you not to get his hopes up, okay? Alex often acts aloof, but his heart is fragile."

Sensing where she was going, I nodded and decided to be transparent. After all, she was my future mother-in-law, even if she did intimidate me at times.

"I know about his past."

Her face paled. "He told you?"

I nodded again. Alex's mom ran her hands through her

hair, her breathing heavy. I couldn't imagine how she must have felt about what had happened to him. "What do you think? Alex never wanted anyone to know. I'm surprised he decided to tell you."

"It doesn't change anything for me. Alex is still Alex, and I love him the way he is."

When she started crying, I wondered if I'd said something wrong. Lexi hugged me hard. I returned the embrace, feeling emotional too. For the first time in months, it felt like she was finally accepting me. Not for the little Elena of years ago, but for me.

"Take care of my son, okay?"

"What did you do to my mom?" Alex entered the kitchen with a suspicious look on his face.

His mom placed a kiss on my forehead. She winked at me, and the atmosphere in the kitchen became lighter again.

"Nothing. Just girl talk."

CHAPTER 25

Elena

Just as Nina and I were leaving the biology classroom, I spotted Alex waiting for us outside. He was strangely nervous, jumping from one foot to the other, his fingers drumming on his arms. His brown hair was even more dishevelled than usual, like he'd run his fingers through it countless times.

"Do you have any plans for tonight?" he asked casually.

"No."

Nina gave me a wry smile before hurrying off down the hall. Did she know something I didn't?

"Then now you do."

"Why's that?"

"Let's go on a date."

A laugh left my lips. Was he nervous about asking me out? I had to tease him, if only a little. It wouldn't be funny if I didn't.

"What a strange way to invite a lady."

"Yeah, I tried to think of a more romantic way, but I can't remember what I had memorized," Alex rambled.

He stopped when he realized he'd said more than he'd

intended, his green eyes widening. This never happened to him. He who was usually calm and composed must really have been in overdrive if he couldn't control his mouth. As he did whenever he was uncomfortable, Alex rubbed the back of his head. A nervous tic I found more and more endearing every day.

"Cute." I giggled.

"It's embarrassing."

"I think it's sweet. Okay, I accept your invitation."

"Great. Wait for me in the parking lot after class."

Unlike usual, Alex turned on his heels and disappeared in the blink of an eye, leaving me alone at lunchtime. For the rest of the day, I couldn't help trying to guess what he had planned. This was the first time in my life I'd been invited on a date. And the cherry on top, it was with Alex. Everything suddenly seemed so real between us. I grinned like an idiot.

At the end of class, I met Alex in the parking lot. I didn't think it was possible, but he was even more jittery than earlier. During the drive, I chatted about everything and anything to try and lighten the mood, without much success. Alex parked his car at the city's indoor ice rink.

"We're going ice skating?"

"No, we're going to plant umbrellas."

I pretended to laugh before rolling my eyes. He was back to his usual charming self, it seemed. "You've got so much personality today."

Alex took a few things out of the trunk and handed me a pair of gloves, socks, and a brick-coloured sweater that caught my eye. The sweater was soft and smelled of washing powder, and a touch of his perfume—something I very much appreciated. I turned to him and smiled. He returned my smile, and for the first time today, he seemed to relax a bit.

"How did you know I like skating?"

"Just a hunch called Sophie."

Once we'd put on our skates, we headed for the rink. I moved slowly, getting used to being on ice again. I did a few zigzags and pirouettes before turning back to Alex. Poor thing. I chuckled as he clung to the edge, holding on for dear life. He frowned.

"Of course you can skate." He sighed. "I was hoping you'd be as bad at it as me."

"If you can do ballet, you can ice skate. It's all about balance."

He tried to move towards me, but his balance was terrible. I held out my hands. Alex was a danger on the ice.

"I'm not going to let go of the edge if that's what you're suggesting."

"Oh come on, don't be a sissy. I won't let you fall. At least, not too often."

Alex rolled his eyes but agreed to take my hands anyway. I guided him slowly. "Maybe for a first date, I should have chosen something more up my alley."

I bumped my shoulder against his in jest, and he nearly fell. I caught him as best I could. Alex wore a disgruntled grimace.

"We're holding hands while skating. Isn't that romantic?"

"I feel like a kid holding his mother's hand."

Although he wasn't comfortable, Alex followed me all over the rink. He fell occasionally, but all in all, it was a very cute afternoon. If all dates were as carefree and fun, I wanted to go on more.

Back in the car, I kept Alex's sweater on. Every now and

then, I'd notice him watching me with a smile. Now I just had to find a way to keep it.

"Thank you for this afternoon. I loved it."

"The day isn't over yet."

I whistled, impressed. "When you organize, you go all out, don't you?"

"You'd better get used to it if you're going to be my girlfriend." He winked at me before starting the car.

"I can't wait."

We entered a small pizzeria. The smell of olives and tomato sauce made my mouth water. The dimmed lights gave the restaurant a cosy air. I was pleasantly surprised. For someone who'd never been on a date in his life, Alex had managed like a boss. The day was perfect.

A waitress took our order. A pizza capricciosa for me and a pizza pepperoni for Alex, with extra garlic bread. Enough to chase vampires away.

Reaching for the salt, Alex spilled his glass of Coke on the table. A waitress hurried over to clean up the mess before bringing him a new glass. My friend pinched the bridge of his nose and sighed. His nerves had returned full force.

"Alex, what's going on? You've been nervous all day."

He let his head fall into his hands, and I could no longer see his face, so I touched his leg under the table. His head shot up.

"You okay?"

"Yeah. I just ruined our first date because of my panic."

"Why are you getting so worked up?" I asked, taking a sip of my Sprite. "It's just me."

He shrugged, looking defeated. "I guess I wanted to try to impress you and try to be romantic. It didn't turn out the way

I planned. This is the first time we've seen each other since..."

Since Alex confessed his feelings for me. He was still having trouble adjusting, the two of us having just reached an important milestone. A step neither of us had taken before, but Alex wasn't on the same page as I was. If I thought about it, we'd been on many dates already. That didn't make our outings any less exciting. It had just given me a head start.

He crossed his arms. "Why aren't *you* nervous? You're as calm as ever."

I nibbled on a piece of garlic bread, unsure of how to continue. "For me, nothing has changed."

His gaze darkened and I felt a small pang of guilt form. "I told you I was in love with you. That doesn't change anything?"

I had to tell him, didn't I? "Alex, I have a confession."

"I'm listening."

I bit my thumbnail, hoping I wouldn't ruin our date. "You won't like it. Uhm, how should I put this? Actually, I knew you were in love with me before you said it..." I squeaked, unsure of myself.

Alex choked on his Coke, only to be shaken by a coughing fit. Would he survive this date? "What?"

"Yeah, I know you tried to hide it for a few months, but I knew."

His fingers tapped on his arm. "Don't tell me I was unconsciously giving you enamoured looks."

"At times, but that's not what gave it away. You told me."

"No, I never..."

"Greek statues," I cut him off.

His cheeks turned red like his sweater. The way things

were going, the answer was no: he wasn't going to survive the evening. Alex pointed an accusing finger at me. "That's why you let it go when I told you I didn't want to talk about it. You didn't insist."

"Correct. I didn't want to embarrass you further."

"And now?"

I put my hand on his, and Alex smiled. How was it possible that such a handsome man could be so adorable at the same time? "Now it's different. Now I can gently make fun of you and all the crap you said. You were so eloquent when you first told me how you felt."

Even though I was teasing him, the atmosphere between us became lighter. The waitress brought our pizzas, and as she left, I grinned with all my teeth. Alex leaned back in his chair.

"Talk. I know you're dying to tell me."

"See the Greek statues? Well, you don't look like them at all. You're prettier and you've got a much better ass. Are you icing? Because I want to put you on top and lick every part of you."

Alex hid his face behind his hands, and I giggled even more. At the time, his confession had turned my world upside down. Now it gave me a daily dose of serotonin. It wasn't romantic, but it was fun. And it was perfectly us.

When our pizzas were finished, Alex dropped me off at my front door. "Don't forget to give me back my sweater."

Yeah, right.

"What?"

"The sweater you're wearing. Don't forget to give it back."

I glanced at the brick-coloured cloth. He was never getting it back. Alex had only lent it to me so I wouldn't get cold at the rink. But the sweater was soft, and it smelled of Alex.

"I don't know what you're talking about."

He gave me an amused look. "What are you playing at?"

"Can I keep it, please?"

I placed my hands around my face in a kawaii position. Suffice it to say, Alex was not impressed.

"Why would I give you my sweater? As far as I know, I can't take one of yours."

"I know they wouldn't fit, but I'm sure that my style would suit you perfectly. Now, can I keep it? I look so cute and hot wearing it. It would be a waste if I gave it back."

Eventually, he'd give in. I just had to keep pleading with my eyes. Alex didn't know how to say no. He crossed his arms.

"Careful, your head won't fit through the door if you continue like this."

Let's change tactics.

"Are you saying you don't find me absolutely adorable in *your* sweater? That would be a lie. I've seen the way you look at me."

For a few seconds, Alex held my gaze. Then he lowered his eyes. Victory was mine. He exhaled loudly.

"I can't tell if you're telling the truth or bluffing. Fine, keep it!"

I hugged Alex and inhaled his scent. He hesitated, but eventually returned my embrace. He was still adjusting to this new situation, whereas I'd had all the time in the world to get used to it. Still, it was surreal to be able to hold him in my arms like this.

"Thank you for today. I enjoyed it more than you think."

"You're welcome."

Alex pulled me tighter against him. If I could be stuck in a time loop, I wish it would be this moment.

CHAPTER 26

Elena

Like every Thursday afternoon, we met at the Partea. This time, it was Alex's turn to order for the group.

"What do you want?" he asked.

"A classic bubble tea with tapioca pearls," I said, grinning from ear to ear. "A large one."

Calories don't count when it's good. At least, that's what I told myself.

"I'll have a mango bubble tea," Nina added, her attention on her phone.

Alex raised an eyebrow before replying, "Get your own."

Nina sputtered in protest. Sophie let her head rest in her hand—she was used to it.

"What kind of favouritism is this? Elena gets chivalry from you, but we don't? Bros before hoes!"

Alex let her simmer, pretending not to care about what she was saying, but his gaze was playful. He was pulling her leg, and Nina didn't even realize it, too offended. After a while, he seemed to take pity on her. "I'm kidding. Of course, I'll order for you."

Sophie and I giggled.

"He was going to order for you, no matter what."

"He fooled me, didn't he?"

"Just a little."

I brought my thumb and forefinger together. Nina let her head drop against the table so hard that I feared she had hurt herself.

"Elena?"

I turned to face the speaker, surprised to find Robin standing in front of me. I hadn't seen anyone from the dance school since my accident. Going there as a visitor would hurt too much.

"Robin!"

His face lit up. "I knew it was you."

He hugged me before I had time to respond. The Elena from a year ago would have had her heart racing. Today's Elena returned the embrace without losing her nerve. Robin stepped aside, all smiles.

"We're all looking forward to your return to the studio. When will you be back?"

"The doctor has forbidden me to dance while I'm revalidating. I'm still waiting for his approval."

The dancer sat down in Alex's seat. Some of his sand-coloured curls were unruly. It was weird not to want to run my fingers through them anymore. Nina watched us with an inquisitive eye, but I ignored her while Robin and I chatted.

"The studio feels empty without you."

My heart clenched. I'd managed to focus on other things, and yes, by other things I meant a taciturn boy who made my head spin, but I missed dancing. Seeing one of the members of the hip-hop club reminded me of that emptiness I'd been trying to ignore for months. I joked to keep the mood from getting gloomy.

"Of course, I'm the best."

Robin ruffled my hair. "I can't say you're wrong. We should grab a drink sometime, what do you say?"

I opened my mouth to agree when Alex placed another chair on my other side and sat down. The hand he let rest on my thigh didn't go unnoticed. Robin wasn't impressed, his smile unwavering.

"Whenever you want," Alex said, holding Robin's gaze.

The tension was palpable, but only on one side. Robin rested his elbows on the table, leaning towards us. Alex's hand became heavier.

"Don't worry, Alex, I'm not going to steal your girlfriend."

A small part of me wished Robin had been interested in me. After all, he'd been my crush for years. On the other hand, if I'd kept obsessing over him, I might never have found Alex. Just the thought of it gave me goosebumps.

"That said, the day you screw up, I'll find you."

I mentally prepared myself for Alex losing it. Instead, he just nodded. Robin stood up, and I followed him to the exit. From the corner of my eye, I could see Alex not letting us out of his sight.

"I was happy to see you."

"Me too."

Robin hugged me one last time and whispered, "I didn't expect you to choose a guy like Alex."

Even if it was rather blunt, he wasn't wrong. "Why?"

"I thought you'd choose someone more like yourself. Someone with your passion for dance."

"Weird, right? And yet, Alex is exactly my type."

He ran a hand through his curls. Alex was my type, but

Robin was still a tiny bit my type, too.

"There was a time when I was your type," he murmured, smirking.

I swallowed hard. "How do you know that?" I squeaked, mortified.

"You're too transparent when you love someone. I hope he takes good care of you." He winked before leaving the Partea, leaving me red as a peony in the café.

I took a deep breath and went back to my friends, who were all watching me. Sophie with astonishment, Nina with incomprehension, and Alex with displeasure.

"I can't believe it. I'm gone for five minutes and you get hit on by someone else!"

"Robin wasn't hitting on me."

Alas. My ego would have appreciated it if he had. Alex was seething; his neck turned red.

"You could have told him you were taken."

I knew I shouldn't, but I wanted to annoy him a little more. "I am? Since when?"

"Not funny," he grumbled.

"Are you jealous?" I asked innocently.

Alex clenched his jaw. He was so jealous. *I love this.*

"I'm not jealous." Alex went back to the counter to get our drinks. He returned to the table without looking in my direction. I kissed his cheek, but Alex continued to ignore me.

Nina rolled her eyes.

I wrapped my arms around his neck and pressed my cheek against his. "Are you done?"

"I've already told you, I'm not jealous."

I gave up. Nina and Sophie glanced at each other, but remained silent. Perhaps I'd taken the joke too far.

"Yeah, and I'm the queen," I mumbled.

Even though he had been scowling mere seconds before, he laughed. "What an honour, Your Majesty."

The sky began to darken. Once we'd finished our drinks, Alex offered to take me home.

I was about to accept when Nina interjected, "We'll bring her back."

"I can do it," said Alex, grabbing his car keys.

"We'll bring her back," Nina repeated in a tone that indicated she didn't want to be contradicted.

I wanted to retort that I could very well choose who I wanted to go home with, but I kept my mouth shut. What was going on? Alex accepted and left the café. Only a couple remained at the other end of the room.

Nina turned back to me. I gave a questioning glance at Sophie, who looked just as lost as me. "Can I ask you a question?"

It wasn't often that Nina took a serious tone. I already knew I wasn't going to like what happened next. I nodded anyway, waiting to hear what she wanted to ask.

"Don't you feel like you're leading Alex on?"

My heart skipped a beat. This was the blow I'd been waiting for, only worse. I had expected an unpleasant question. This one had the same effect as a punch in the stomach. Sophie's instincts kicked in.

"It's none of our business," said the little blonde. "You shouldn't ask such things. Lena, ignore her."

"I just want to understand," Nina replied. "Alex follows her around like an enamoured puppy. I'd like to know why you're giving him hope if you have no intention of going out with him."

That was indeed what I was doing, wasn't I? I let him run after me, making promises that hadn't led anywhere. We'd finally set things straight, gone on our first date, and that was it. Nina was right.

Her gaze softened, which made me feel even more guilty. Everyone looked at me like I was this little thing that would break at the slightest unpleasant word.

"I'm not blaming you. I just want to understand what's going on in that head of yours."

How was I supposed to make them understand what was going on in there? The more I thought, the less clear things became. I took a deep breath, running my hands through my hair. I tugged at a few strands.

"I don't want to start a relationship with Alex while my life is a total mess," I began, uncertain. "He's already seen things he shouldn't have. If we date now, he'll only be more concerned, and I don't want that for him. I don't want that for myself, so if I can spare Alex, I will."

There it was. Nina put her hand on mine.

"Don't you think that's his choice to make?"

She was right, once again. I should give Alex the choice instead of making these kinds of decisions on my own, but I couldn't do it. I couldn't inflict my life on Alex, just as I couldn't inflict the consequences on myself. I looked down at my hands, unable to meet my friends' gaze.

"I don't know. If we were together now, he'd feel even more like he has to save me. I don't think that's a good idea. I don't want him to feel like he has to fix me when that's my job."

The image I had of my life was that of a broken vase. I couldn't expect anyone else to try to put the pieces together.

Alex was already doing too much. If Alex fixed me, I wouldn't know how to live without him or his magic glue. I couldn't give that power to anyone. If he ever realized that I wasn't good enough for him and decided to leave, there would be nothing left of me.

When we were together, I tried to look confident. In reality, I was just as scared as Alex was, if not more so. I already knew I wasn't good enough for him, but I still wanted to do my best to become better, for him and for me. That way, the day he'd realize all this, I wouldn't be completely destroyed. Alex loved me now, and I trusted him, but that didn't mean forever. One day, he'd figure out what he was worth, and apart from a wounded heart, I had nothing to offer him.

"You're crying," Sophie remarked. "Well done, Nina."

Sophie pulled me against her and stroked my hair like a mother would. The kind of mother I didn't have. I squeezed my eyes shut. I didn't feel like crying in a café, even if no one was watching.

"I'm sorry," Nina murmured.

***

Alex

Alex had texted Elena to see if everything had gone well with Nina, as the situation had seemed rather tense. For several hours, she'd been offline. That didn't feel right. Normally, she was very responsive.

The doorbell rang, and Alex went to check. It was past

ten at night. Who the fuck would come at this hour? Alex was surprised to see Elena in front of him. What was she doing here, and where had she come from? She was drenched from head to toe by the rain.

He stepped aside to let her in. Alex handed her a towel and a pair of pyjamas. She must be freezing. Instead of leaving to change, Elena stood with her clothes in hand, staring into space. Her eyes were red, like she'd been crying.

"Are you okay?"

This question shook her out of her trance. She looked around Alex's room, surprised how she'd ended up there. What had happened with Nina to make her so upset?

"Yes."

"Tell me."

"I'm fine."

"If you want us to work, you're going to have to be honest with me."

This struck a chord. Elena lowered her eyes without saying another word.

"Go get changed. We'll talk later."

Without retaliating, Elena disappeared into the bathroom. Five minutes later, she emerged. Unlike usual, she stayed close to the door. Alex patted the spot next to him on the bed, but she hesitated. What could have happened to make her suddenly so suspicious?

"Alex, do you feel I'm leading you on?"

"Why are you asking me this?"

"Answer me."

"Not really."

Her shoulders slumped. Had she really walked all the way out here in the rain to ask this? Alex had thought things were going well between them. Until Nina seemed to have sown the seeds of doubt. They went round and round in circles.

"So a little."

He came to stand in front of her and tucked one of her orange locks behind her ear. In a similar situation with someone else, Alex might have thought he was being led on like a fool. Elena was different; he knew her. And he knew she loved him, even if she wasn't ready to go any further yet.

"I don't think you're leading me on. You've been honest from the start. That doesn't mean the wait isn't long at times."

"Sorry…"

"Don't be. I know your feelings are genuine."

Alex spread his arms, and Elena clung to him. He felt the tension in her body dissipate. If she was here, he knew they'd be okay. Whatever was going to happen, Alex knew they were meant to be together.

"I love you," she whispered.

"I know. I love you, too."

CHAPTER 27

Alex

"Yo, Lena! We're going to the beach next weekend. Want to come?"

Elena, who was resting with her head on Alex's lap, opened one eye to look at Nina. In the last few days, she'd become clingier. Not that he minded. Whenever they were together, she found excuses to touch him. The fact that she initiated the physical contact herself was new. It felt so good.

"Uhm, it depends. I'm not going camping or sleeping in the sand if that's what you have in mind."

The princess was not a fan of nature.

"No," Sophie assured her, laughing. "My grandparents have a flat there."

Alex knew she wouldn't be able to refuse. Nina and Sophie had wormed themselves into her life, and they had no intention of letting Elena slip away. She was part of the trio now. Nina looked at her with a kicked puppy face, and Elena agreed.

"Okay, I'll come. How do we get there?"

"Alex can drive us," Nina suggested, grinning.

Alex blinked once before sighing. "Did you really just include me in your plans without asking?"

"You can't refuse! Don't you want to go to the beach with Elena?"

She waggled her eyebrows and Alex rolled his eyes. Nina knew what she was doing. Of course, he would love to go to the beach with her. Seeing her lying in the warm sand in nothing but a bikini was a sight he didn't want to miss. *Don't think about that now.* He shrugged.

"Yes, but I had no intention of including you in the equation."

"Meany."

Nina pouted, and Sophie patted her head in sympathy. Elena sat up to face Alex.

"You don't have to come."

Alex pursed his lips. "Why's that? Are you planning on hitting on other guys? Is that why you want me to stay?"

She tucked a strand of orange hair behind her ear with an innocent expression. This girl was a demon with the face of an angel.

"Maybe. What happens at the beach stays at the beach."

Alex flicked her on the forehead. "Do that and you can take the bus to school."

Elena fell against him and held his arm. "I don't know how to flirt with you, so how am I going to do it with others?"

"Not the answer I was hoping for."

***

Nina and Sophie were already in the back seat when Elena added her suitcase to the trunk. Alex watched in amazement. They were going to Oostduinkerke for a weekend, yet they'd all taken enough to travel for a month.

"How long are you planning to be away?"

"A woman always has an outfit for every occasion," Elena replied, closing the trunk.

Once the car was loaded, Alex drove off. Elena took something out of her bag, and Alex had to look twice, and still, he couldn't believe it.

"What's Neighomi doing here?"

"Neighomi goes where I go. It's not up for discussion."

The dancer swept her long hair back over her shoulder while the ridiculous stuffed animal rested on her lap, its glittery gaze riveted on the road. Nina poked her head between their seats to see the unicorn.

"A plushie!"

"It's so cute," Sophie added.

Elena hugged the unicorn tighter. Alex was starting to regret buying that thing. He'd bought it as a joke, but Elena had grown attached to the silly country-singing unicorn with a purple mane. Maybe he should have listened to Audrey's advice and bought a stuffed pony instead.

"It's a gift from Alex."

"That explains a lot," Sophie laughed.

Throughout the journey, the girls sang along to a Disney playlist Elena had put together. At times, they tried to get Alex to sing with them. The excuse of having to concentrate on the road saved him.

When they arrived at the apartment, Nina ran into the living room and threw herself onto the leather sofa. The apartment was spacious and soberly furnished.

"Wow! Your place is gorgeous."

Sophie picked up Nina's suitcase and disappeared into a bedroom. "Let's set up the beds."

Elena and Alex followed her into a room with two bunk beds. Alex watched the beds, doubtful.

"I don't care what you do, but I sleep with Lena," he said, letting his backpack fall on one of the lower beds.

"And risk having the beds creak at night?" Sophie shot back, her arms folded. "I don't think so."

Alex sighed. He always felt more at peace when she slept next to him. The little blonde left the room to fetch some sheets. Elena put Neighomi on the bed above Alex.

"Seriously, why did you bring that thing with you?"

"Be nice. Her life isn't easy. She's mute now."

"Did you take the batteries out?"

"You can't imagine how annoying it is to hear her singing and giggling through the night."

She took her toiletry bag out of her suitcase, along with a beach towel, before turning back to him with a smile.

"I like having her with me. It's reassuring because she reminds me of you."

Alex frowned. Sure, it was sweet that she was keeping Neighomi close to her, but at the same time, he wondered.

"But I'm here, so you don't need it."

"A girl always needs her unicorn. You wouldn't understand."

***

At the beach, Nina and Sophie removed their clothes and shoes before rushing to the water. Elena and Alex laid out the towels and parasol. Once settled, Elena positioned herself under the parasol with a dog-eared version of The Silmarillion. Unlike the others, she kept her clothes on. The most surprising of all: she was wearing long pants in the sweltering heat. Alex left her alone at first, but noticed how often she glanced at the water.

"You don't want to swim?"

"I think I'll skip this year."

She did her best to look carefree—it didn't fool Alex. What was bothering her? Elena had the body of a goddess, sculpted by countless hours of dancing. What could possibly make her so self-conscious?

"What are you trying to hide?"

She looked up from her book, her lips pursed. "Of course, you figured that out." Elena put her book away. She knew Alex wouldn't let her go until she'd come clean. "I guess I don't want people to see certain parts of my body."

"Do you really care what strangers might think of you?"

"Fine! There are certain parts of my body that *I* don't want to see."

Alex knocked his knee against hers. "Regretting old tattoos?"

A laugh left her lips. "I wish. I still have a big scar on my knee from the accident."

"Are you ashamed of your scar?"

"I'm not ashamed of it, but it reminds me every day of what I've lost. When it's covered, I can almost forget it's there. And it's ugly. I don't want you to see it."

That explained why she never wore anything but long

pants or dark stockings.

"Are you really going to waste your vacation because of a scar? I wouldn't judge you for something like that."

Elena hesitated, then finally gave in. She took off her clothes. Once she was wearing only her white bikini, all her self-confidence evaporated. Alex found himself unable to react. Elena was even more beautiful than he'd imagined, and he *had* imagined what she'd look like. Her body was muscular yet curvy in all the right places. Her pale skin looked incredibly soft, and he had to restrain himself from reaching out. He looked down at the scar. The damaged skin ran the length of her knee. Elena sought Alex's gaze, hoping to find comfort there.

"Don't worry about it. It's not as bad as you think."

"You're saying that to make me feel better."

"Yes, but I mean it."

Alex wanted to devour her. That mark only made her more beautiful. How could she not know? He bit his tongue. She wasn't ready to hear that. Not yet, anyway.

Sophie returned, dripping from head to toe. "Oh boy. You didn't tell me you were that hot."

Perfect.

"See?"

"What?" Sophie wondered.

"Her scar."

Her mouth turned into an oh. Elena stirred under the attention.

"I hadn't noticed."

"Listen to Sophie."

***

Elena was applying a fresh layer of sunscreen. The more she rubbed every inch of her skin, the more agitated Alex became. He couldn't stop staring at her; she was gorgeous, even when she wasn't trying. Her smooth skin, her shiny hair... The more he looked at her, the harder it became to look away. She was half-naked, and right there, only inches away from him. In front of this siren, his self-control was crumbling. Alex wanted her. He wanted all of her. And he couldn't help wondering what she tasted like. He wanted to kiss her. Everywhere.

Realizing that he was fantasizing about her, he raised his head. His neck and cheeks flushed at the mischievous grin Elena gave him. Alex cleared his throat and stared at the ice-cream truck. He did his best not to lose face, but he knew Elena understood. She knew what kind of images were playing in his head. She knew how much he wanted her. Because he'd been ogling her like a starved dog in front of the most delicious buffet. Elena turned her full attention to him. Her eyes sparkled.

"Am I turning you on?"

Sadistic as she was, Elena positioned herself behind him, pressing herself against his back. Every inch of bare skin, every curve, every breath. He felt everything. Elena placed several small kisses on his neck. Alex took a deep breath. A shiver ran down his spine, and his hair stood on end.

"Want me to take care of you?"

Her voice was deeper, like melted chocolate. Alex bit his lip. She wasn't serious, was she? A warmth formed in his belly, and he knew he had to do something while his head was still clear. At least, clear enough. Not touching her was torture. If he let himself be tempted, he wouldn't be able to stop. He abruptly moved away from Elena and stood up. She fluttered her eyelashes as if nothing had happened. This was all a game to her, and Alex was at her mercy.

"We're going swimming."

Without giving her time to reply, he headed for the water. He really had to cool down. Out of the corner of his eye, he spotted Sophie staring at him, confused.

"Alex, wait!"

Elena ran to catch up with him, but he refused to waste any time. He needed to take his mind off things, and a cold sea was exactly what he needed. Alex closed his eyes and let the waves rock him. He knew Elena was waiting for him to speak. All of this was new. Never before had a girl managed to get him so worked up. He'd always liked control, but every time Elena was around, he couldn't think straight. He wondered if she felt the same way. She had her own centre of gravity, and there was nothing he could do to get away from her. Hell, he didn't want to. He loved her too much to go back to how his life was before.

Alex let his head fall back. He couldn't run away from her forever. When he turned back, she was smiling at him—all traces of mischief long gone. She threw her arms around his neck and her legs around his waist. Instinctively, he placed his hands on the small of her back. Although the water was cool, he felt Elena's warmth invade him. In the distance, children were laughing, but Alex was unable to concentrate on anything but the siren in front of him. If she started singing, he'd follow her underwater. Without warning, Elena placed her lips on his. For a few moments, Alex was stunned. For months, she'd been the one holding back. Now Elena was taking the lead, and Alex didn't know what to do. She backed off when Alex still wasn't responding.

"Why aren't you kissing me back?" she asked, her head cocked to one side.

"Why are you kissing me in the first place?"

"Because I love you."

Since when was she so outspoken?

"But you wanted to take it easy..."

"So you don't want me to kiss you?"

"No! I mean, yes!"

Alex grumbled. Every time she was with him, he scrambled for words. Her chest shook with silent laughter.

"I want you to kiss me every day. All day long, as much as you want to. I just don't want you to feel like you have to do anything if you're not ready."

Elena rested her forehead against his.

"In that case, you'd better get ready."

"I think I'll survive."

Elena kissed him again, and this time Alex kissed her back, all tension gone. Their kisses were soft, light, and full of love, and that was all he needed right now. When they drew apart to catch their breath, Elena placed a final kiss on his cheek. An idea occurred to Alex.

"Oh, no! No, no, no! Alex, don't."

She tried to free herself from his embrace, but before she could break away, Alex pulled her under. Once back above water, she glared at him, and Alex laughed. She had the charisma of a wet puppy. Elena tackled him, and they splashed around like children. Alex couldn't remember the last time he'd been so carefree, but he was now. If only they could stay like this forever.

Elena's face suddenly fell. Panic invaded her features.

"Oh no..."

"What did you do?"

For several long seconds, Elena seemed to be caught in a dilemma she couldn't resolve. She looked up at Alex with a grimace.

"You've got to help me."

"What?"

"My top came undone. Help me close it."

Alex laughed even harder. Could it be that karma had caught up with her? He had to tease her a little. "I've been asked to undo a bikini before but never been to lace one up."

Elena frowned, which only made his fun increase. He quickly tied the bikini strings, and she ran to the beach without looking back.

"Hey, wait!"

Still grumbling, she grabbed her bag and stormed off towards the seawall. Sophie and Nina watched her leave.

"What's going on?"

"She's jealous," Alex replied, crossing his arms with an amused look on his face.

***

Ever since the bikini incident, Elena had mastered the art of eluding Alex. She'd give him discreet glances, but as soon as he turned to her, she'd act like nothing had happened. At first, Alex had thought she needed time to grumble, but evening had come, and Elena was still pretending he wasn't there. He hadn't expected her to be so jealous and territorial, but he loved it.

"Your sweetheart is still mad, I see."

Sophie sat down beside him on the sofa. Alex was going to have to find a way to make it up to her if he wanted her to talk to him again before the weekend was over. Making up with this mermaid would be the best part of his day. He was already hers. She just had to understand that.

"I know. I have a plan."

They prepared to go to a tapas bar. The girls had all decided to get ready, so Alex had little choice but to follow suit. He pulled on a black shirt and rolled up the sleeves. This would have to do. While they were getting ready, he checked one last time that his plan was well thought out.

When Elena walked into the room, Alex was unable to react. The only word that came to his mind was *breathtaking*. Elena was wearing a mid-length brown satin dress that hugged every part of her body perfectly, and white heeled sandals. Her long hair was wavy, and she'd done her eyes up. Elena had walked straight out of a dream. When she saw him staring at her, she lowered her eyes, uncomfortable. He wanted to compliment her, but as he opened his mouth to speak, Nina and Sophie left the bathroom. Although they were both beautiful, he couldn't take his eyes off the ballerina.

On the way to the bar, Nina and Sophie chatted as if nothing had happened while Elena continued to carefully avoid Alex. Whenever he came near her, she started walking beside Sophie. Alex smiled. Even though she'd been grumbling for hours, she held her head high like a real princess.

The atmosphere in the bar was cheerful. Out of the corner of his eye, Alex noticed that Elena regularly gave him furtive looks. He enjoyed the quiet while the girls chatted. When she got up to go to the bathroom, he knew he had to act now. Alex followed her and waited. As she came out, she was surprised to see him. Elena tried to walk past him, but Alex held her back. She put as much distance between them as possible and leaned against the wall. She seemed to realise that he wasn't going to let her slip away, so instead she glared.

"Are you done sulking?"

She looked everywhere, except in his direction. Her hair looked so soft and silky. Alex wanted to grab a curl and play with it.

"I'm not sulking."

"Oh really?"

Elena sighed. She ran her hands through her hair, carefully avoiding his gaze. "Maybe a little."

"Wanna talk about it?"

"No."

Alex placed his hands on the wall, caging her. As he'd expected, she lowered her eyes.

"Talk to me."

Elena finally looked up at him, her gaze uncertain. His siren was breathtaking, and all he wanted to do was lose himself in her blue eyes. And kiss her. Now that he'd had a taste of it, staying away from her had become even harder.

"Put yourself in my shoes, Alex. I wanted to impress you, and my top came undone. It was *so* embarrassing. And you had to allude to other girls. How should I have felt? I thought we were having a moment..."

She bit her thumbnail. How was she so cute? Alex thought

of a way to make her feel less embarrassed. The only thing he could come up with was to embarrass himself in turn. If it were for her, he didn't mind.

"You don't have to impress me anymore. You're already the icing on my cake."

Caught off guard, Elena burst out laughing. Alex leaned in to kiss her, but against all odds, she turned her cheek.

"Don't think you've won me over that easily. I'm still mad."

"Follow me."

"Where are we going?"

"Out."

"But what about Nina and Sophie?"

"They'll have fun without us."

Sophie knew about his plan. Alex took her hand and pulled her out of the bar. Elena waved to her friends without retaliating. Once outside, she let go of his hand.

"Where are we going?" she repeated.

"It's a surprise."

Elena crossed her arms.

"I don't like surprises."

"I know, but trust me. You'll like this one."

Alex held out his hand. For a few long seconds, Elena hesitated, then shrugged. She gave him her best smile and linked her fingers with his, her other hand on Alex's arm.

"Okay."

They walked in silence. When they were together, even the silences were pleasant. He enjoyed the warmth of her palm in his. Alex guided her towards the beach, where people gathered in front of a small stage. Musicians were already playing.

"A concert?"

"You'll like what they're about to play."

Another band took to the stage and began to perform. The small crowd went wild, and Elena followed suit. She sang and jumped like every seventeen-year-old was supposed to. The musicians played Maroon 5's *This Love*, and Elena turned back to Alex, surprise and adoration written all over her face. While she enjoyed herself listening to one of her favourite songs, Alex admired her. He'd be willing to pay to see her so carefree more often.

The band went on to play several Maroon 5 songs, with Elena dancing. When the last song was over, Elena returned to him, smiling widely.

"Thank you."

"Having fun?"

"I love it. There's just one thing missing to make it perfect."

She placed her lips on his. Before he could kiss her back, Elena stepped back to look at him.

"How did I get so lucky to find you?"

Feeling his heart beat faster at these words, Alex kissed her back. He wanted to convey everything he felt, and Elena understood what he wasn't saying. The music grew slower. Alex put his arms around Elena's waist. They rocked in each other's arms, enjoying the music. *Mission accomplished.*

***

A buzzing energy floated around them. A mixture of happiness, anticipation, and a large dose of want. Alex felt electrified. He glanced at Elena, and she smiled; she felt it too. As they drew closer to the apartment, her pace quickened, and all Alex could do was follow while laughing. It took a moment for his eyes to adjust to the apartment's dimness. Elena placed her palms on Alex's chest. Her warm breath gave him goosebumps. Alex pulled her in for a kiss. Their kisses became hungry and messy, their teeth clashing. Elena jumped into his arms and encircled his waist with her legs. The moment Alex placed his hands on her ass, she moaned before kissing him harder. All he wanted to do was rip off her pretty clothes. Without ever breaking the kiss, Alex took her to the bedroom and laid her on his bed. Elena sat back to watch him. Her big eyes looked at him with desire. The moonlight filtering through the window caressed her skin, making her look like porcelain. Alex felt the muscles in his abdomen tighten. *Damn*. He wanted her so badly, and she was lying there, right under his fingertips. The only thing he had to do was reach out.

Elena wasted no time and drew him into another kiss. Everywhere her fingers touched him, his skin burned in the most delicious, exquisite way possible. Elena positioned herself above him. Alex froze, unsure of what he was supposed to do. He'd never let a girl dominate him physically. He'd always been unable to let anyone else have control during sex. When Elena kissed him again, all resistance disappeared. If she were an ocean, he was a sailor who willingly let himself be swallowed by the waves. Her slender fingers undid the buttons of his shirt, one by one.

The sound of a key unlocking a door snapped them out of their trance. Elena's eyes widened as she froze. Her chest heaved hard; her eyes still misty. Alex motioned for her to move. Nina and Sophie walking in on them was something he'd rather avoid.

"Go! Before they see us."

This brought her back to her body. Elena climbed onto the ladder without making a sound. Alex sighed. He already missed her, and she was barely a meter away from him. If Sophie and Nina hadn't come home so soon, how far would they have gone? Now that he'd had a taste, he wanted to know what it felt like to go all the way with her.

With Elena, everything was so different. Everything was special. It wasn't just sex. Alex wanted to be with her, body and soul. He wanted to cherish her, love her, and have her by his side. His feelings still scared him, but she was worth it. No one else had ever been able to make him feel so alive.

Nina and Sophie tiptoed their way into the bedroom, and Alex hurried to the bathroom, needing a cold shower. He had to stop thinking about how perfectly her body fit with his

Back in the room, he waited for sleep to take him. It was a lost cause. When he heard a soft snore, Elena climbed out of bed and crawled under Alex's comforter. He moved aside to make room for her, and she pressed herself against him. Her fingers traced invisible patterns on his arms, and Alex relaxed. In the arms of this siren, peaceful sleep took him under.

***

From the terrace, Alex watched the sea caress the sand. The door opened, and Nina plopped down beside him, gazing out at the horizon.

"Hey."

They enjoyed the peace and quiet. It had been a long time since Alex and Nina had been alone together.

"I see guys made up. I'd be surprised if you hadn't."

Not only had they made up, they'd become even closer.

"I'm glad you found her. You seem happier with her by your side."

"I thought you said she was leading me on?"

His harsh tone surprised him, not Nina. She'd known Alex all her life and was not impressed.

A few weeks earlier, when Elena had asked him in a panic if he felt she was leading him on, he'd been mad. Even now, he still couldn't understand why she'd said such a thing. She was Elena's friend, after all.

Nina was playing with a lock of hair.

"I know. For a while, I thought she didn't know what she wanted and was giving you false hope. It didn't seem fair to you. I understand now why she's taking so long."

Elena had talked about her life with them? Pride swelled in his chest at the progress she made.

"She told you?"

"Among other things, yes. She's good for you. I feel like my childhood friend is finally back. You changed after your trauma. But you seem to feel joy again, and I know Elena has a lot to do with that."

Speaking of the devil, Elena appeared on the terrace. Not wide awake yet, she rubbed her eyes. She was still wearing her dress from the day before, and her make-up had run, making her look like a panda. It was strangely cute. Alex moved aside to make room for her on the bench. Elena sat on his lap instead.

"The bench isn't good enough for milady?"

She rubbed her head against his chest like a kitten would.

"Oh, shush. You had your tongue in my mouth a few hours ago. Stop whining."

***

On the way home, Alex let his hand rest on Elena's thigh. Such a simple gesture, yet so meaningful. It didn't go unnoticed by the two gossips in the back seat.

"You're closer than usual," Sophie observed, looking very calm, too calm. "Has something happened we should know about?"

Of course, she'd figured it out. Sophie knew a person in no time. Elena glanced at Alex, smiling conspiratorially. A lot had happened in the last two days.

"Lots of things."

"You did *it*?" exclaimed Nina. "In Sophie's grandparents' apartment? I can't believe it!"

Elena and Alex rolled their eyes.

"No, not *that*!"

They could have if the two girls hadn't come home so early. Alex sighed. Their relationship had moved so fast, and he wondered what that meant for them. Although Elena wasn't saying anything, she wasn't holding back as much as she used to. It gave him hope. If she'd been ready to take that step with him yesterday, maybe she was finally ready to be with him for good? As if she could hear his thoughts, she winked at him. They were going to have to discuss all this, but that was a question for later, when they were alone.

"Nina, not everyone is as impatient as you are," Sophie scolded her.

Nina let herself fall back against the seat with a theatrical air. It was no coincidence that she and Elena had found each other.

"Why should I wait when I know it's going to be a good time? I don't like wasting time thinking ahead. I want a boyfriend, too!" Nina exclaimed, pouting.

Sophie gave her a sidelong glance. In the trio, she was the mom, while Nina was the hyper kid and Elena the unpredictable teenager.

"You'll get bored with him after a few weeks."

"I know."

"What do you mean, you'll get bored?" Elena asked, turning back to her friends.

"Princess Nina hopes to find Prince Charming by kissing frogs," Sophie explained, analysing her orange nail polish.

"But all frogs turn into toads," the princess muttered.

"What if you kissed a toad instead?" Lena asked. "Maybe he'd turn into a prince."

The girls looked at each other before bursting into laughter.

"Now there's an idea."

***

Alex was stressing out. Ever since they'd gotten out of the car, Elena had been acting as if nothing had happened. She looked so calm, while he felt so agitated. There was an elephant in the room, but Alex wondered if he was the only one to see it. After a moment, he snapped. He had to know.

"We need to talk."

"About?"

She didn't look up from the pile of clothes she was taking out of her suitcase. How could she act so normal? They'd been closer than ever these days. Were they going to keep up with the momentum, or were they going to go back to the way they'd been before the trip?

"What are we?"

"We're Elena and Alex. What else is there?"

"I'm serious."

"So am I."

"Look, what I'm trying to say is—"

Elena cut him off. "I know what you're trying to say. But I don't know what you want me to tell you."

She abandoned the idea of unpacking and sat down on her sofa, finally giving him her full attention. Her face exuded serenity. So why was he so anxious?

"Are we dating?"

"Officially? Not yet. Unofficially, most certainly."

"That doesn't answer my question."

"Let's say we make things official once my life is less of a mess, but already try to make things work? Can you live with that?"

"You're making it hard on yourself. I'm already crazy about you, no matter what you do."

"Can you live with that?" Elena repeated, pleading with her eyes.

Alex wanted more. Of course, he wanted more. The last few days had been incredible. Alex hadn't been this happy since his life before... And being happy was addictive. As long as nothing was official, he'd always have this feeling that Elena was going to slip through his fingers. But Alex didn't have much of a choice, not if he wanted to be with her. And there was nothing he wanted more than her, even if it meant waiting a little longer. Alex was completely at her mercy, and he never wanted Elena to let him go. The torture was too sweet.

"If I accept, can I kiss you without permission?"

Elena positioned herself between his legs, her palms on his cheeks. She brought her mouth close to his without touching it. Her breath caressed his face.

"You never needed permission."

Elena closed the distance. The more they kissed, the more intoxicated he became with her. As she sat on his lap, Alex let his fingers slide down her thighs without breaking the kiss.

"Elena, can you... Oh, you're busy."

Alex froze at the sound of his future mother-in-law's voice. Elena placed a kiss on his nose.

"Hi, Mom."

Elena faced her mother, laughing, while Alex disintegrated on the spot. His head and neck heated with embarrassment. Holding on for dear life and what little dignity he had left, he pulled his hands away from Elena. Maura gave him an icy look. Usually, he didn't care what others thought. This time, it was different.

"Hi, Maura."

"Alex. Shouldn't you be getting home? I'm sure your mom wants to see you."

"I won't be long."

Elena let her arms rest around his neck. She smiled at her mother, showing no sign of embarrassment or regret. The two women stared at each other, and Alex felt a pang of pride rise in him. Elena was standing up to someone without looking down.

"Mom, stop tormenting him."

Maura gave them a tight smile. The mother-daughter relationship hadn't improved.

"Stay as long as you like."

Once Maura had left, Alex got up.

"You're leaving? I had plans for us."

This was the second time they'd been interrupted. Alex wasn't one to believe in signs, but it was clear that the timing wasn't right yet.

"I think we should wait a little longer."

Elena was about to retaliate, then thought better of it. She frowned. How could she be so adorable? Or how could he be so in awe when all she did was breathe?

"Didn't you say you wanted to be with me?"

"Being with you is more than sex, darling. I can wait."

Elena dropped a kiss on his cheek before returning to her suitcase.

"Good answer, though you're still staying with me tonight. That's not negotiable."

"The lady is demanding."

She winked at him teasingly. "You better get used to it if you want to be with her."

Since Elena had come into his life, those dark days he'd grown accustomed to had become brighter. Was this fate? If so, fate was a woman, and her name was Maura.

CHAPTER 28

Alex

"Are you serious?"

"What?"

"Love, we're going to a party. Your outfit will stand out."

Elena was wearing a denim skirt and a V-shaped sweater in fine white wool. She glanced at her reflection in the mirror, but saw nothing wrong with it.

"I don't see the problem with this outfit."

This style suited her perfectly. As always, no matter what she wore, Elena had an elegance that was all her own. It was also the first time she'd worn clothes that didn't hide her scar. For that reason alone, Alex wished she'd kept that skirt on. But he felt nauseous thinking about the hands that might touch her.

"I'll choose your outfit."

Alex headed for the wardrobe to choose something else, but Elena blocked his path. The dancer crossed her arms in front of her chest, pouting.

"No, thanks! I'll keep my clothes."

"You don't want to go to this kind of party wearing a skirt.

Please."

Seeing Elena give in, Alex rummaged through her wardrobe. He found a pair of skinny jeans with lots of holes and tossed it on the bed. Continuing his search, he saw a black lace crop top with oriental motifs, and knew it was perfect.

"Now change."

Elena looked at her new outfit sceptically. Finally, she grabbed her clothes and left. After what seemed like an eternity, she reappeared. Her make-up was simple, consisting of a cat eye and red lips. Yet that little bit of extra colour made her look even more elegant, and just as seductive. Her lace top offered a plunging view of her cleavage, and Alex didn't know where to look. This was going to be an awfully long evening. Elena was beautiful, and he was about to launch her into a sea of hungry sharks.

***

Elena

"I still don't get why you insisted on this outfit. It's not like I was planning on hooking up tonight."

Alex chuckled, opening his car door for me to sit down. As always, he was the perfect gentleman. In the back of my mind, I was plotting the death of the person who invented skinny jeans. My pants were so tight I could hardly move.

"As if you know what that means."

He started the Polo. I sighed; Sophie and Nina were right. I really did have a too-pure image. It was time to rectify that.

"Unlike what you think, I know what it means. It's just not my cup of tea."

Alex gave me a sidelong glance, seeming to realize the turn the conversation had taken.

"Are you telling me..."

I bit my thumbnail. *Oh, dear.*

"It was a mistake, but yes."

"Do I want to know?"

"Well, do you?"

I really had to stop sabotaging myself.

"I gotta admit I'm a little curious."

Oh my... The only way to end it was to spit it out. I cleared my throat. Even Alex looked nervous. But he deserved to know.

"It happened last year. I was invited to New Year's Eve by Oscar, from my hip-hop class. And there was this guy I liked, Robin."

He turned back to me. Of course, he understood who I was talking about.

"Oh, no, you don't! Please don't tell me it's Robin Lafont!"

Robin is the guy everyone knows. Talented, good-looking. He has it all. And like most of the girls in the club, I couldn't resist his charm. Looking back, I realize that the only thing that interested me about him was his looks. Who could blame me? I was just a girl with hormones.

"Unfortunately, yes. Anyway. Robin had suggested we play beer pong, and since I wanted to get closer to him, I agreed to join in the game. Oscar and I teamed up, and lost. We had to empty all those glasses, and that was that. I don't remember much of what happened next. Not the first time

I'd dreamed of."

This admission kept him silent just long enough for him to digest the information I'd just given him.

"Uh... okay. But did you hook up with Robin?"

Or not.

"No, Oscar," I confessed, my complexion rivalling that of a peony.

My friend's eyes widened like saucers. "Oscar? Are you serious?"

"What? Oscar is cute!"

I tried to rectify the situation as best I could. It was all in vain. The only thing I'd managed to do was dig my own grave, so I could die of shame afterwards. Alex shook his head.

"I'm sure he's gay."

"He is. He told me a few weeks later."

"I shouldn't be laughing, but this is hilarious," Alex said, unable to keep a straight face.

He was taking it much better than I'd feared. Not that he had any right to resent me for having a history. I watched the landscape go by.

"That's not the worst part," I continued.

"Huh?"

"Yeah... I slept with him again after New Year's, before he came out."

He opened his mouth, but no comment came out. He was just laughing.

"It was so awkward... we stopped in the middle of it, it was too weird."

Alex laughed until he had tears in his eyes. It was embarrassing to tell him, but somehow I preferred him to know everything about me. Even my worst moments.

"I'll admit, I didn't see that one coming."

"Why's that?"

"I thought you'd be the type to wait until you met the right person."

In itself, I didn't mind being seen like that. There was nothing wrong with waiting, but something still bothered me.

"Who should I have waited for, Alex? For you? You didn't wait for me either."

"That's not what I meant."

"No, but it's what *I* mean. We're still figuring things out."

"I'd like to point out that we would've had sex if your friends hadn't come home."

I choked. How could he talk about it so calmly when I was sitting there, burning on the spot because of embarrassment?

Alex put his hand on my thigh, his gaze focused on the road.

"Just so you know," my friend admitted in a calm voice, "if I'd known it would be you, I would have waited."

At the party, everyone was dancing to techno blasting like it was the best time of their lives. It was horrible. Goodbye Dido, Ed Sheeran, Damien Rice, and Birdy. It had been an honour. The sound was too loud, and I was sure that once I left that evening, I'd be as deaf as my grandfather. To think Alex used to come to parties like this, and Kelsey would kill to be invited to one. I wondered what was wrong with me. A party like this wasn't the place for an introvert.

"Alex, I forgot to ask, but whose birthday is this?"

I'd agreed to come when he'd asked me if I wanted to join him, simply so I could spend more time with him. If that meant following him to a party I didn't care about, so be it.

"Tiago's."

Fuck. What the hell had I gotten myself into again? What if Kelsey were here? How would I react to her? I hadn't prepared enough possible scenarios to face her. I wasn't ready. Alex motioned for me to follow. Just what I needed! Kelsey and I were already in a cold war, but on top of that, I was at her boyfriend's birthday party. I really couldn't find a better day to go out, huh? Hopefully, I wouldn't run into either of them. If I could avoid them, maybe my evening wouldn't be entirely wasted.

We entered the living room, and I immediately spotted an empty sofa pushed into a corner. I tried to sneak away. My plan was discovered when Alex grabbed me by the back of my leather jacket. *Shit.*

"Where are you going?"

"Uh... sit? My knee is sore," I lied.

I hadn't had a sore knee in weeks, I just wanted to hide in a corner and wait for this evening to be over. Damn it. What had possessed me to try and be like everybody else? I didn't want to be like everyone else! I wanted to put on the clothes I liked, listen to the music I liked, and do the things that interested me. There was nothing for me here. The introvert in me was scared to death, and I had a mad desire to run away.

"Stay close to me."

Without giving me time to reply, Alex turned around. Turning my head, I spotted Kelsey. She was alone, but radiant. Luckily, she hadn't seen me. I grabbed Alex by the sleeve before it was too late. I hadn't prepared myself mentally for this.

"I want to go home," I begged.

"We've just arrived..."

"Kelsey's here. I'm not ready to face her."

"If you think like that, you might never be." He sighed.

"I want to go, please."

Alex ran a hand through his hair, which naturally remained spikey, and sighed again. Still, he nodded.

Just as we were about to leave the living room, someone shouted, "Alex!"

Tiago. I wanted to run away, but Alex held me back, again.

"Leaving already?"

They shook hands and chatted about God knew what. After a few minutes, Tiago finally gave me his attention. His eyes lingered a few seconds too long on my cleavage, then his gaze lit up, making my unease return full force. Now that I could see Tiago from this close, I understood why Kelsey always looked at him with drool dripping from her mouth. Tanned complexion, sky-blue eyes, and curly brown hair. Not to mention a smile worthy of a toothpaste ad. Tiago was the stereotypical hunk, which broke his charm. Alex was much more to my taste. But my opinion was biased. What could I say? I'd developed a preference for darker men.

"Who's this?" asked Tiago, pointing at me with his chin.

I didn't like the fact that he turned to Alex to ask this, as if I were a doll incapable of answering. I may have been an introvert, but I could talk. Ten points off for Mr. Handsome.

"That's Elena, don't you remember her?"

"We've been in the same biology class for five years," I said, rolling my eyes.

He rubbed the back of his head, unsure of how to react. Tiago tried to dispel the unease by offering us a drink.

"What can I get you?"

"Nothing. We were just leaving…"

"Oh, come on! Just one drink."

Alex and I looked at each other. Could he see my panic? Apparently not, for he merely shrugged and nodded. Things weren't going the way I'd planned. I had no choice but to stay at this stupid party.

We walked to the bar where Tiago handed us a cup of beer. I watched the liquid, avoiding tasting it. Between my drunken father and my latest misadventure, I'd learned to be wary of alcohol.

Alex beckoned me to drink. It was easy for him; he was used to drinking like a fish and smoking like a chimney. I hesitated, still staring at the liquid. The last time I'd touched beer had been during that infamous game of beer pong. And needless to say, the aftermath had been anticlimactic. I took a deep breath and took a sip. One drink wasn't going to kill me. My past mistakes weren't going to be repeated.

The taste was gross, just as I remembered it, and I spat my sip back into the plastic cup. This time, I wasn't going to force myself to swallow beer to try and impress someone. The two boys bent over laughing. *Shame*.

"I'll go get you something else," Tiago offered as he took my beer back, still chuckling.

Alex gave me a mocking smile, and I pouted. This was all his fault.

"What?"

"You never cease to amaze me."

He gently pinched my cheek. Before I could bat his hand away, Tiago handed me another glass.

"What is it?"

"Vodka Redbull."

We settled into one of the soft sofas. People continued to wiggle to the noise that was getting on my nerves, and Tiago headed back to his group of friends. After a while, Alex left to join him. He assured me that he wouldn't be long, but as soon as he was gone, I was overcome by loneliness. This was going to be a very long evening indeed. I took a sip of my drink. I just wanted to spend a nice evening with Alex. *Such an epic fail.* I raised my glass to myself.

"Cheers."

CHAPTER 29

Alex

When Alex turned back to the sofa, Elena was gone. He couldn't see her anywhere.

"Where's Lena?"

"She went upstairs with someone," Tiago replied.

Not wasting any time, Alex climbed the stairs two by two and searched each room, his senses on the alert. Was Elena planning to spend the evening with someone else? Just thinking about it made him sick. It couldn't be true. After all they'd been through, he couldn't accept it. *She's not like that.* He ran to the second floor and heard her voice.

"No, don't."

Alex entered the room, and his blood ran cold. Fear clawed its way up his spine. Vincent had Elena pinned against the wall. How had he managed to get in? Had no one noticed? Elena tried to free herself, to no avail. Vincent turned his head towards the door and smiled.

"Alexander, what a nice surprise."

Red tinted Elena's cheeks. Was she drunk? Elena stared at him with round, wet eyes, her gaze full of regret.

"Alex, I'm sorry."

"She's beautiful."

When his former coach stroked her cheek, Alex felt something break inside him. Without thinking, he grabbed Vincent by his sweater and pulled him back, coming between him and Elena. Tears rolled down her cheeks when Alex touched her face.

"I'm so sorry."

"Are you okay?"

She nodded. Alex fished his keys out of his pocket and handed them over.

"Get in the car. I'll be there in a minute."

Elena staggered out of the room.

"We're alone at last. I wasn't sure we'd ever see each other again."

"What did you do to her?"

"Nothing. I just wanted to talk."

Rage pulsed through his system, and Alex pushed him against the wall. He'd never thought he'd come face to face with Vincent again, let alone in a position of strength. For years, that face had haunted his nights, driving him to madness. But Elena was right. Alex was stronger now. His former coach could no longer hurt him. Now that Alex looked into Vincent's eyes, he felt nothing but disgust and anger.

"You destroyed years of my life. I won't let you destroy someone else's."

"I only wanted what was best for you."

Alex saw red, all the bad memories blurring his vision. He threw a punch at his tormentor, then another, then another. Standing over the man who had destroyed his childhood, he let all his rage and pain escape.

"Alex, stop." Elena tried to pull him back, but he was too far gone. "Please, stop!" she yelled. She knelt beside him, her hand on his shoulder. "Please, I'm begging you. You're better than him."

Alex turned his head towards her, and his arms went limp. Seeing Vincent's inert body on the ground and his bloodied face, sadness threatened to swallow him whole. She was right. He didn't want to be like this anymore. Acid tears burned his eyes. Feeling suddenly powerless, he dropped down beside Vincent.

"Come here."

Elena wrapped her arms around his shoulders as he burst into tears.

"It's over. You're okay."

His whole body trembled. For long minutes, she continued to stroke his hair, reassuring him. And for the very first time, Alex understood how much she loved him. He clung to that thought. She was the light at the end of the tunnel that made him lift his head. Elena watched him. All traces of alcohol in her system seemed gone.

"Let's go?"

She stood up and held out her hand. As always, she was there to help him up.

***

As they drove to the police station, Alex couldn't help but wonder. He had to, because he couldn't understand on his own.

"Why'd you follow him? You know he's dangerous."

"I'm... I'm sorry."

"Why did you do that?"

Elena rubbed her cheeks with the back of her hand.

"He said we'd talk about you. I needed to know."

"Know what, damn it?" he exclaimed.

"I had to know why he hurt you."

"Elena, he's a paedophile. He's sick! No matter what he'd have told you, you could never understand him."

She lowered her eyes. After what she'd just done for him, Alex tried to control his temper. He owed her.

"I know you meant well, but some things are better left unknown. Please don't ever do something like this again. I don't want you to go through what I went through."

Alex could never forgive himself if anything happened to her. Elena had suffered enough. She didn't need any more trauma. Entering the police station, Alex motioned for her to take a seat as he made his way to the reception desk.

***

Elena

Alex followed one of the policemen into another room. I tried to stay calm, but my nerves were getting the better of me. The policewoman at reception smiled and offered me a coffee, which I accepted.

"Is that your boyfriend?"

Why did I still insist that Alex and I weren't together? After all we'd been through, we were more than friends. I had wanted to keep him out of my crazy life, and now I was involved in his. So what was the point in denying what had become inevitable?

"Kind of. Is he in trouble?"

"I don't think so. It all depends on the victim and whether he wants to press charges or not. The fact that he's come forward and that there's history will cushion the consequences."

I wouldn't have used the word victim to describe Vincent, but I couldn't objectify in front of a representative of the law. Alex and I were in a delicate situation. It was best to keep a low profile.

"Do I also have to make a statement?"

"Do you want to?"

"If it helps Alex, sure."

The look she gave me was kind.

"How did a young girl like you end up in a situation like this?"

"I was in the wrong place at the wrong time, and decided to stay."

Once we'd taken our statements, we left the police station. The dashboard indicated that it was past three in the morning.

"Can you drop me off at home, please?"

"It's late. Don't you want to stay at my place? I can drop you off in the morning."

"I'd like to go home. I need to think."

The restlessness I'd felt the last few hours continued to take its toll. I needed to distance myself from Alex—I needed to put my thoughts in order. This evening had been so exhausting, I didn't know where to start. All traces of the alcohol clouding my mind had dissipated, giving way to a heart-breaking emptiness.

"I'm sorry you had to see that," Alex sighed as he pulled up in front of my house. "You must have been scared."

I'd been absolutely terrified when Alex had pounced on Vincent. But my fear had soon been replaced by something else: envy. Tonight, Alex had finally faced his ghost. Even though he'd been overwhelmed by anger and sadness, he'd managed to snap out of it. He had stood up to the person who had destroyed him just a few years earlier. Alex had won. It was time for me to face my own demon and stand up to him, too. But how?

"Elena, say something."

My heart sank. What was I supposed to do? Now that Alex had faced his past, I could no longer be the shackle that kept him from moving forward. I had to make a choice. Either I chose to move forward and be with Alex or I could stay in a life where I would never feel safe. Which meant giving up on Alex and our future together. Either way, I had to face this internal war, even if I knew I wouldn't win. Unless luck was on my side.

"Why do you look so sad?"

"I love you, Alex."

"This sounds like a goodbye."

Instead of answering, I pressed my lips to his. As always, his mouth was soft and warm. If I could, I'd never stop kissing him.

"Don't go," he pleaded.

I inhaled his scent one last time before getting out of the car.

"See you later."

Tell me everything

I entered the house. Without bothering to take off my shoes, I dropped onto my bed. Overcome by the silence of the night, new tears burned my eyes. I put on *To My Youth* by BOL4 and cried my eyes out. What was I supposed to do? Despite having prepared myself mentally, I had arrived at one of the biggest turning points in my life, and I was scared. My phone screen lit up, displaying Alex's number.

"I'm sorry, Alex," I murmured.

Feeling that the restlessness inside me increased, I stood up. I knew what I had to do if I still wanted to be able to watch myself in the mirror later.

For the first time in three years, I entered my brother's room. On his bedside table stood a picture of us as children. My father was carrying me on his shoulders, while my mother and Mick were holding hands. Those moments where my family had been happy seemed so distant, as if they were a dream instead of a reality. My tears welled up. I missed him.

"Wish me luck."

I took a sweater from his wardrobe and slipped it on. Closing my eyes for a moment, I took a deep breath. This night had taught me one thing: fate was fickle, but some things were inevitable. There was no way I was going to let my life depend on others. It was time to get rid of my handcuffs, like Alex had. I deserved better. My determination was ironclad. I plugged in the stereo and turned up Metallica's *Fade to Black*. Mick's favourite band, and right now, I needed all the support I could get. My thoughts turned to Alex. *Please wait for me. I'm coming.* I waited, listening. There was noise on the stairs, footsteps coming closer. *This is it.* Frank appeared in the doorway; my mother hot on his heels.

Mom stared at me. She knew as well as I did what was about to happen.

"What's this?" my father asked, a nasty sneer on his face. "What the hell are you doing here?"

The room, the music, the sweater... My father was unsettled when he saw all these links to his dead child. There was only one intruder amid all these memories: me. Mick was gone; I was still here. Frank came towards me. Mom rushed to stop him. It was too late, and I had no intention of stopping it.

"Frank, stop! This is a misunderstanding, right, Lena?"

Her eyes shot me a desperate look. I knew what I was doing, or at least I hoped I did. I knew the risks. It wouldn't be the first time.

"Take off that sweater immediately."

His tone was chilling. I swallowed.

"No."

"Take it off, or..."

"Or what? I'm not afraid of you anymore."

I wasn't afraid—I was terrified. But my determination was bigger. Or was it recklessness? Frank seemed taken aback by my attitude. For years, I'd kept my head down and taken the blows without flinching. This time, I would hold my head high. Tonight would be the last time. He headed for me, and Mom was stupid enough to try and stop him. We all know what happens next: a man hits his wife to get what he wants. Mom rolled to the floor, a trickle of blood running down her nose. Even though I felt guilty, I had to go on. I had to get us out. For her sake and for mine.

"Asshole!" I shouted. "This is between you and me."

And Frank went on his way. There was no trace of fatherly love in his eyes, nor the slightest hint of regret. We stood at a crossroads, and I hoped that from here on, our paths would finally part. I took a deep breath. *This is going to hurt.* He grabbed me by the throat, tightening his grip. Mom was distraught, and I gave her a look that I wanted to reassure her. *Please do what you have to do.* Mom quietly left the room. Now all I could do was hope that I had enough time left. I could hardly breathe. My lungs burned more and more. I wanted to scream with all the air I had left, but my windpipe was being crushed. No one would hear me, like the mute girl from my past. My head started spinning. *Hold on, Lena.* New voices approached, but the sound was already fading, as was my father's angry face. Black spots blurred my vision as my mother entered the room, followed by my neighbour and his son. They came straight for my father, but I never saw them arrive. Unconsciousness had already swallowed me.

CHAPTER 30

Alex

Alex had been trying to reach Elena for hours, to no avail. In the car, her gaze had been sad but determined. That night, she had made an important choice, one that concerned them both. But more than anything, a choice that would define her future. She had kissed him. A kiss that felt like goodbye. Knowing it might be the last time drove him mad. Alex tried to call her again and again. He knew she was ignoring him. Elena had her phone with her; her Spotify was on. For over an hour, she'd been listening to the same song over and over. When he saw that it was *To my youth*, Alex knew something was up. She always listened to it when she felt like her world was falling apart. He let his head fall back on his pillow. The pillowcase still smelled like the cherry blossom perfume she loved to wear.

From the start, Elena had made it clear that she had a choice to make: fight to move on and be with him, or stay stuck in the life she'd led so far. Why did everything have to be so complicated? He wanted to be with her, no matter what her choice was. Even if she decided not to fight. Things were never that simple. Not for Elena. She found it important to get through this stage of her life before starting another. And now that she'd moved in one direction, Alex knew he'd lost her. All his fears had come true. Elena had decided to move on without him, leaving him alone and miserable. But he didn't know how to give up. After all they'd been through together, he didn't want to. Even if he had to fight or get down on his knees to convince her to stay, he wouldn't let her go without doing everything he could. So Alex kept calling, expecting to hear her voicemail again. Against all odds, she picked up.

"Hello?"

It wasn't Elena, but Maura.

"It's Alex. Is Lena there?"

"Yes."

"Can I talk to her?"

"Not right now, I'm afraid."

Alex heard her breath tremble, as if she were searching for words. The silence felt endless.

"I'll give you the address of the hospital. Come and see us whenever you like."

Without giving him time to reply, she hung up. For a while, Alex remained inanimate, unable to react. *The hospital.* Elena was in the hospital? What could have happened in such a short time? They'd only seen each other a few hours ago. The worst possible scenarios ran through his mind. He grabbed his keys and dashed down the stairs.

"Where are you running to?"

Lexi poked her head out of the kitchen and frowned. As always, she knew something was wrong. Alex couldn't pretend when it came to Elena.

"What's wrong?"

"Lena is in the hospital."

"Why?"

He felt so powerless. "I don't know."

His mother quickly embraced him. "Drive carefully."

Arriving at the hospital, Alex bumped into Maura near the elevators. Her eyebrows shot up in surprise. Dark circles dug the skin under her eyes. She looked ten years older overnight.

"When I told you to come, I didn't mean right now."

Elena's mother beckoned him to follow her to the cafeteria. At first, he walked in silence, expecting Maura to explain, but like her daughter, she was the type to lose herself in her thoughts to the point of forgetting the world around her. Alex jumped from one foot to the other. He wanted to run and join Elena, but Maura was taking her time. Long seconds passed before she realized Alex's agitation. Maura smiled sadly.

"There's no point in hurrying. She's unconscious."

His anxiety rose a notch. How bad had the evening gone?

"What happened?"

"I don't know."

Tears glistened in her blue eyes. She who was always so stoic was on the verge of collapse. Maura put down her cup of coffee; her hands were shaking too much.

"In the middle of the night, Elena turned the radio in her brother's room up to maximum. Frank and I went to see what was going on, and she started provoking him," she explained, running a hand through her auburn hair. "It was as if she wanted him to attack. I thought he was going to kill her. Why would she do such a thing?"

Maura burst into tears. Alex felt his heart drop. Elena had decided to face her demons, just as he had done earlier. She had made her choice. Alex was her choice. He'd never thought it possible to feel as miserable as he did now. The person he loved most had risked her life to be free. To be with him. Maura looked up at him.

"Alex, why would my daughter do this?"

"She wants to be happy."

***

Lexi paused in his doorway.

"There's someone at the door for you."

Alex's heart raced. Was it Elena? Had she finally woken up? Lexi shook her head, a sad look on her face. She, too, was waiting for news on her condition. When he'd gone to the hospital, Elena had been unconscious. Maura had forced him to go home, promising to call as soon as she woke up. He'd insisted on staying, but she hadn't let him.

Alex went to the front door. One look at the person standing there, and he shook his head, ready to close it.

"Wait!" Kelsey begged, taking a step towards him.

Alex crossed his arms; he'd never liked her. That pest had made Elena so sad. He didn't want to waste his time with her. Especially not now.

"Please, at least tell me how she's doing."

Worry distorted her harmonious face. For an egocentric bitch, she sure looked bad. Alex looked over her shoulder and noticed Tiago waiting in his car. Alex had wondered for months what he saw in her. He loved one-night stands and easy relationships, and yet Kelsey had been with him for ages. Alex didn't get it. She was shallow and selfish, the exact opposite of Elena. Sweet, sweet Elena. His eyes burned, and he took a deep breath. Tiago nodded encouragingly. Alex rolled his eyes, then stepped aside. Kelsey widened her eyes, but hurried into the house before he could change his mind.

They settled on the sofa, and Alex waited for her to talk. Her presence alone put him on edge.

"How's Lena?"

"She looks like someone who almost got killed by her own father. How do you think she's doing?"

Kelsey's hands trembled. When she realized Alex was watching her, she hid her hands between her thighs.

"What happened? Frank's always been crazy, but he never tried to kill her before."

Alex huffed.

"You seem strangely shaken for someone who willingly let her best friend down in a situation like this."

Kelsey's eyebrows went up. He wasn't going to spare her. She deserved someone to give her a piece of mind.

"You show up here whining supposedly because you're worried about her, but where were you when she needed you most? Don't think I didn't see how you treated her. When she was at her lowest, you let her down because it was the easiest thing to do."

Kelsey shook with sobs, and her face twisted. Suddenly, there was nothing cute or harmonious about her face anymore.

"You're right. I was awful."

Alex had to strain his ear to understand what she was saying, she was crying so hard. Was she having regrets?

"I was so hurt that I ignored Elena's feelings, even when I knew she needed me. I was mean and selfish, and I'm sorry. She didn't deserve that."

"Then why did you leave?"

Huh. She cared for Elena in her own weird, unhealthy way.

"She looked too much like Mick."

"You... resented her because she looks like her brother?"

It was twisted. Like, really twisted. Alex was speechless. Elena really knew how to surround herself with peculiar people.

"I didn't resent her, but she reminded me of him constantly. Her smile, her eyes... Mick was my best friend for over ten years, and he was my first love. I tried to be there for her, but I couldn't grieve for her brother. How could I move on if she constantly reminded me that I'd just lost one of the people I loved most?

"You realize that she, too, lost one of the people she loved the most, right?"

Kelsey lowered her eyes, but nodded nonetheless. She bit her thumbnail nervously. A bad habit he'd seen far too often in a certain ballerina.

"Do you think she'll be able to forgive me?"

"Maybe, but know that you'll be torn to pieces. That's for sure."

"By Lena?"

"I don't think so."

"... by you?"

Alex sniffed. Even though she'd told him everything that had been on her mind, Kelsey still seemed afraid of him. She should be. He wasn't going to let people hurt Elena anymore if he could stop them.

"Not if you treat her right."

The girl frowned, unsettled, but straightened her shoulders. There was a certain determination burning in her eyes.

"I guess I'll get what I deserve."

She stood up, and Alex walked her to the front door. Kelsey turned back to him. She offered him a sincere smile.

"Thank you for your time. Let me know when she wakes up."

Alex nodded, trying to return the smile. From the corner of his eye, he noticed that Tiago was smiling too.

"I will."

***

Elena didn't wake up, and the doctors were becoming less and less confident about her condition. What if she didn't wake up? What if the after-effects were too great and the doctors had been negligent? Things were not going according to plan. Of course, she wasn't dying, but her sleep could still last for a while.

Maura was at work, leaving Alex alone in the hospital. His head weighed a ton, and his eyes burned. All these months, he'd had this feeling that something bad would happen. Even so, Alex hadn't been prepared for this. He missed his friend. His whole life had revolved around sports and going out. Around surviving. Nothing else had ever mattered until this dancer found her way into his life, becoming the person he loved most.

"Where am I?" croaked a faint voice.

Alex's head went up, and he met Elena's confused face. Without wasting time, he ran down the corridors to call the nurses.

***

Days passed without Alex being able to go to the hospital. Elena waking up had been a delicate situation, and the doctors had asked him not to disturb her. When he entered the hospital room, she was asleep. The purple marks that decorated her neck were turning yellow. Once seated, all the tension of the past few days subsided. His eyes were tingling.

"Why are you crying?"

Alex gasped. Elena's face lit up when she saw him. Despite the still visible bruises, she was glowing. Alex rubbed his eyes with his sleeve.

"I'm relieved you're finally awake."

"Trust me, so am I." She sighed, a wry smile on her lips.

"What you did was irrational and dangerous. There were other ways to get out of there."

Elena let her head fall back against the pillows.

"I know. I guess the mix of alcohol and sadness didn't help me think clearly. At least now it's over."

He wanted to say how reckless she'd been to risk her life like that, how worried he'd been. Seeing her alive and relieved, it didn't matter anymore. All that mattered was that she was here, now.

"How do you feel?"

"Like someone who almost died of asphyxiation. The

hospital food, on the other hand, is disgusting. As soon as I get out of here, let's get some bubble tea."

She beckoned him closer, and Alex took her in his arms. He still couldn't believe she was back, even if she'd only been unconscious for a few hours. Elena hugged him back. Everything would be all right for them.

"I really thought you weren't coming back."

"Of course, I would have come back. I'll always come back for you."

Alex raised his head. His tears flowed more freely. He always felt vulnerable with her, in the best way possible.

"Don't be so cheesy."

"But you're very taken with my cheesiness."

Elena gently rubbed his cheeks, never ceasing to smile.

"I mean it, Alex. You're my better half. Nothing can keep me away from you."

When his tears kept falling, Elena laughed, ruffling his hair.

"What a softy! You look like I'd just told you your puppy died."

"I'm sorry, I..."

"Never be sorry for having feelings."

Alex lay down beside her. Now that she was here, he wouldn't let her go.

"Where's Frank?" Alex wondered.

He had to know. Elena rested her head against his shoulder.

"In jail. He won't get out in the next few months. And then he won't be able to approach us, according to the lawyers."

"Is that what you were trying to accomplish the other

night?"

Elena nodded. She'd managed to get the bastard away from her for good. All by herself.

"So, it's all over now?"

"Yes."

Alex kissed her temple, and Elena pressed herself against him.

"I'm proud of you."

CHAPTER 31

Elena

Nina, Sophie, and Alex had come to visit me at the hospital. The last few times I'd been here, I'd always been alone. It was good to know I had friends who cared now. We played Cluedo without Alex. Since he'd arrived here half an hour earlier, he hadn't looked up from his iPhone. Something was bothering him. I wanted to ask what was going on, but I knew Alex wouldn't talk while my friends were around.

Alex looked up at the door and smiled at someone. I turned my head to see who was there and felt my heart clench.

"Hi," Kelsey said, giving me an uncertain smile.

I found myself unable to react. I'd avoided her for months. Seeing my former best friend gave me a strange feeling of unease. Out of the corner of my eye, I could see Nina's gaze darken, but it wasn't her behaviour that caught my attention. It was Sophie's. She placed herself between my bed and the door, arms folded.

"Come any closer and you'll be in for a rough time."

"Chill. I'm not here for you," Kelsey retorted, rolling her eyes.

"I don't think you get it," Sophie repeated as she approached Kelsey. "Go near her, and I'll knock you out."

Nina stood next to Sophie, imitating her pose. The only difference was that Nina was almost a head taller than Kelsey. Despite my friend looming dangerously over her, Kelsey just looked annoyed. She glanced at Alex. He simply shrugged.

"Told you so."

Wait, what? He knew she was coming? Kelsey ignored the two pairs of angry eyes fixed on her, looking straight into mine. My breathing quickened. Even though lately I tended to find myself at the centre of several conflicts, I still preferred to avoid any confrontation. But when I saw the determination on my former best friend's face, I knew I had no choice but to confront her. Kelsey clicked her tongue.

"Elena, if you don't let me speak, I'm going to make a scene in the hall. And you know I will!"

"Come on, guys, let's be reasonable," Alex interjected, trying to calm things down.

"Even I wouldn't do that," Sophie replied.

"I would."

Dark Nina was back, and she was advancing dangerously toward Kelsey. Alex got up, and for a moment, I thought he was going to pull Kelsey away. Against all odds, he stood beside her and put his hand on her shoulder. She silently questioned him, and he nodded. Sophie, Nina, and I were speechless. How long had Alex and Kelsey been getting along? And since when did Alex defend her? He turned his attention back to me.

"Let her talk."

"You want Lena to forgive her after she abandoned her?"

Sophie asked, arms still crossed.

"It's up to Elena to decide if she wants to forgive her or not. It's none of our business."

Sophie glanced at Nina. The brunette nodded reluctantly. "He's right."

"Lena, I'm just asking you to listen to her. You know you'll regret it if you don't."

Why did he always have to be so mature? Sometimes I had the impression that Alex was much older than a nineteen-year-old. I wanted to say no. What could she possibly tell me that I didn't already know? I wanted to be able to move on without the weight of the past holding me back. Alex sat on the bed, my hand in his. His warmth spread through my body, giving me courage. Finally, I nodded.

"I'm listening."

***

I'd never realized how comfortable the couches at Stacey's were. The last few years, I'd spent so much time being stubborn that I didn't even realize how cosy her office actually was. I curled up in one of her soft blankets that smelled of cotton flowers. Stacey smiled. This was the first time since I'd been her patient that I tried to get comfortable.

"How are you?"

"I'm okay."

The last few days had been trying, to say the least. Between the altercation between Alex and Vincent, my father, who had tried to strangle me, and Kelsey, who had returned out of nowhere, I didn't know what to process first.

Frank and Vincent were both in trouble, so I tried not to make myself sick by thinking about them too often. As for Kelsey, I wasn't sure what to do. I'd promised her I'd think about it, but I still wasn't sure whether I wanted her back in my life or not. Too much had happened for me to decide now. Despite the avalanche of events, I could finally see the light at the end of the tunnel.

Stacey took a deep breath.

"Your mom told me what happened. That was a dangerous bet. You should have told me about your father's violence. I could have helped you."

It was worth it. Those who choose freedom rarely regret it. If I had to go through the same thing again to get my mother and me out of there as quickly as possible, I'd do it without the slightest hesitation.

"I have no regrets."

"How are you holding up? Even if you came through it unscathed, it was a traumatic situation."

When I fell asleep, I could still feel his hands around my neck. A few weeks weren't enough to forget.

"I'm still afraid. When I hear a door in the house slam, I still fear it's him, even when I know that's impossible."

It was hard to get used to the fact that he'd raised his hand to me without hesitation, but deep down, I knew things had to go this way. Although this revelation sucked. At least now I could get on with my life without his shadow looming over me. Had he tried to kill me, or had he just wanted to hurt me? Had he been drunk, or had he been lucid? I didn't know. It didn't matter anymore. Frank was no longer part of my life. I was free, and my future had never looked brighter. I just needed time to heal.

"What about Mick?"

"I miss him every day. But the fact that I miss him doesn't feel as painful anymore. I no longer feel like I'm suffocating when I think of him."

"It's amazing. You're finally becoming the person you were meant to be."

Stacey sat down beside me and put her hand on mine. Her eyes turned into crescent moons.

"Who am I meant to be?"

"A strong woman."

CHAPTER 32

Elena

The clock on the wall ticked nervously, each sound echoing in my head. Anxiety had been gnawing at me for days. Jade squeezed my hand. Her smile was calm, as if she knew what was going to happen. She didn't look worried. The door opened, and the doctor beckoned us in.

"Hello, Elena, how are you?"

"Good, for now."

He sat down at his desk and looked at my file. Doctor Petit asked a few questions about my recovery from the operation, but I couldn't make out the look on his face. His smile was as warm as ever, but I couldn't predict what he was going to say. He stopped talking and watched me in silence. Eventually, the doctor stood up and took my hands. My heart was pounding in my temples.

"Don't worry. Your career is not in danger. Your results are excellent."

I turned back to Jade, wide-eyed, unable to answer. My aunt hugged me. Unable to hold back, I burst into tears. Jade stroked my hair until my tears subsided. Doctor Petit led us to the hospital entrance before attending to another patient.

Ella and my mother, who'd been waiting in the cafeteria, bombarded us with questions. Jade gave them all the details, while I silently enjoyed the good news. I could finally dance again.

***

The lights went out and the curtain rose. Silhouettes of dancers stood on the stage, waiting for the music to bring them to life. This was to be the best day of our careers as ballet students. From the crowd, I could feel the buzz of anticipation. When the show began, I held my breath. They were all dancing with such grace and passion.

I'd been away for over six months. With everything that had happened, it felt like a lifetime had passed. A twinge of sadness bubbled to the surface when one of the other girls in my class performed my solo. If I hadn't had my accident, I could have been on that stage. Maybe I would have been spotted by a professional ballet school. Maybe not. But several things were certain: I wouldn't have gotten to know Alex, nor would I have reconnected with my family. And above all, I wouldn't have been able to accept my brother's death and free myself from my father. All these little miracles had one thing in common: Alex, the person who had taught me to love myself and to never give up. The person I'd come to love more than anything.

Once the show was over, the audience went wild. The teachers presented a bouquet of flowers to each final-year student, giving a speech on the performances.

"And last but not least, we'd like to thank Elena Fleureau.

Even if you couldn't make it tonight, you're still part of the team and we'd like to thank you for all the years you've spent with us."

All eyes were on me as I made my way down to the stage. I accepted the flowers my teacher offered me, grateful and moved.

Some of the dancers in my class were approached by scouts, and I was so proud of them. Everyone in this room has worked so hard to be here today. It took blood, sweat, tears, and a lot of passion to make it happen. And they had succeeded.

The room began to empty, and I looked at my bouquet of white roses. It somehow felt like they didn't belong to me.

"Elena! I'm glad to see you're still here."

Marya, my dance teacher, and a man in his early thirties approached. The man looked at me with great attention. I'd seen him talking to Pauline, a girl in my class, a few minutes earlier.

"This is Dimitri."

"Pleased to meet you."

His grip was firm. I tried to shake his hand just as hard.

"The show was beautiful, wasn't it?"

"Yes, it was breathtaking."

His Russian accent was barely perceptible.

"I was disappointed not to see you on stage tonight. I looked forward to your performance."

That wasn't possible. My name had been removed from the program after my accident. I turned back to Marya. She, too, was surprised by this revelation.

"Let's have a drink," Dimitri suggested.

We followed him to the bar. Marya and Dimitri were

having wine. As I was underage, I stuck to a flat white. Dimitri kept his focus on me.

"You've had a very interesting dance career despite your young age. You've skipped a class and won a lot of competitions. We've been following your progress for a few years now. What do you plan to do next?"

"I'm going to continue dancing. My doctor told me that I can resume my sporting activities full-time."

I plastered a smile that I wanted serene on my face—quite the opposite of the shock his words had given me. Marya congratulated me and raised her glass in my honour. Dimitri played with the rim of his wine glass. His gaze was inscrutable.

"Several months off are not very promising in a dancing career. Do you think you can catch up?"

He was testing me. *Just you wait*. I was a good dancer. No, I was a great dancer, and nothing could hold me back this time. I was ready to take my life back. I looked up at him and held his gaze.

"I have no doubts."

Dimitri nodded and turned back to my teacher.

"I'm curious. All right, Marya, what do you think?"

"Elena is my best student; she always has been. She'll amaze you. I just know it."

I stared at Marya, mouth agape. They weren't saying what I thought they were saying, were they? Dimitri smiled at me at last and raised his glass in my direction.

"I'll be watching your performance at the Vaganova Academy entrance exam. Dazzle me."

Vaganova, the academy of my dreams.

"Pinch me. I think I'm dreaming."

Marya pinched me, but nothing changed. Dimitri was still there.

"You'll still have to retake your final year at the conservatory," Dimitri added, taking a sip of wine, "but I have faith in you."

***

I held my bouquet of flowers to my chest as I watched the sun set over the horizon. The light bathed the basketball court in a soft, orangey glow. I still felt like I was dreaming; everything felt so surreal. Life was smiling at me at last.

Footsteps caught my attention. Alex was standing a few steps away from me. The sunlight made him seem to glow from within, like an angel. Maybe he'd been right all along and was an angel placed on my path. I stood up and handed him the bouquet. Alex took the roses with a smile.

"You really like giving me flowers, don't you?"

"They were given to me at the dance show," I confessed.

My nervousness fuelled his.

"Then why are you giving them to me?"

"I don't deserve them, but you do."

"I'm not sure I understand," he said, running a hand through his hair.

I beckoned him to sit down, and Alex settled on the bench, keeping the flowers in his lap. I nibbled at my thumbnail while I cleared my head, pacing back and forth. My mind was going in all directions, I didn't know which way to turn.

"I went to see the show I was supposed to be in. Marya

gave me these flowers to thank me, but they felt wrong. This year has been incredibly hard, and I realize that if I've managed to get through it, it's because of you. So, I want you to accept my flowers."

Alex nodded.

"It feels like we're at a crossroads and that things are about to change, aren't they?"

I could only nod in agreement. Everything was going to be turned upside down from now on. But damn, I was ready for these changes! Alex frowned, looking worried. I really hoped I wasn't going to screw things up.

"Alex, I have to tell you something."

"Okay, talk to me."

He clutched the flowers to his chest as I had done a few minutes earlier.

"I saw my doctor this week. I'm allowed to dance again."

"Truly?" he exclaimed. "I'm so happy for you!"

Alex leapt to his feet and took me in his arms. His embrace gave me that warm feeling I'd come to associate with him. He made me feel special and loved. Now it was time for me to return the favour. My heart quickened to the point where I could feel it pounding in my throat. I swallowed hard. I stepped back enough to look him in the face. Alex bit his lip. He was having trouble deciphering me, and it was making him panic. I could see it in his eyes.

"I've got something else to tell you."

"Which is?"

I took a deep breath. There was no way I was going to chicken out this time.

"Be my boyfriend?"

For a brief moment, he looked at me, unable to react. Alex

shook his head and grinned.

"What? I'm sorry, but I didn't quite hear that."

I rolled my eyes but played along. I resumed with more confidence:

"Alexander Niessen, be my boyfriend."

Alex hugged me again, tighter this time. He peppered my temples and face with kisses.

"If you insist, I think I'll accept."

THE END

What now?

Thank you so much for picking up this book! If you loved it, please leave a review on Amazon and/or Goodreads. It helps me out a lot!

If you want more of Alex, you can find him as a side character in *Be my forever*, where he is as meddlesome as ever ;)

Love,

Josie

About the author

Josie Winters has been imagining stories since kindergarten. Her favourite books to write are the ones about characters with emotional baggage and quirky personalities.

When Josie's not writing, you can find her nestled on the couch with her cats, reading swoony love stories.

If you want to know more about when Josie's next book will come out, or what she's up to (it's no good, that's for sure), take a look at her TikTok or Goodreads page.

Connect with Josie here:

TikTok: @josie.n.winters_08

Goodreads: Josie N. Winters

www.ingramcontent.com/pod-product-compliance
Lightning Source LLC
LaVergne TN
LVHW030342070526
838199LV00067B/6406